The Count
of
Mount Collier High

ISBN 978-1-329-84594-7

The Count

of

Mount Collier High

David W. Gordon

Claymore 1745 Press

2016

ISBN 978-1-329-84594-7

First Printing: 2016

ISBN 978-1-329-84594-7

Claymore 1745 Press
New York

Claymore1745@yahoo.com

Ordering Information:

Special discounts are available on quantity purchases by corporations, associations, educators, and others. For details, contact the publisher at the above listed address.

U.S. trade bookstores and wholesalers: Please contact Claymore 1745 Press via email at claymore1745@yahoo.com.

Lulee –
I owe you more than I could ever repay.

To Porthos and Aramis
All for one, and one for all

Acknowledgements

The greatest stories always seem to be driven by betrayal, love, and revenge. No greater example of this exists than *The Count of Monte Cristo* by Alexandre Dumas.

When I embarked on reading the novel for the fourth time, I mentioned it to a student of mine who said they had never heard of it. I was saddened by that fact, especially, since she was a stellar student and an avid reader. Children have a vague sense of *Zorro*, but not *The Scarlet Pimpernel*. They know Batman, but not Edmond Dantés. I thought it was disgraceful that kids didn't read some of the great classics and that they had no idea how the things they loved today were so informed by these treasures that had been written a century or more earlier. Why didn't they read this stuff? Maybe it was the length of the book, the vocabulary, or just that the material was dated, I didn't know. That is when I decided to do something about it.

The book you hold in your hand is an attempt to rectify all three of the above dilemmas. *The Count of Mount Collier High* takes the basic plot and characters of Dumas's classic, *The Count of Monte Cristo*, and brings them to life in a modern high school. It shortens the story considerably, not because I felt the original needed to be trimmed, but rather to make it less intimidating and more accessible to modern sensibilities. Regrettably, the second generation of characters from the original classic won't appear in this rendition due to the youthful nature of the main characters. Despite that, every attempt has been made to keep the heart of the story and the characters intact within the walls of Mount Collier High.

I grew up loving the adventures that Alexandre Dumas gave the world. This novel is an attempt to do him homage and to keep his stories alive and well in the hearts and minds of today's readers. I hope that I do him proud.

As with all great efforts in life, they are never accomplished alone. I want to thank my wife, Lulee, for her tireless efforts and her willingness to sacrifice so much in getting this novel published. Also, much gratitude goes to my early readers who volunteered to read and comment on the manuscript: Lindsay Macchio, Shaun and Lisa McGee, Michael Courtney, Sofiya Filoppova, Luisa DiNardi, Mr. Woodrow, Nicholas Oliverio, Margaret Fox and JoAnn Bronschidle. Thank you for all of the help and constructive criticism.

Chapter 1

The Homecoming

Edric Davies could hear his name over the din of noise. The team bus had not even pulled into the parking lot of Mount Collier High School, but the timber of chants had already begun to undulate through the seats. His freshman basketball team still had not come down from the euphoric high of their stunning victory. In the game their rival, the Rams of Catalan Valley, had gone down to a last second buzzer-beater thrown by an eighth-grader.

The team's star player, Jason LaClair, had blown out his knee early in the fourth quarter. The Spartans were down by sixteen, and they had lost the one player who had any hope of bringing them back from the brink of disaster. Into the mix came an eighth grade kid to take LaClair's place, a bench warmer, who would play out the remainder of the loss and try not to let it become a massive embarrassment. The team drove the ball to the top of the key, but was forced back by a tough zone defense. They passed it out to the young eighth-grader who arced a three from the corner and sunk it. The large section of visiting fans, once silent and deflated, gasped audibly and filled with expectant air. The Rams took the ball to mid-court only to have an errant pass stolen from them. The Spartan player took the breakaway and sunk an easy layup, and those same visiting fans leapt from their seats and roared, for it was the same player who sank the earlier three-pointer. Suddenly, there was hope.

The minutes ticked by and the sixteen point gap was slowly, painstakingly reduced until there was seconds left. The Spartans, down by one, fed the ball to that hot young player and pinned their hopes on him. He did not disappoint. The ball swished through the net as the buzzer sounded and the visiting fans hugged and high-fived one another while the home fans stared in horrified silence. The game was over. The Spartans had stunned the Rams with an eighth grade bench warmer.

The air brakes puffed out a squeaky cry as the bus came to a halt in front of the high school. Edric sat as his teammates poured off the bus, blending into the awaiting mass. Some, as they passed him, tousled the curls of Edric's stark black hair or gave him a gentle punch on the arm. Edric waited for them to pass before he stood, gathering his bag and tossing the strap over his shoulder. He looked out of the open rectangular window at the sea of blue and gold clad classmates and parents. They were clad in an array of school t-shirts and hats, all emblazoned with the school's Spartan mascot. Many of them, maybe a third, he guessed, had war paint on their faces. They were the loyal remnants of what was once a disappointing homecoming weekend that had serendipitously turned into a spectacular victory. It was as if the Spartans had won the day at the Hot Gates of Thermopylae, despite the odds, and all of Greece was celebrating with them.

A large hand slapped against the lower portion of the window, jarring Edric from his revisionist history daze. The shock of the noise or maybe the size of the imposing hand had sent Edric back from the window. The school mascot was dressed in a puffy Spartan costume with over-exaggerated muscles and a big head. He was jumping up and down, ramping up the crowd and smacking the side of the bus, rattling the thin yellow metal that held it all together. Edric allowed himself a nervous laugh as he watched the mascot bounce up and down and throw his hands up into the air, encouraging the spectators to cheer louder. Edric stepped into the seat and thought about sitting back down. Instead, Edric used both hands to push in the window locks and slide the window up. His teammates never closed their windows, rather leaving them for the driver to deal with instead. He closed the windows in the seats to his front and back before he headed to the door. He smiled at the driver, a portly man in his fifties who had a slow, southern drawl that never quite fit in a town like this. "Enjoy it, Edric. You deserve it," he said in his thick accent as he offered a fist bump to Edric. "Thanks," Edric replied, blowing it up with him and then taking a deep breath before heading down the stairs.

As Edric emerged from the bus the congregation exploded. Cheerleaders lined both sides of the path, their hair tied in blue and gold ribbons and pom-poms swishing high in the air. Before his foot hit the concrete curb, Edric felt himself being lifted up. Two seniors, who had suffered an earlier heartbreaking loss to the Rams, were waiting near the door and had grabbed him by the arms and lifted him onto their shoulders. They carried him down the path marked by the cheerleaders as if he were a knight walking under drawn swords.

The crowd chanted his name, "Edric! Edric!" He looked out at all of the adoring faces and found he knew many of them. Never in his life could he have imagined this would all be for him. There was Jennifer Kelly, a bright and very hot senior, who used to babysit him, cheering and yelling his name. She looked like she was in her twenties and dressed like a scantily clad sorority girl. Edric saw John Barker, a burly wrestler in eleventh grade who worked at the lumber yard with him. His fist was raised high in the air and he wore the proud smile of an older brother looking upon the success of the younger. Then, there was Frank Macintyre, a fellow eighth-grader who was yelling and cheering louder than any dozen members of the admiring faction. Edric pointed at his best friend, appreciating his efforts. He was deposited onto his feet and endured a drubbing of back-slapping admiration. Still, he hadn't found the one face he was looking for, though she had found him.

Meagan Dumas came barreling out of a gaggle of girls and nearly knocked Edric over as she crashed into him. She hugged him, wrapping her arms around his athletic frame and he immediately felt awkward, wondering if he smelled. He didn't hug back, rather holding his arms tight to his side, hoping that any stench that might emanate from his armpits would be held in check.

"Congratulations!" the girl said, beaming as she released her hold on him. "You were awesome!"

Edric took two small steps back and bowed his head in embarrassment. "Thanks. The team played well today."

The crowd around them continued to chant his name, slap him on the back and otherwise cheer Edric on. One guy passed him and threw his arm around him and said, "Kiss her already, man," and then walked on as if he had merely suggested the obvious.

Suddenly, Meagan became shy and it was her turn to avert her eyes. She turned slightly away from him and her long brown hair helped to hide her flushing cheeks from his view.

"I'm sorry," Edric said quickly, then added, "about all this . . . and that guy . . . what he said, I mean." He did want to kiss her, he thought; maybe just not with all of these people watching.

Edric was having the best day of his life. So, in between the back slaps and the cheers, he decided to press his luck and see just how great a day this could be. "Would you, maybe, want to go out sometime?" he half asked and half yelled, praying the din of the crowd would not suddenly quiet and leave him screaming at her. Thankfully, the crowd did not relent and his voice carried just enough volume to do the job.

Meagan whipped her perfectly highlighted tresses around. Edric was mystified as the gentle curls bounced and settled on her shoulders. Then, he saw the smile on her face and it told him everything he needed to know. "That would be cool," she said, trying in vain to hide her own happiness.

"Okay," Edric said, nodding his head, impressed that his luck had held strong.

"I'll text you later," Meagan replied, waving goodbye with her fingers and quickly disappearing into the sea of girls she had come out of.

Edric watched as the crowd engulfed her and chatted about what had just transpired. He wanted to let out an enormous cheer but, he held it in check. He walked towards the locker room and was slapped, shook, and high-fived at every step. He smiled, feeling like there was nothing more this day could give him that would make it any better.

Edric wasn't the only one who had watched Meagan walk away. Frank Macintyre wasn't cheering anymore. He had watched intently as Meagan left. When she had drifted out of sight Frank shifted his focus to Edric. His face had twisted into a perverse scowl. If looks could kill, Edric may well have simply exploded where he stood.

Chapter 2

The Status Quo

The locker room at Mount Collier High School looked like it belonged to the Oregon Ducks or the USC Trojans. Oak cabinets with ornate hooks, individual showers and a state of the art sound system were but a few of the simple pleasures it had to offer. It had all of the trappings of a big time college locker room, courtesy of some very wealthy boosters and alumni who had ensured that the school would attract the best players. Edric had been shocked when he made the freshman team. To say he didn't fit in with his team would be to suggest that Edric fit in at the school at all. Edric often joked that he was "poo." That is to say he was so poor; he couldn't even afford the r at the end of the word. In this town, wealth was measured with zeros and commas that most basic calculators couldn't handle.

Edric understood where he fit in. He was the servant class of sorts. He lived on the side of town where everyone who had jobs did. The rest of the sprawling, hilly area was reserved for the inherited wealth or those families who lacked the scruples to care how money was acquired.

The energy of the day was beginning to subside and give way to routine. The team was going about its business and heading to the showers or preparing to head home. The locker room had a low buzz of noise, nothing like the preceding moments that had made Edric feel like a rock star. He appreciated the quiet now. Edric stripped off his white away-jersey and tossed it in the laundry bin for Mr. Winston to wash. To the other players, he was some unseen custodian, but to Edric he was a sweet old man who had given him some great pointers on his game. Mr. Winston had practiced with Edric every day for two months. He had made Edric killer in the paint and nearly as deadly from the three-point line.

Edric smiled at the thought of how far his game had come. He headed off to the showers as the quiet of the locker room was broken by some classic AC/DC that the coach pumped in via the sound system. It had become one of the many and varied rewards heaped on the team after a victory. Yet, what they received paled in comparison to the varsity squad: T-shirts, hats, free meals at local restaurants and more. The administration violated the law and money covered it all at Mount Collier.

Edric didn't care. He just wanted to play ball. He was still secretly enjoying the day as he walked towards the showers. He cared very little about the win or his role in it. What made this day special was that he had finally gained the courage to ask Meagan out and she had said yes! Yet, that "yes," was now beginning to panic him more than he cared to admit. Where would he take her? How could he ever afford to impress her? He wondered if Mr. Moore would let him pick up a few more hours at the lumber yard so he could make some extra money.

Abruptly, Edric slammed into what felt like a wall. His head rocked back and he shook off the pain as he tried to figure out what had happened. Standing before him was freshman Brett DiVinceo, the team's center, the tallest, and most aggressive player, they had. The kid looked like Thor, from the Avengers, but behaved like Ivan Drago from Rocky IV. He was thick, muscular and sported long blonde hair that was always tied back into a neat ponytail. With him, retreat was always the better part of valor.

"Sorry, Brett." Edric proffered, trying to move around the number two player on the team. With Jason's injury, Brett was positioned to be the new team captain or maybe even make a move to JV.

Brett was wrapped in a towel and his broad chest with flecks of hair offered proof of his excess testosterone. He stepped in front of Edric, denying him the ability to pass. "You played well today, kid," he said, but Edric wondered if he really meant it.

"Thanks," Edric replied, moving to the opposite side, only to be blocked again this time by Brett's thick arm slapping against the aqua colored tile wall of the bathroom.

"My man, don't forget who the star of this team is, okay," Brett said with a sadistic smile. He slapped Edric on the arm harder than any friend would do. Satisfied that his message had been sent, Brett walked away triumphantly.

Edric showered, feeling uneasy about the attention he now had upon him. He dressed hurriedly, looking forward to getting home and telling his father everything that had happened. He wished his dad could have been at the game, but Edric understood why he had to work. The garage his father owned was a struggling business even at the best of times. When work came in, his dad had to make sure it was done fast and done right. Otherwise, customers would go to one of the many businesses owned by Mr. DiVinceo. The man owned more than half the town and probably a tenth of the county. He had garages, restaurants, lumber yards, movie theaters and more, every one of which offered rewards for wins. Edric's dad was a perpetual David to the town Goliath. The only difference was that no amount of stones could bring down the wealthy elitists of Mount Collier.

He rounded the corner of the bathroom and headed for the door. Brett was still at his locker and Edric could have sworn that he saw one of the varsity players just leaving.

"Was that Zaire who just left?" Edric asked.

"Nope. Nobody here but us, dude," Brett answered, stuffing something in his pocket without looking up.

Edric blew the whole thing off and headed home, happy to tell his dad the good news. He decided he would save Meagan's answer of a "yes" for last!

Chapter 3

The Relationship

Edric walked along the unending corridors of the adjoining high school with his gym bag slung over his shoulder. The halls were not altogether familiar to him since he was still in middle school. Though the two buildings shared a campus, office space, and cafeteria between them, no amount of hallways could make them feel connected. When a student crossed through the office annex from the middle school into the high school, it was as if Alice had emerged into Wonderland. This world was bigger, yet it felt to Edric as if it was collapsing in on him. The lockers were larger, the pathways longer and more meandering. Sometimes he wondered if the architect made the high school like a maze on purpose. He wanted to head out the south exit, but he was becoming more certain now that he had made a wrong turn.

The high school was so massive that it was divided into a series of four houses, each functioning like its own independent school within the annex that was only a part of the sprawling campus. Each of the houses had its own assistant principal who functioned like a lord over all who were assigned to their domain. The principal was rarely seen, assuming the role of useless figure head for the entire building. Students could be standing right next to the man and nobody would have recognized him. He, like so many others, reveled in the anonymity that the vast numbers of faculty and students provided.

Edric made a right, hoping it would put him back on track. Instead, the path soon led him down a hallway full of student art. There was a pointillism piece that showed the local mountainous landscape done by a girl that Edric thought must have taken dozens of meticulously patient hours to complete. A few watercolors of the same scene and then a work that seemed to be inspired by Picasso that Edric assumed was on the same subject but could not make heads or tails out of it.

He moved through the hallways, lit only by the fading sun that was falling fast below the horizon. He found a sign outlined in bright yellow that pointed to the left and to the administrative offices. That, he knew, would take him to the south exit. It was his yellow brick road and he merrily took the path.

The trek took him past the Spear House offices. The school had four houses, Spear, Shield, Sword and Armor. The student government had chosen the names when the decision was made to subdivide the high school instead of building a second one. When Edric had moved to town with his father after his mother left, he joked that the high school probably had its own sorting hat to go along with the houses, too.

Spear House was the home of the infamous Mr. Vincent Germaine. He had been the assistant principal here for two years and everyone knew he had his eyes on a larger prize. He wanted to be principal and probably even superintendent someday. He was as mean as he was ambitious. While other assistant principals meted out justice with an eye towards student growth, Germaine considered only one thing; his career path. Edric had met him once. He watched the man make a sophomore cry at basketball tryouts. Germaine had pulled the boy aside for some reason and when he returned he was red faced and choking back tears. It had cost the kid a shot at varsity and Edric had pitied him.

The light was on in Germaine's office, but the curtains were drawn. Edric wanted to slip past without being seen. If spotted, Germaine would find some reason to discipline Edric or, at the very least, to unleash some pent-up rage on him. Edric walked on the far side of the hall, hugging against the brightly painted brick. His shoulder snagged on a poster taped to the wall and Edric bent down to pick up the paper. He thought he could hear voices in the office. It sounded like Germaine and a female student. Edric felt he recognized the voice, but it was too muffled for him to be sure.

Suddenly, Edric heard the door to the office pull away from the door jam. Light from the office flooded the hallway. Edric dashed into the nearby stairwell nearly tripping up the stairs. He would go the long way. Better that than to be seen by Germaine at this hour.

Edric gained the safety of the stairs. He paused, focusing on his feet so that his steps would not be heard.

Then, he realized he was right. He had heard two voices.
One was Germaine, but the other was Jennifer Kelly,
there was no mistaking that. He had grown up with that
voice since he was seven. She was his childhood crush
turned awkward babysitter.   He shuddered at the
memories and strained to listen. Edric couldn't make out
everything they were saying. Jennifer had thanked him
for something and he had told her not to worry and
something about being quiet. There were other sounds
too. What sounded like kisses and giggling to him.
Then, Edric heard steps coming up the stairs and he made
a light-footed dash to the upstairs hallway. He moved as
fast as he could towards the opposite stairwell so he
could head back down and escape the labyrinth of the
school and go home.

Jennifer Kelly reached the top of the stairwell. She
watched as Edric disappeared around the corner. She
rested warily on the midnight-blue lockers that adorned
the walls of the school. She was certain he saw her leave
Germaine's office. He didn't wait for her, though. That
made her all the more nervous about what Edric might
suspect.

Chapter 4

The Men of Honor

The Saturday morning alarm came hard and fast for Edric. He awoke to the blaring beep, smashing his hand down on the snooze button because it was easier to reach than the off button. Edric pulled the pillow over his head for a minute before begrudgingly throwing off the sheets. He needed to be to work at the lumber yard in forty-five minutes and he was starving.

Edric stumbled into the kitchen and poured milk into a large mixing bowl. His *Honey Nut Cheerios* were left on the table by his father and he sprinkled them in without opening his eyes. His father had come home late from work last night and they had spoken for a few minutes before Edric had gone to bed. What one ate for dinner, the other ate for breakfast.

"I'm proud of you, son," his father said. He hugged him and held him tightly, then added, "Don't let it go to your head though, okay kiddo." He understood that was what passed as celebration in this house. Where other kids would be taken out to dinner or bought extravagant gifts, Edric lived with a man who offered measured praise and high expectations. Even as an eighth grader, Edric knew he got the better of the deal.

Edric rhythmically shoveled the cereal into his mouth and finished his breakfast with all do haste. He had precious few minutes to waste before he needed to be at work. It wasn't as if Mr. Moore would have been angry; he was a kind-hearted man who had a deep respect for hard work. Edric shared the man's feelings. He had too much respect for Mr. Moore to ever be late. He took one last large spoonful of cereal and dumped his bowl in the sink while he chewed. He was dressed and out the door a short time later.

He jogged the three blocks to Moore's Lumber and entered through the automatic doors in the front. Normally, Edric would have slipped in through the back gate. Mr. Moore always left it open in case one of his employees needed to borrow a tool or grab some supplies when the store was closed. It was one of the many reasons employees loved working for him. Today, the store was already open so there was no need to go through the back. Edric regretted that decision almost instantly. As soon as he walked in, a customer greeted him. "Way to go, Edric!" the man said, pointing his finger at him. He dropped a dollar into the small plastic jar that had a handwritten label, "Julie's Dowry" on it and said goodbye.

"Hi Julie," Edric said to the pretty girl at the register. She smiled at him and flicked her brown eyes upward, suggesting Edric do the same. He did. Hanging from the gray beams of the warehouse ceiling was a Spartan yellow banner with blue lettering. It read, "Way to go, Edric!"

"Dad wanted to do something to celebrate," she said somewhat apologetically, moving her long bangs away from her eyes. Julie was Mr. Moore's daughter. She was a senior at Mount Collier High and was headed off to college to study Secondary Education. Her father had suggested a college fund jar, but Julie thought the dowry bit was more fun. Mr. Moore couldn't let it go and commented on it all the time. "You're too pretty to need a dowry," he would say, or, "With your brains, a guy should pay to marry you!" Edric agreed with his boss. Nevertheless, Julie never changed the jar.

"Is he always this embarrassing?" Edric asked, already knowing the answer to his own question.

Julie flicked her head from side to side, her long brown ponytail swooshing back and forth as she did. "No!" she replied, "Usually, he's worse!"

The store loudspeaker chirped and Mr. Moore's gravelly voice came on. "Ladies and gentlemen, we have a celebrity in our midst! Let's all give our own, Edric, a round of applause for saving Homecoming from being a complete disaster last night!" The store erupted in applause and Edric had no place to hide. Even Julie was applauding as she giggled at the discomfort and embarrassment that stretched across Edric's face.

Mr. Moore hung up the phone he was using to make his announcement and rounded the edge of the central-service counter. He was in his early fifties with a small belly and an enormous heart. He wrapped his arms around Edric, lifting him in the air and twirling him around. "We're all proud of you, Son," he said as he set the young man down. Soon, Edric was being patted on the back, fist bumped, and high-fived by customers and staff alike. Uncomfortable with the attention, he tried to make his way out to the yard as quickly as possible.

Edric worked the yard with one other kid, a junior named John Barker who was a shoo-in for an ROTC scholarship. Mr. Moore hired good people and treated them well. In turn, they treated their employer even better. They gave him a hard day's work, probably harder than they would have worked for someone else who could have paid them more money but wouldn't have appreciated their sweat nearly as much as Mr. Moore did.

Customers were notorious for trying to steal product from the yard. The two boys tried to enforce the policy of customers waiting at the front gate. The problem was that Mr. Moore wouldn't let them shut the gate. He felt that it made the place look like it was closed. Instead, the boys tried to assist customers load their cars while watching the gate and any unsupervised customers who had slipped into the yard. The morning began with some water softener bags loaded into a minivan and a cranky contractor who was tossing lumber back and forth, looking for a board so straight it couldn't possibly exist. John came over to lend a hand. He was restacking the boards as fast as the contractor could toss them. Edric turned away, trying not to laugh as the two men worked at cross purposes. He saw another car head over to the pine shed.

"You okay here, John?" Edric asked and John waved him away as a piece of lumber came within inches of hitting him in the face. "Good luck," Edric said and headed off to the pine shed.

"Hello. Can I help you find something?" Edric asked the man who had entered the shed. He was in his thirties, in jeans and a t-shirt, but didn't look to be a contractor. He sure wasn't a regular that Edric could identify.

"No. I'm fine. I don't need any help," the man replied, continuing to fish through the racks of wood. Whenever a customer tried to get Edric to go away, he got suspicious.

"Could I have your ticket," Edric asked, suspecting that the customer had not yet paid.

The man reached into his pocket, but didn't take out a ticket. "Here you go," he said, holding out a twenty-dollar bill to Edric. "Not how I roll, Man," Edric said and pointed the man to the back door of the store. "Come on, kid," the man pleaded, but Edric wouldn't hear it. "Go get a ticket or get out," Edric said, growing angrier by the minute.

The remainder of Edric's day was uneventful, though long. When closing time came, Edric and John were pretty-well exhausted. Edric closed and locked the gate and said goodnight to John. He headed inside and then headed upstairs to see Mr. Moore. He knocked on the office door and opened it part-way. "Mr. Moore, can I speak to you a moment," Edric asked, peaking his head into the small office.

"Sure. Come in. Come in."

Edric sat in an old spinning chair with one of the arms emitting exposed foam.

"You have some concrete in your hair," Mr. Moore said without looking up from his computer screen.

Edric rubbed his head a bit and answered, "Hazard of the job, I guess."

"What can I do for you, kiddo?" Mr. Moore asked as he turned his chair to focus on Edric's needs.

Edric adjusted uncomfortably in the chair. Mr. Moore smiled genially at him. Edric hung his head, feeling ashamed to ask for more hours, knowing how difficult Mr. Moore's finances had become. Edric decided he would find some other way. Suddenly, the door swung open and Julie came in.

"Hey, Dad, the yard is wrapped up and the registers are done. Anything . . . Oh, I'm sorry. I didn't know you were busy."

"It's okay, Honey." Mr. Moore said, taking the register receipts and a small stack of cash from his daughter. "Edric just popped in to ask me something."

Edric squirmed in his seat.

"Oh, he wants more hours," Julie said matter-of-factly.

Edric hung his head in utter shame and embarrassment.

Julie noticed the shift in his body language and smiled. "He asked that girl out I told you about," Julie said to her father.

"Meagan, right?" Mr. Moore queried.

Edric gave her the evil eyes, but she just giggled. "Yup," Julie replied and shut the door behind her.

Mr. Moore took several twenties from the small stack of cash and put them in front of Edric. "Show her a good time."

Edric shook his head wildly. "I can't take that, sir," Edric argued as he pushed the money away from him.

"Consider it a loan then," Mr. Moore said. He understood the boy and played to his pride. He knew Edric would never accept charity. "You can work it off in the next couple of weeks. God knows the yard could use a good cleaning. Maybe, you can organize the lumber stacks and the cull bins?" He rose, took the money in his hand and walked over to Edric. "You are young. Be happy. Enjoy this. There will be time for work and worries later." Mr. Moore gently took Edric by the hand and put the money in his palm. "I was young once, too, you know."

"I . . ." Edric began to say, but was quickly cut off.

". . . Can say thank you and good night," Mr. Moore demanded. "I have a family to get home to and you have a date to plan. Now go!"

Edric got up and walked towards the door. "Mr. Moore, I don't know what to say." Then, without another thought, Edric crossed the room and gave the man a hug. "Thank you."

Chapter 5

The Complicated Relationships

Edric had no idea what he should do. Should he wait for her at her locker? Then, the thought struck him, "Was that being too presumptuous?" Just as quickly he wondered, "What if I don't and she expected me to?" Confusion reigned within him. Edric paced the tile floors of the hallway like the Road Runner trapped in Wile E. Coyote's first successful trap. Every time he thought he had committed to a course of action, his mind would get the better of him. Meagan had agreed to go out with him, sure; but, did that mean she was his girlfriend? Edric grinned uncontrollably at the thought that Meagan Dumas could actually be his girlfriend.

Edric decided that he would hover around the area of her locker and try to make it look like he was just passing by. His locker was two hallways in the opposite direction, and their first period class wasn't "on the way" for him to be passing by it. Still, it was the best he could muster, so he was going with it. Edric did three loops before he saw Meagan at her locker, surrounded by her entourage.

"Hey," Edric said, faking nonchalance as best he could.

"Hi," Meagan replied bubbling over with happiness at his presence.

"Darn," he reflected, now feeling like he should have waited at her locker. That thought, however, didn't last long. The sneers and glares from her friends had told him that even passing by had been a mistake. He didn't come close to their social status. A rank established in Mount Collier by three things; money, last name, and the ability to look out for number one, in that order. One girl scoffed at him when he smiled at her. Two others tittered and whispered to one another.

Meagan's enthusiasm for him waned in direct proportion to her friend's reaction. She put her head down and Edric understood that she wasn't about to risk the delicate place she held in the social strata defending her choice to go out with him. Edric didn't want to give her any reason to back out and so he departed as gracefully as his shame would allow.

"See you first period," he blurted as he darted down the hall.

Meagan's grip on her position within the school was far more tenuous than she cared to admit to anyone. Her parents were in the midst of a messy divorce, not exactly shocking news for a kid in this community. The problem was how much money her parents were spending to destroy one another. They would prefer the house, the cars and all that they owned go up in smoke before the other got it. That seemed to include Meagan herself. She was the biggest pawn in the whole game. Her mother wanted her to adopt her maiden name; Claire, a wealthy and well-respected family of snobs that claimed to date back to some successful gold prospectors. How they really earned their fortune was the subject of quiet gossip. Thus far, Meagan had avoided that mine field by telling her mom she would think about it, but it was too hard to do in the middle of a school year.

Her parents had taught her the most valuable lesson of Mount Collier; look out for number one. Meagan did just that when she had said yes to Edric. She liked him. He was kind, sweet, good looking, a great athlete, and he was about as gentle and honorable as anyone could be. How she was going to balance dating him and satisfying her friends was something she had yet to work out. Frustrated, she headed to first period determined to apologize for how she had behaved.

Edric's phone was blowing up with text messages throughout first period. If he looked at her, he knew it would be over for him. Any chance of focusing on classwork would disappear. Still, he could feel his phone vibrate in his pocket and had lost count as to how many had come through. He watched the clock, counting the minutes until pass time, where he would be able to check it. When the bell finally rang, Edric practically ran into the hallway. He went around the corner into the stairwell to the basement level. He reached into his pocket to take out his phone when Meagan came over and playfully punched him in the arm.

"Why are you ignoring me?" she asked feigning hurt feelings. "Sorry about this morning," she added, looking down and not elaborating on it.

"Nothing to be sorry for. You didn't do anything," Edric assuaged her guilt. "That was you sending all those texts? You are not supposed to use your phone in class. You could have gotten caught!"

Megan scoffed at that, "Please! Mr. Wright doesn't care. As long as you don't interrupt his lecture, he doesn't care what you do."

"True," Edric conceded.

"If you read your texts," she chided, "I was asking what you wanted to do on Friday."

That was a relief. Edric was happy to hear that she still wanted to go out with him. He had counted every penny he had available. The plan was to invite Meagan to the mall for their date. He could afford a meal and maybe a virtual reality ride, or skating at most. That would be the extent of his limited funds. Still, he hoped it would be enough to make her happy. "Can I take you to the mall?" Edric responded slowly, trying to check his excitement. He did not want to seem overly eager.

Meagan put her hand to her lip and shook her head, "No!" she blurted, "That's too expensive." In any other town in America, going to the mall would be an utterly lame and very cheap date. In Mount Collier, the mall was where the wealthy teens strutted around as if they were on parade. There, the children of the elite could showcase how an accident of birth made them somehow superior to everyone else.

Edric wondered if that was her real concern. She was right; it would be expensive for him. What she had not said was that they would likely be seen by other students. He desperately wanted this, but he didn't want it if she was ashamed of him. He gently pushed the issue, "I'll meet you in the food court. Is six o'clock okay?"

Meagan watched the edges of his face crinkle into that cute smile he had. She didn't want him spending so much to impress her. She didn't need him to try. Meagan went to tell him no again, but she remembered something her mother always told her about how fragile a man's ego could be. Reluctantly, Meagan replied, "Sure. That will be great." Then, she kissed him on the cheek and walked away, the smack of her lips echoing in the empty stairwell.

Edric brought his hand to his cheek and caressed the spot she had kissed. He watched her walk away and his heart bounded at the thought that she would be with him this weekend. If things went well, maybe she'd choose to stay with him. He realized he was young, but a lifetime with her was something that he could easily envision. In that, Edric was very much unlike his peers. He wanted, yearned for, a girl who wouldn't flee at the first sign of trouble. Though he wouldn't admit it, his mother's departure loomed large in his life.

She had left when he was young. He barely remembered her. Sometimes, Edric thought that the images of his mother came more from pictures and home video than from actual memory. Still, there was a gap in his life, a chasm of loneliness. That was the problem. He knew where it was, just not how to fix it. Being with Meagan seemed to make it hurt less.

Edric and Meagan spent the next week in sort of a pseudo-relationship. For her part, Meagan did all she could to let Edric know how excited she was that he had finally asked her out. He couldn't even begin to count the number of texts she had sent him detailing one time or another where she thought he might ask. Each one ended with her disappointment and each consecutive one began with her renewed hope. By Wednesday afternoon, he took to turning his cell phone off during class so the constant vibrations didn't tempt him. Still, just knowing those little notes were waiting in cyberspace for him was a source of insane distraction.

Edric was not a totally naive kid. He understood that their relationship existed in the shadows. He hoped that was a situation that would be temporary. Someday, she would warm to the idea and then they could be out in the sunlight together. For now, Edric respected her need to be coy. He didn't push to hold her hand in the hall, nor did he try to sit with her at lunch. Sometimes, she would send him a text that would say, "You're staring at me," or "Stop being so cute," with hearts and smiley face emoji's. When she thought no one was looking, she would brush up against him in the halls. Her fingers would extend, gently sliding across his, even holding him for a brief second before falling away.

Within their burgeoning relationship, Meagan seemed to become bolder with every passing moment. Edric's excitement for Friday grew as her comfort with him did. He felt more and more certain that Meagan would not cancel or stand him up. So, he grew bold as well.

~

"What are you doing this weekend?" Edric asked his friend Frank as he sat at the lunch table.

"Not sure yet. Whatever it is, I'll be sure to piss off my father," Frank said with a sarcasm that Edric was certain would be fulfilled. Frank was a product of one of the wealthiest families in town. He thumbed his nose at societies' structures like only an uber-wealthy teen could. He was brazen, arrogant, and quick-witted. He had a comeback for every comment, a plan for every situation, and a quiet disdain for social status granted by wealth. He respected only the keen mind and those with the willingness to use it. Edric always wondered if his friendship was an act of defiance or a genuine appreciation for talent. He lacked the courage to ask Frank which of those was the root of things.

"You going out with Meagan this weekend?" Frank asked nonchalantly.

Edric's mouth was agape. "How did you know?"

Frank averted his eyes and replied, "I'm not blind, you know."

"That obvious, huh?" Edric conceded.

"To anyone who bothers to pay attention, yes," Frank said, as if the revelation was a trifle. "Don't fear, nobody else cares to notice you."

Edric wasn't sure if that was a dig at him or not, but he wasn't about to fight over it. Frank seemed edgy today. Edric assumed it was another battle with his father and let the comment slide. Frank was perennially fighting with his father. The last one he had witnessed was particularly nasty and focused on Edric himself. He recalled the words exactly as he had heard them.

"You really shouldn't fraternize with the poor. People will start to think you want to be one of them. Let Davies be with his own kind. I don't want him skulking about our home anymore."

Still, Frank was a good friend to him. They hung out often, never letting the social strata define what they could do or would accomplish together.

"I'm taking her to the mall," Edric added.

"I guess lumber pays well," Frank raised his eyebrow incredulously.

"Mr. Moore is really good to me," Edric didn't tell Frank about the money. There was a part of him that felt ashamed that he needed help to take Meagan on a date.

"Lucky you," Frank said with obvious derision in his voice.

Edric was taken aback. "What's eating you, man?"

"Nothing," Frank responded curtly. He got up from the table and tossed his tray into the garbage. Half of the uneaten food went in the receptacle; the other half sprayed some poor student who happened to be walking by. Frank stormed out of the cafeteria leaving Edric to wonder what exactly was wrong with his friend.

"Wow! You sure know how to piss people off," a voice from behind said.

"Hi, Jennifer," Edric said without turning. He knew the voice better than most.

"Can we talk?" she asked, taking the seat across from him.

"Are you going to snap at me too?" Edric asked, a hint of sarcasm in his voice.

"That depends," Jennifer replied, the flirty eyes that Edric had spent his childhood dreaming about batted back and forth. "I know you saw us together," she said, suddenly serious.

"Wha . . ." Edric tried to feign confusion, but she knew him too well.

"Please, don't fake it. You suck at it. Remember, I used to babysit for you," Jennifer chided him. "I know you saw us. I just need to know what you plan to do with that information."

Edric grimaced. He hated to be reminded of that fact. She was four years older than him, but that hadn't stopped a lengthy childhood crush. Now, she was a senior sitting across from an eighth-grader wondering if he was going to destroy her reputation. Edric was far more worried that she might be involved in something she didn't want to be in. "What do you want me to do?" he finally asked.

"Stay quiet," she answered quickly, a firmness Edric had remembered when he was denied the right to stay up later.

Edric furrowed his brow. "You sure about this?" he asked. "What you're doing with him, I mean? The kids hate him."

"They don't know him like I do," she said defensively.

"It's against the law. He's an administrator and you are a student," Edric said contemptuously, not hiding his frustration.

"So," she said, though Edric got the sense that he was getting through to her.

"Look, I won't say anything. It's your life and you are the smartest person I know. Just, be careful. You know it can't last. I really don't want you to get hurt, okay?"

Jennifer went to respond, but said nothing. Instead, she got up and hugged him.

"Hey, I don't need any rumors to start," Edric joked.

"She's a real catch," she said, referencing Meagan, "but you're better. Thanks. I'll think it over."

Edric watched her walk away. He was worried about her. Jennifer was confident and intelligent, but Edric suspected she was in too deep. She was playing a risky game; one where she might not be able to see the danger until it was too late.

Chapter 6

The Date

The Mount Collier Marquis, a massive four-floor complex of extravagant shops and experiences, was the central hub of the student experience in the town. Every student went there, but not every student spent there. The mall was full of Prada, Dolce, Michael Kors, Burberry and all the others. It housed an inside ice skating rink, a go-cart course, paint ball experience, laser tag, theater, and six virtual reality rides. Everything about the place was what some called high-end, while others in the town saw it as pretentious, arrogant, and wasteful. The management company was meticulous in its efforts to fashion a product that spoke to the "right" clientele. Even the food court was carefully crafted to ensure only the best offerings, not even a single fast-food restaurant allowed.

Frank sat down in the food court and pouted. He flopped his chin into his hands, careful to keep his fingers far from his hair. He had been working on his relationship with Meagan for the last two school years and now, Edric had undone it all. Since sixth grade, Frank had toiled endlessly in an attempt to get Meagan to see him as more than just a good friend. He planned to drown his sorrow in some great sushi, but he had no appetite for food just now. He stared at the rolled tuna in rice, looking for answers in his spicy tataki roll and finding none.

"Stuck in the friend zone, huh?" a voice cut the quiet of his self-pity. Frank looked up to see his peer, Chris Sullivan walking towards him. Chris pulled out a chair and sat across from him. He was a lanky, gangly kid that seemed to be coming out of puberty in fits and starts rather than all at once. Chris was known to tumble over his own feet or anything that was within striking distance for that matter. The kid was everything Frank was not. Frank was graceful, good looking, and the tumultuous days of puberty were firmly behind him. Like Edric, Chris was a working class kid. Still, Chris was popular at the middle school with most kids. He didn't seem to mind laughing at himself or having others laugh at him, which happened with alarming regularity. Today, however, Frank was in no mood to laugh.

"Go away, Chris," he muttered.

Chris folded his arms and leaned his bony elbows on the table. "Sucks, doesn't it?" he observed.

"Yup," was all Frank could muster.

"She know that you're into her?" Chris asked.

"Are you just incapable of minding your own business?" Frank lashed at him.

"Where's the fun in that?" Chris suggested.

"Look," Frank pleaded, "It has not been a great couple of days for me. Let's leave it at that."

Chris left the subject alone and pointed far off down the wide pathway of the mall. "Check out who's competing for most miserable." Frank followed the index finger to its intended target and saw Brett DiVinceo stomping towards them.

Brett's week could have gone better. For days, he had walked through school feeling like a water balloon trying to navigate through halls full of pins and needles. A week ago, he walked those same halls as if he owned them. It was his name they whispered. He was the freshman who was going to get called up to junior varsity. He was the ninth grader who had upperclassmen paying attention. Now, all he heard was the name of Edric Davies. He had been supplanted by an eighth-grader and that was something he could not tolerate. Brett had not decided on a course of action, but he was determined to knock the kid down a peg or two.

Frank watched Brett trudge towards them, oblivious to their existence. Brett always scowled like he had decided to ram his head through a brick wall and would do so in a matter of moments. His was not a friendly face. Today, that countenance was especially cranky.

"Hey, Brett," Frank called as he got closer.

He took three more steps before the sound of his name seemed to sink in. "Hey," he responded, and then looked at Chris like he was a pebble in his shoe.

"Where's your pal?" Brett directed the question at Frank, rage dripping from his lips.

"Who?" Frank huffed, "Edric?"

"Yeah. You know who I mean," Brett seemed to grow angrier if it were possible.

"You think you hate him? Try having the girl of your dreams stolen from you," Frank said, blowing him off.

Brett sat at the table and slapped his arms down on it. His big mitts folded over one another, he looked at the two of them. "So then, this is sort of a hate Davies Club?"

"Wow! I've never been a member of a fan club," Chris acted overly surprised and excited. "Sounds sort of geeky to me, but if you guys want to make it a thing, who am I to say no."

Brett tried to ignore him as he let loose his feelings regarding Edric. He ranted about his play on the basketball team. He complained about his looks, the sound of his voice and even his choice of deodorant. Nothing associated with Edric Davies was positive in Brett's eyes. Chris egged him on, asking inane questions about trivial aspects of his looks or actions, enjoying how Brett would rail against them. Frank would interject and agree on some of the more salient points. The addition of Brett at the table seemed to be like pouring lighter fluid on a campfire. Frank got hotter by the moment. Finally, Chris decided if this went on any longer one or both of them would have an aneurism.

"Some Friday night date," Chris observed. "I've seen more attractive couples!" He suggested the two of them seemed perfect for one another, holding his hands out to suggest some form of coupling between them.

Frank watched as the temperature gauge slowly began to bubble over as Brett's face went from pale to pink to a deep shade of crimson. Every comment Chris made seemed to bring Brett closer to physical violence. Frank could feel his own frustration building too. "Why don't you find some other people to annoy," Frank said, trying to get Chris to leave.

"Wait! Shut up! Do you see that?" Chris exclaimed, pointing as he did.

Brett went to punch him, but Frank grabbed his arm, impeding his progress. It seemed that Brett would turn his anger upon Frank, but Chris kept saying, "There! Right there!" Instead, Brett repeatedly looked around; searching for whatever Chris wanted to distract them with. He figured he could wait until Chris had embarrassed Frank before he pummeled him.

Frank, however, didn't need to ask what Chris had seen. He knew exactly what, or rather, who it was.

~

Meagan arrived late. She had tried on at least seven outfits, rejecting every one of them in quick succession. The first was too trashy, the next, too conservative. She could not find just the right mix of clothes to say, "I'm totally into you, but I am not easy." That balance proved to be far more difficult than she had imagined. Typically, she went to school with a single mission; look hot and make everyone jealous. All of her weapons were one dimensional. She combed through drawers and closets, hoping she could assemble something that wouldn't say, "I'm a slut." She had settled on an electric blue skirt with rhinestone edging and a white t-shirt that allowed a hint of her bra to show through. It was a mix of casual but suggestive. Not exactly what she wanted, but it would have to do if she were going to make her date with Edric tonight.

Across town, Edric tossed another shirt onto the pile of rejects. "Yeah, Dad, but I can't show up looking . . ." Edric stopped before he finished the thought.

"Poor," his father finished it for him. "You are not poor, kid. We just aren't rich, is all." His father handed him forty-dollars. "Don't argue!" his father demanded that he take it. "That shirt is fine. Get in the car already!"

Edric hugged his father. "Thanks, Dad."

Meagan's arrival at the food court was hurried and she glanced around frantically, hoping he had not decided that she stood him up. Meagan spotted Edric over near the frozen yogurt stand. He waited patiently, with a small bouquet of fragrant lilacs in his hand. Meagan could feel her cheeks flush. She wanted to go straight over and kiss him. She wore a perfume scented like lilac. It was her favorite and he clearly had noticed. "Don't you dare," she told herself, fearing she might send the wrong message. She waved, gaining his attention and the two fast-walked towards one another.

Edric chanted his father's words over and over in his head as he approached her. "She said, yes, didn't she?" his father had reminded him.

"Hi." Edric beamed.

"Hi." She repeated.

"You look great," Edric blurted, holding out the flowers. "These are for you."

"Thank you! They are beautiful," Meagan replied. The gesture was sweet, but poorly thought out. What was she going to do? Carry around a bouquet of flowers all night. "Boys don't think ahead," she thought. Several women passed by and cooed as they noticed the flowers. The attention felt great and Meagan rethought the whole thing. Maybe Edric knew exactly what he was doing. Despite herself, she gave him a kiss on the cheek.

They walked together, circling the food court, trying to decide what to eat. "Do you like Italian?" Edric asked as they passed the fifth in a long line of swanky eateries. Meagan had rejected the first four. In truth, any of them would have been fine, but she was now thoroughly enjoying walking through the mall and holding her bouquet of flowers. She felt like a bride walking down the aisle with every eye pinned on her.

Bistro Siciliano had a façade that made it look as if you were eating outside on an Italian piazza, complete with stucco walls, a brick walkway and ivy colored awnings. The young couple was seated by the hostess as she smiled sweetly at the flowers. Meagan beamed and reached her hand across the table to hold Edric's. His palm was sweaty. His nerves made her feel electrified. They were a couple now, awkward and stumbling through it all, but a couple nevertheless.

Edric was indeed nervous. His budget was so tight that he was doing the math of every possible combination of order Meagan might choose to make. His A in Honors Math came in handy as he multiplied those numbers by 1.0875 in his head to include the tax and then figured in a tip. Then he deducted those amounts from what he had, hoping there would be enough to do at least one of the virtual reality rides with her. What he realized was there were at least six combinations that would allow them to do two rides together. Unfortunately, there were two combinations that would leave him without enough. So, he combed the menu looking for the cheapest item he could eat.

Meagan ordered a small dish of linguini and a water with lemon. Edric's budget fears dissipated. He gently tightened his hand around hers. He didn't know if she had ordered what she wanted or if she chose something cheap on purpose. He couldn't bring himself to ask her either. One way or another, he appreciated it. Meagan brought her free hand to her hair and brushed it back behind her ear. Then, she placed it on top of his hand, so that her hands were both above and below his. Edric said nothing. It wasn't the first time they had held hands. This just felt more natural, not like they were performing or trying to hide from their classmates. He was still in awe that she was here with him. His luck couldn't possibly hold out, he thought.

They sat in silence for a while, basking in the attention. Other patrons would glance and smile at them. People walked by and would not go too far before commenting, "How adorable," or "They are so cute." Meagan listened intently for each comment while Edric studied her face. They were so preoccupied that they never noticed the people leering at them from afar.

"You see them?" Chris asked, pointing through the small planter that shielded their table from view.

"Yyyyes," Frank said, extending the length of the "y" to match his disdain. They had been watching them ever since Meagan had arrived.

Brett stood up to get a better view and Frank pulled at him. "Stop touching me," he complained.

"Do you want them to see us?" Frank asked as if he were talking to a five-year-old. Brett shoved Chris and took his seat.

"What? He takes your spot on the team, so you take mine?" Chris jabbed. Brett gave him the death stare and he feigned an apology. "Sorry."

"Ugh! Look at him trying to pretend he can afford her," Frank bleated.

"Maybe, she's cheaper than she looks," Chris observed. This time it was Frank's turn to threaten with his eyes. Chris shrugged his shoulders, but kept his comments to himself for a while.

They watched with the intensity of hawks as the two ate and flirted. What Chris had thought was blind rage before paled in comparison to the incensed hate that the two exuded now. What was once a vocal expression of disdain had become a silent seething and loathing that Chris had never encountered before. They watched as the two left the eatery and headed for the *Design Your Own Virtual Reality Coaster*.

Now was his chance. Chris decided that his chances at retreat were quickly dissipating, so he got up to leave. Brett's fists were still clenched, and Frank's hand rested gently on his shoulder as if to calm the savage beast. "Fame is fleeting," Chris observed as he took a big step back from the table. "Relax, his won't last forever either." With that, Chris made a bee line for the exit.

"I'm gonna kill that kid," Brett swore and pounded the table with his fist. Drinks and food leaped from the table like a game of *Trouble*. When they returned to earth, liquid merged with solids to create a colossal mess.

"Come on!" Frank exclaimed. "Seriously, man! What good did that do?"

"Made me feel better," Brett brooded. He moved a stack of napkins to wipe up the flow of liquid heading towards his side of the table.

Frank got up and moved two tables away. Brett looked quizzically at him a moment and then seemed to realize that would solve the mess well enough for him. When he joined Frank, Brett noticed a crafty smile on his face.

"Wha . . .?"

Frank did not respond. He waived his hand, telling Brett to be quiet. Reluctantly, Brett waited.

"I have an idea," Frank finally revealed.

Brett leaned forward in his chair and asked, "Are we going to screw him up? Whatever it is, I'm in!"

Frank shook his head and grinned widely. "No," he replied, "We are going to absolutely ruin him!"

Chapter 7

The Betrayal

By Friday, Edric and Meagan had fallen into a predictable routine. They were no longer dating in the shadows. The pair could be found in the morning outside of Meagan's locker. They held hands in the hallway between all but two classes. In the cafeteria, they sat across from one another, flirting as if the rest of the world had ceased to exist. At the end of the day, Meagan would walk Edric to his bus, while she made her mother wait in the parking lot for her. That routine was about to be broken.

"Edric Davies, please report to Mr. Germaine's office," the loudspeaker crackled.

The announcement was repeated twice. A crystal clear request that was anything but a request. Edric had just been ordered to Mr. Germaine's office. Germaine, who had thrived on sadism and torture. A man who satiated his thirst on the tears of children.

"Edric," Ms. Knouff spoke, her hand gently resting on his shoulder, "Did you hear the announcement?" It was ninth period and she was a great way to end a day. She was young and pretty, her voice melodious; laced with a twinge of pity.

Edric shuddered at her touch. She was kind-hearted and, like most of his teachers, she cared deeply about her students. He loved his teachers and he knew that most loved him. Ms. Knouff's motherly touch and pitiful voice told Edric that his instincts were correct. He should be afraid. He nodded and rose from his desk, separating himself from her hand.

"Hey," Brian, the class wise-guy, grabbed his arm and told him, "Good luck! You're gonna need it!" Edric knew he spoke from experience, but the kid wasn't exactly helping him through this. Try as he might, he couldn't muster a sarcastic comment that he could launch back at Brian. He knew one would come to him in the hallway, too little and too late to do any good.

Edric marched down the long hallway that connected the middle school and high school. The shared resources such as office space, auditorium, cafeteria, and gyms were centrally located between the two schools, connected by long, winding hallways. He moved like a condemned man going to the electric chair. His feet dragged, but his mind raced. He had only ever been in trouble once in school. He punched a bully that had been pulling a girl's hair. That was in first grade. Since then, he had been a straight-laced kid who never came close to challenging the rules, much less breaking them. Why would Germaine want to see him, he wondered. As he combed his brain, seeking for a reason, he realized there didn't need to be one. Germaine was a cruel man who toyed with children the same way mean children toyed with insects. Edric was just the unlucky ant under his magnifying glass today.

He arrived at the office and stared at the door. The door was solid, the glass crackled, only allowing an outsider to see shadows within, nothing more. Black letters declared it was the home base of Vincent Germaine, Assistant Principal, Spear House. Edric felt it would have been more appropriately located in the basement of the building so others couldn't hear the screams of his impaled victims! The Gestapo had nothing on this man.

"Sit," his secretary, Mrs. Harris, said as soon as he entered. She was decrepitly old and withered. She looked like she had spent a lifetime sunbathing and smoking cigarettes, her skin wrinkled beyond anything Edric had ever seen. Her hair was thin and wispy, her fingers in no better shape. Edric shook off the eerie feeling she gave him and did as he was told, trying not to stare at her.

Edric sat for what seemed an eternity, listening to the old woman tap on her keyboard. He mastered his shaking hands only to find that his legs began to bounce with nervous energy. Once he settled his legs, his stomach began to make odd sounds. They were so loud that they had gained the attention of the elderly secretary who only glared at him as if to say, "Shut up, I'm working."

"Send him in," Germaine's voice called through the door. The skeleton lady raised her eyebrow at him and Edric rose and walked to the door. He looked back at her to gain permission to enter, but she had already returned to her typing without regard for what Edric was about to endure. Edric wondered if she was some poor little kid's grandmother. Imagine being that kid, he thought! The idea brought a small smile to his face, thinking that his life could always be worse. Edric pushed through the door to meet his fate with a renewed sense of calm.

"Sit," Mr. Germaine ordered.

Edric did as he was told. The seat was a small plastic one that looked like it had been dredged from the leftovers of an abandoned elementary school. Again, Edric smirked. The man and his secretary had one thing in common; they were both curt and rude, he thought. He waited for Germaine to begin, but the man had his head buried in some paperwork on his desk.

"Do you know why you are here?" Germaine asked, finally looking directly at him.

"No," Edric admitted.

Germaine leaned back in his massive black leather office chair and placed his hands together in the shape of a pyramid. "No idea?" he asked again, eyebrow raised, suggesting that Edric may well have been lying.

"No," Edric repeated, shrugging his shoulders this time.

Germaine seemed to study him for a while before he spoke again. "Do you have a cell phone?" he asked.

"Yes," Edric responded and reached into his pocket to take it out before Germaine even asked. Edric held his arm out towards the desk, palm up in supplication, offering the phone to the Assistant Principal.

Germaine pursed his lips and took the phone from Edric. He placed it on his desk, staring at it, though not touching it. "I believe you," he said.

Edric was stunned that a man of Germaine's chilling reputation would say such a thing. "You do?" he asked incredulously.

"I do," Germaine confirmed, leaning forward and resting his elbows on the desk. "Though, I think it may be important you understand why you are here, nevertheless."

Edric waited for him to speak, to explain it all. He could feel his shoulders relax, the tension flooding from them like a shattered dam.

"Did you know that you are a drug dealer?" Germaine asked, a hint of sarcasm peering through the words.

Edric's jaw dropped. He said nothing as his mind struggled to process the accusation.

"I received a letter, detailing your supposed activities on campus and off," Germaine said nonchalantly. "According to this, you make quite a bit of money dealing drugs at our school," he added, holding up a piece of paper and waving it in front of Edric. The print was facing away from him, so Edric was unable to read any of it, despite his best effort. Germaine tossed the letter into the garbage can and folded his arms, sitting back in his chair.

He already had his culprit. Germaine had watched the video footage of Brett DiVinceo planting something in Edric's gym locker. It didn't take a genius to figure out what he put there and who was behind the letter. Still, Germaine wanted to see if Edric had any idea of the animosity that another student held for him. The kid was naïve; totally ignorant of how the dangers of the real world functioned.

The two of them sat silent for a moment. Germaine waiting for a reaction that Edric was too flabbergasted to give. The silence was suddenly broken by the vibrating of Edric's phone.

"I'm glad to see you keep it on vibrate, at least," Germaine commented, reflecting on the least enforced and most ignored school policy of cell phone use. He picked up Edric's phone and glanced at the text he had just received. The name of the sender was familiar to him. "Passcode?" Germaine asked casually. A bead of sweat began forming in the corner of his widow's peak, despite the cool office air.

"5309," Edric responded without consideration for his privacy. He was certain of his innocence and growing more comfortable with the idea that even Germaine knew he was, as well. Germaine gave him a quizzical look at the four digit number and Edric smiled. "My dad's favorite song," Edric explained, the classic eighties tune of Jenny immediately taking over in his brain.

Germaine read the text to himself. *"You are right. This has to stop. I'll break it off when I see Vincent next and I'll talk to my dad. He will know what to do."* He read it again and then again. This wasn't happening! It couldn't happen! Jennifer was about to ruin him. Destroy his career. Jesus! He would probably go to prison, he thought, terror nipping at every extremity. Then, suddenly, he felt teeth rend his flesh, as if he were in the clutches of a great white shark who had found a fat seal. Germaine felt bile bubble up like water in an unwatched pot about to overflow onto the stovetop. Edric knew! He knew and was encouraging the girl to end it. Worse yet, he was telling her to expose it to her father. Germaine casually swiped his finger to the side and hit the red trash button, deleting the text strand. He realized that only solved a small portion of his problems. He had a plan for such an eventuality. He just never thought he would have to use it.

"Would you excuse me a moment," Germaine asked politely. Edric nodded as the Assistant Principal left and shut the door behind him. He was stunned by the man he had been confronted with. The pit bull was a poodle as far as he was concerned. Mr. Germaine had been nothing but nice, fair, and totally sane. Edric realized that he was still sitting forward, his shoulders raised. His whole body was taut, like he had just been in a car accident. He allowed himself a massive sigh, feeling his muscles slowly relax.

It was a long time before Mr. Germaine returned to his office. He held a stack of papers under his arm and Edric's phone in the other hand. He sat down and Edric noticed that the man looked a bit gray, as if he had ingested some bad shellfish or something.

"Are you okay?" Edric asked, concerned.

Germaine shuffled the papers, oblivious to Edric's question, making several stacks on his desk and facing them towards Edric.

"Mr. Germaine," Edric said, trying to get his attention again.

"Wha . . . Oh, I'm fine, thank you for asking," he finally replied, a plastic smile cementing across his face. "I just have some things I need you to sign," he added, handing Edric a pen.

"Sure," Edric said, excited to get this entire thing behind him.

Germaine pointed to lines here and there, flipped pages for Edric and excitedly jabbed his finger at a line Edric had missed. When he was all through, Mr. Germaine scooped up the paperwork and cradled it to his chest like he had saved an infant on train tracks from impending doom.

"So, what was all of that I had to sign?"

The question seemed to drive the man instantly insane. Mr. Germaine slammed the paperwork onto his desk and began screaming at Edric. Shocked, he leaned back in his tiny chair, almost tipping the thing over to avoid the onslaught being directed at him now. Germaine accused him of being a notorious drug dealer, of risking the lives of children and peddling death! Edric tried to defend himself only to be met with an increased rage he never imagined possible. Edric began to cry; he was confused and terrified.

When Germaine had finished his ranting and raving, the door to his office opened. The HS resource officer entered. He was a big massive Deputy Sheriff that Edric had only seen from afar. Edric read the name tag, Collins, and was hopeful the man could do something about the raving lunatic in front of him.

"Sir, please . . ." Edric begged rising up to his feet.

Collins slapped his hand on his shoulder and forced him back down into the little chair. He dropped a large zip-lock bag on the desk. Edric could not identify what was in the bag, but he knew enough to know it was drugs. Edric realized quickly that Collins was not here to help him, but rather Mr. Germaine.

"Deputy Collins, could you give me a moment with this young man," Germaine requested politely.

Collins nodded and left.

Germaine turned to his computer and opened a window. He pressed play on the screen and Edric watched as Deputy Collins silently removed the bag of drugs from his gym locker. "Before I bring him back in, there is something you need to understand," Germaine began. "This is happening. There is nothing you can do to stop it. These are simple facts that, the sooner you face it, the easier this will be on you."

Edric still didn't understand what was happening. He did, however, realize that whatever he signed wasn't going to be good for him. What he was being told to "face" remained a mystery, but it was growing darker by the second.

Germaine came around his desk and sat on the corner of it, looking down at Edric. "If you choose to fight this, you will lose. I will become angry. I will take that anger out on your father," he threatened, a sadistic smile forming at the corner of his mouth. "You know I can ruin his business with a few words. Imagine, the whole town thinking that your father allowed you to deal drugs right under his nose, out of his garage."

"That's not true!" Edric yelled, his anger overcoming his fear.

"Oh, but truth is a matter of perception," Germaine cackled. "You can disappear quietly and no one will suspect, or you can fight a public battle. What do you think the town will believe?" The Assistant Principal leaned towards him and added, "Who do you think they will believe?"

Edric opened his mouth to argue, but no words came out. His thoughts were of his father. He envisioned the garage as a ghost town, people shunning the place whether they believed the accusations or not. The town valued pretense over honor, image above friendship. He saw unpaid bills piled high, and his father's pride unable to ask for help as his world collapsed around him. With a word, Germaine could destroy everything the man had worked to build. Edric said nothing because he knew any fight was already lost.

Satisfied, Germaine opened the door and invited the school resource officer in again. He handed the man some paperwork and a sealed envelope. "This is for the Commandant. Make sure the driver understands," Germaine ordered. Collins nodded his enormous head and awaited further instructions.

"Deputy Collins will escort you from the school grounds," Germaine began. "You are being reassigned to another school. Deputy Collins will take you home so that you can inform your father of this."

Edric no longer tried to control his tears. He sobbed at the thought of having to tell his father. Innocent though he was, he would have to find a way to convince his dad not to fight this. There was only one way to do that though. Edric knew he would have to lie to him. He knew he would have to make his father believe it was true. Edric had to convince the man that his own son was a drug dealer. How he was ever going to do that was beyond him. He felt dizzy. Somehow, the world had been put into fast-forward and Edric was just trying to catch a glimpse of anything to help him understand.

"He will then take you to the bus depot where you will be reassigned. Any questions?"

Edric had thousands of them. He asked none.

"Goodbye, Mr. Davies. We shall not see each other again," Germaine turned his chair and looked out of his window. The tight lines of his perfectly manicured hair blending with the edges of the molding.

Edric rose and looked around like a man being escorted to the gas chamber. Germaine would not look at him. There was no mercy to be found in him anyway.

Through foggy eyes, Edric pleaded with Deputy Collins, but there was no hope of aid there either. They passed the decrepit old secretary at her desk. She kept her head down, tapping away at the keyboard, as if his life was not ending. He wanted to scream! Desperate for help, he did just that. "Help me!" Edric pleaded. He thought she might have stopped typing for a moment. A second or two at most passed, then the click of keys began again and her head never moved. She could not be bothered to look at him, much less provide comfort to the condemned.

Chapter 8

The Goodbye

Deputy Collins walked Edric to the door of his house and handed him the stack of papers that Mr. Germaine had given him. "Give these to your father," he instructed. "I'll give you ten minutes, no more," he added, as if he were doing a tremendous favor for Edric. Deputy Collins then proceeded to set a timer on his watch. He folded his burly arms and stood at the door, staring off into space.

Edric hesitated to open the door, knowing what would have to happen once he went inside. Collins glanced again at his watch and that spurred Edric to act. He burst into the home and yelled, "Dad!" There were so many should haves running through his head. His father should be home. The garage had been slow this month. Edric should have been at work by now. Mr. Moore would be worried, he thought. This day should not be happening. He ran into the kitchen. Not seeing his dad, he dashed towards the stairs and almost collided with his father.

"What are you doing home?" he asked, a twinge of concern in his voice. Then, his father noticed the puffy red eyes and Edric's body shaking. "What's happened? Are you all right? Edric, tell me what is going on," his father's words came faster than bullets fired from a machine gun.

Edric had not planned how to handle any of this. Even if he had, standing in front of his father now would have changed it all. He had promised himself that he would lie. That he would tell his father it was all true. Edric would do this to protect him. He would sacrifice himself for his father. It had been a good plan. Now, seeing his concern and love, those well-laid plans melted away. He felt his father's hands take his shoulders and drag him forward. Edric's face disappeared into the man's chest and his strong arms wrapped around him. "Whatever it is, I'm here for you," his father said as he kissed his son's head.

Edric gently nudged his way out of the embrace. Steeling himself, he went to speak, but, finding no words, he merely handed his father the paperwork. His father sat on the stairs and began to read. Edric glanced at the photo of his mom that his father blew a kiss to each morning. She had abandoned them when he was only three, but his father still loved her. He had never dated another woman in more than a decade. He had never allowed a mean word to be spoken about her. All he would ever say was, "It was hard on your mom. Sometimes, people don't know how to fight for the things they love, so they run. That doesn't make them bad people. They just need some strength and not everyone can find it all the time." As Edric grew older, he understood she was never coming back. His father was never one to admit that.

Edric stood, waiting for his father to read all of the paperwork that Edric had signed. All of the paperwork he should have read before signing it! Edric felt stabs of pain, like sword thrusts every time his father saw his son's signature on the page. He watched as his father rubbed his thumb over the fluid strokes of the pen in disbelief. When he had read it all he stood and looked at Edric. A long hard stare that seemed to compare the son in front of him to the boy he had read about in that paperwork. Finally, his father spoke, "We're gonna fight this."

"Dad, please don't argue this," Edric pleaded, knowing his father's character too well. Fighting for the people he loved was his defining characteristic.

"Is it true?" his father asked as if he had suddenly been hit in the gut by a baseball bat.

Edric felt that same thud as his father's face contorted into a mix of shame and disbelief. If he said nothing, it was as good as admitting that the accusations were true. He knew that was what he needed to do. His father would be crushed at the betrayal, but he would survive. He would lose his son, but maintain his business and home. If Edric denied the accusations, his father was sure to fight for him. As his father's eyes welled with tears, Edric succumbed. He had never lied to him before. Edric could not do so now. "Dad, you shouldn't even have to ask."

"Why, then?" his father screamed, confusion and frustration fueling his rage. "Tell me why I shouldn't fight this?"

"Germaine, that's why!" Edric yelled, raising his voice towards his father for the first time in his life. He softened it immediately, realizing that emotion was getting the best of both of them. Edric knew he had to be careful here. He had to find a way to make his father understand. He was trading a small portion of his life for that of his father's. That was a price his father would never allow, but one Edric would pay willingly. "You know what he is capable of," Edric paused and then added, "They have video of the drugs coming out of my locker."

His father paused at that. The town had a long history of victims when it came to Vincent Germaine. The Miller kid had killed himself after falling into the man's crosshairs. Information had leaked about his proclivities and few had any doubt about who had been behind it. The Coopers just up and moved when their boy was accused of plagiarism and pulled off the football team. Nobody won when they challenged this guy.

Edric watched his father's eyes as they processed the truth. "Dad, just let it go. Please. It will be okay, I promise." His father looked doubtfully at him. "Come on Dad, I'm sure it's just a different type of school. I'll be home soon." Then, Edric added the one thing he was certain would make his father think twice, "I want there to be something to come home to." They couldn't afford a legal battle. They couldn't afford the garage to go under.

His father took him into his arms and hugged him tightly. He kissed his son softly on the cheek. "When did you become such a brave man?" he asked, his voice full of pride. He kissed Edric again, this time on the forehead. There wasn't enough time or space for the affection the man felt for his only son. They meant the world to one another and it was difficult to find the words or actions to encompass those feelings in so fleeting a span of time. They fell towards one another again in a final hug. "I'll find a way, son. I promise. I'll find a way," he whispered.

"Don't," Edric replied. "Promise me, Dad."

They held the embrace. Their tears mingled as their arms separated; Edric stepped out of the house where Deputy Collins was waiting for him. Collins opened the back door of the patrol car and placed his meaty hand on the small of Edric's back, guiding him into the seat meant for criminals. A seat that would take him away from Mount Collier, for how long, he did not know.

He looked back at his father, standing in the doorway and mouthed, "Promise me," and then added, "I love you," to him. It would be the last time the two saw each other.

Chapter 9

The Empty Space

Meagan needed Monday to come. Now that it had finally arrived, she was devastatingly disappointed. Edric wasn't waiting for her at her locker this morning. His desk was empty. Meagan made three passes past the door of his third period math class just to be sure he hadn't come in late. She hadn't heard from him all weekend. None of her texts were responded to. She had called his cell three times and even left a message at his house. All she knew was that he had been called to Germaine's office on Friday afternoon and had not been seen or heard from since.

"I heard he got expelled," a rich girl named Tasha announced to the entourage that surrounded her locker. She pulled her books out and handed them to one of the hanger-on's and then checked her reflection in the small mirror stuck to the interior of her locker. She remarked with satisfaction, "You know it has something to do with that game performance, right? He couldn't be that good."

The emphasis on the word *"that"* cut at Meagan. He was *"that"* good. Is. She tried to correct her thought process. Is. He wasn't past tense. This would all have a simple explanation. She was sure of it. Meagan stormed past the gaggle of gossipers as they stared at her.

"That was his girlfriend," one whispered.

"Bet she knows what he was up to," another pronounced.

Meagan quickened her pace, feeling a thousand eyes pawing at her, seeking, searching, trying to see something that just wasn't there. She began to run. She felt desperate to escape from a thousand staring eyes. It was a gauntlet of claws, the wealthy and poor both glaring in judgment, tearing and rending at her flesh. At Mount Collier, they all turned on each other like ravenous animals, seeking the first sign of weakness to attack.

Meagan burst through the bathroom door and headed into the first stall. She leaned against the wall and began to cry. The judgment of her middle school peers seemed to waft through the air. It followed her wherever she ran. Meagan's confusion and fear pummeled her. The bell for the period change rang. She could hear the shuffle of students in the hallway heading to and fro. Her chest ached, but her sobs were masked by the noise in the hall.

She began to flick the charm that she wore on her wrist. It was a simple silver heart strung on a red elastic band. It was cheaply made, but Edric had bought it for her as their date ended. Meagan knew he had spent the last of his money on it. Gently, she held the heart between her fingers, remembering how sweet he was to her. He made her feel like a princess.

Meagan spent the next two periods in that bathroom stall hiding from the world. Eventually, she would have to face the questions that had no answers and the students who secretly thrilled at her pain. All she wondered now was, "Where are you Edric? What happened to you?"

~

"Edric Davies?" Mr. Duncan repeated the roll call again. The man was in his late sixties and held tightly to his regimented ways. Kids often referred to the elderly history teacher as "Flunkin' with Duncan," because you could get away with almost anything in his class, but the tests were impossible. Yet, his stories were fascinating. The man knew more about history than any library this side of the Mississippi. It was easily Frank's favorite class. Frank allowed an eerie grin to expand across his face as he recalled that Edric often saw himself as a competitor for top marks in the class. Another fringe benefit of eliminating his friend from the school. Frank would be unchallenged at the top of the class now, an unrivaled king among pawns.

That wasn't the main reason for seeing Edric off, though. The central impetus for his actions now dominated his thoughts. That target was currently missing. Frank's eyes lingered on an empty desk two rows over and three seats up. Meagan was also missing from class. He listened as Mr. Duncan called her name, "Meagan Dumas," twice, before marking her absent. He had no idea how long Edric would be out. Had Germaine suspended him for a week? A month? Maybe for the rest of the year? Frank could only cross his fingers and hope he had that long. Until he was certain, he would treat time as a precious commodity. Frank intended on using every second wisely.

His plan was simple. Be there for Meagan in her grief. Fuel whatever rumor surfaced about Edric through his less than honorable cohorts. Charm her. Buy her things Edric couldn't even afford to dream of. When Edric returned, it would be too late for him.

His thoughts turned to the boy who thought him a friend. Edric was nice. Kind and caring. Hard working, though naïve. All the qualities that Frank had used to argue in favor of Edric's friendship with his father. Still, Frank could think of no great man in history who held such qualities. Greatness was fueled by ambition, prestige, cunning, and strength of action. "You should never have played in my world," he thought.

It was his world. Frank shaped it to his will. If events did not unfold to his liking, he manipulated them until they did. Money bought influence. Influence brought power. Power aided in the growth of wealth. Control that cycle and you could control the world. To Frank, there was no greater lesson in history than that.

He listened to Mr. Duncan's lesson on Abraham Lincoln as Commander-in-Chief. He noted how Lincoln was careful to ensure that the rebels fired the first shots of the war, rallying men to his cause of preserving the union. Lincoln boldly suspended the writ of habeas corpus, hired and fired more generals than Frank could count and shrewdly expanded the goals of the war when it served his ends. Lincoln's words were silk, but his actions were often steel.

Frank took the lesson to heart. Be silky in the eyes of Meg, steely in the hearts of his enemies. There was just one problem. She was missing.

"Mr. Duncan, may I use the bathroom?" Frank asked, spearing the man's lecture just as it reached a crescendo. The man waved him out of the room and Frank scurried to the door. He hit the quiet hallways and wondered, "Where are you, Meg?"

~

Brett DiVinceo was on a celebratory tour today. His Monday had started like any other one, until Frank had texted him that Edric was not in school today. "It worked?" he had responded. Frank had called him and torn him apart about putting stupid ideas in writing. Still, even getting chastised by someone younger and smaller than he was could not dampen his day. The letter had worked. It had led the administration to search the locker where he planted the drugs Frank had provided. He was sure of it. Edric Davies was suspended, maybe even expelled. He was off the basketball team and out of the way! Normally, he would have pounded anybody who talked to him the way Frank had, but the guy had found a way to rid him of a problem that he couldn't punch his way through. That was worth a bit of patience in Brett's mind.

Brett had decided to cut a few classes and spend the afternoon in the middle school cafeteria. He headed down the passageway during pass time to avoid being noticed. The central hallway allowed for shared use of the gym, office, and auditorium space. It also allowed free access to both campuses, especially if one was willing to skip a few classes. Still, it wasn't without a few risks. Mr. Germaine was always on the prowl. Being caught by him would be a nasty bite, but Brett felt emboldened today. He wasn't about to get caught on this most glorious of occasions!

~

Vincent Germaine had his secretary clear his schedule for today. He wanted to be out amongst the students with his ear to the ground. Germaine had found that the greatest currency in the entire world was information. With it, one could predict the probable future and prepare for its coming. Without it, a man traveled blindly through the world, exposed to every danger.

He gathered that information by listening. One could slither through the halls and hear who hated whom. He could linger around a corner and learn the weekend plans of the moneyed and well-connected of the town. It was always helpful to have such trivialities available when some arrogant and powerful board member tried to cut off the upward mobility of his career. To be able to share a nugget at just the right moment could shift the course of the future, his future. Germaine made information his stock and trade.

That was how he had come to own the loyalty of Deputy Collins. The man had found himself hopelessly involved in a tryst with a young, attractive art teacher. When Germaine assembled the video footage in a montage that would have made even the boldest man blush, he invited Deputy Collins into his office for a viewing. It was easy enough for the law enforcement officer to understand what Germaine wanted and what Mrs. Collins would receive if Germaine's demands were not met.

He had roamed the halls during pass time. He popped in on those classes well-known for group work or cooperative learning where students would have time and opportunity to discuss topics far from their lessons. He learned that Thomas Kenny spent Saturday night drunk on his father's whiskey. There was also a party this coming weekend at the Johnson's house as they were away in Munich for the month. The house staff lived in fear of the daughter, a girl named Melissa. Stories that could all be useful given the circumstances, though not what he was seeking. He had yet to hear anything about Edric Davies.

He was certain that the next location would bear fruit. Germaine headed to the cafeteria. On a normal day, he would hover around the edges of the large open hall. When keen sight or hearing would lead him to easy prey, he would swoop in and remove the student. Once isolated in his office, the child would spill their guts and Germaine would consume anything of value for use at a later date. Today would be different. He hoped he would not have to pull a kid aside for discussing something connected to Edric Davies. As soon as he walked in, his ears perked up.

"Yeah, he's not absent, you know," Brett DiVinceo blew so much wind he could sail Columbus's entire fleet. Germaine knew him to be a braggart and a buffoon, though a talented athlete. He was also likely behind the letter that had accused Davies of dealing drugs on school grounds. Regardless, he could prove that Brett had broken into and planted the evidence in the gym locker. Brett was guilty of something at the very least, though outing the boy did not serve his purposes. Germaine pondered that series of events and wondered if he owed the boy a debt of gratitude instead. Nevertheless, he went to remove the upperclassman from the middle school cafeteria where he did not belong.

"Davies was doing dope," Brett feigned a whisper, though his voice was as loud as usual. Germaine stopped in his tracks and turned from the conversation before he was spotted. Maybe the rumor mill would serve him well, he thought. Several gawky teens surrounded Brett at the table. The boy sat atop the table like a king ruling over his court. "No way he coulda been that good without a little juice in the veins, you know what I'm sayin'?"

Brett did not linger long at the table. He moved fluidly through the cafeteria as if he not only belonged in it, but owned it. The boy was oblivious to Germaine's presence and to the danger he was in, if the Assistant Principal decided to act. He moved from table to table, speaking to whoever might listen. His celebrity status as an upperclassman gave his words undeserved weight. He never lingered long at any one place or with any particular student. He navigated the various territorial waters of the cafeteria like a skilled captain and the engine that was Brett's speech left a wake of gossip and wonder behind.

Germaine lingered far enough behind to hear the various reactions to the seeds that Brett planted. Some grew into tall oaks as students bobbed their heads in agreement and said they always knew there was something fishy about that performance. Other seeds wilted, or barely grew, with students commenting on Brett's arrogance or idiocy in equal measure. Yet, Germaine was growing more and more satisfied that his name and the name of Jennifer Kelly was nowhere to be found on the lips of students. No connection whatsoever was being made to the disappearance of Davies to either of them. He was unafraid, but would remain vigilant, watching and waiting for anything that might turn up.

Mr. Germaine was not the only one watching Brett flit from table to table. Chris took note of the visit from the upperclassman as well. He also noted how Mr. Germaine, a man who was well-known for raining down indiscriminate justice on anyone who violated the rules, watched the same scene unfold. That he did nothing but watch, confused Chris. That was a question that needed answering.

Of all of the questions swirling around the campus, Chris had scant more information than other students. Chris knew full well who was behind what had happened to Edric. He could also pinpoint the why. As the rumor of Edric's drug involvement permeated the cafeteria, Chris was already beginning to regret egging Brett on about Edric. Hopefully, Edric would be back tomorrow and all the drama would be behind them. Somehow Chris didn't believe that would be the case. Brett was too stupid to attack Edric with anything but his fists. Still, Chris couldn't shake the feeling that Brett was somehow involved in all of this.

What had happened to Edric, how it was done and when it would end were all mysteries to him. Chris didn't like mysteries. He liked solutions and he was determined to find the answers to his questions. He knew just the two guys to start with.

~

John Winston was sure he knew what happened to Edric. He had been a custodian at the school since long before Vincent Germaine started as a teacher. He was here when the jerk angled his way into getting the Assistant Principal job. Winston had remarked to his wife that with this guy, it wasn't who he knew but rather what he knew, that got him the job. Germaine was a collector of sorts. He rooted around like a pig through the trash, collecting all the dirt he could on people and then used it as leverage. Winston was certain that Germaine was behind Edric's sudden fall from grace.

The custodian jangled his keys until he found the right one and opened the Assistant Principal's office. Winston went about his daily chores, emptying the waste bin and making sure the windows were locked. Looking at a photo of Vincent Germaine and his fiancé, he grumbled a few words that he would never have said in front of the students. Winston picked up the man's coffee cup, with the platitude of "Teachers make everything possible," and studied it for a moment. Then, he reared his head back and made a guttural noise as he worked the phlegm from deep within his nose. He let it fall slowly from his mouth, swirling the cup around as it drained from his lips. Winston looked inside the mug. Satisfied that the owner would be none the wiser, he placed it back on the desk and turned off the lights. "For you, kid," the old man muttered, locking the door behind him.

Chapter 10

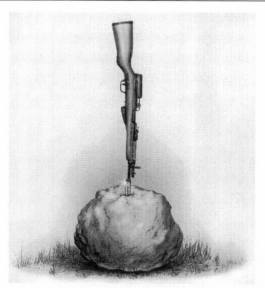

The New Kid

Deputy Collins had escorted Edric to the bus garage in silence. They waited together in silence. Edric boarded the bus alone. The driver simply ignored him. Edric had tried to engage the man in conversation, if for no other reason than to calm his own nerves, but the portly and somewhat disheveled driver never did more than grunt at the occasional passing car. "How long is the drive?" Edric asked. "That guy drives like a nutcase!" He tried to find common cause with the driver to no avail. After several failed attempts, Edric surrendered and sat back in the uncomfortable black plastic seat as his fear and confusion took root.

"Why?" Edric wondered to himself. It was the question he had asked a thousand times over the last several hours. He was exhausted. He had slept little on the long trip. Edric could not even begin to calculate how long they had been driving. Still, "why" was the only word that seemed to resonate in his mind. Mr. Germaine knew he was innocent; he was sure of that. He had said it. Then, just as quickly, Germaine had threatened his dad's livelihood. That was something Edric was certain of too. Germaine was ruthless and powerful enough to destroy his father's business. He would bring low everything that his father had sacrificed to build. Edric signed the confession to protect his dad, but none of this answered his question. "Why?" Edric muttered aloud, knowing full well that he would get no answer.

The small bus came to a stop in front of a thick stone wall and the door squealed open. Edric took a deep breath and rose slowly, his cramped muscles fighting him every step of the way. He walked slowly towards the door. Before he exited, Edric turned to the driver and said, "Thank you," more from habit than actual appreciation. The driver grunted and looked away, muttering something under his breath. Edric swore it sounded like "Good luck, kid." His feet dragged as he stepped from the bus onto the cracked concrete sidewalk. Edric's eyes traveled along the ground to the wall before him.

Flattened rocks, stacked upon each other, stretched at least twenty feet into the air. It was daylight again. Edric had travelled through the night, but he could not see the sun rise beyond the thick stones. Those at the bottom seemed to strain to hold the weight of their compatriots above them. They looked old and worn, gray and cracked with age. Yet, there was clear strength to them still. They held a formidable wall on their shoulders. It seemed that no matter the burden asked of them, these stones would endure it. Edric kneeled down and brushed his hand over one of the lowest stones. It was smooth to the touch despite its appearance. He tried to jiggle it a bit, out of curiosity or fear, but it might as well have been cemented in place.

"Stand up, boy!"

Edric was stunned by the voice of the man who stood before him. A massive dark-skinned African-American man with a square jaw and arms thicker than Edric's body stood before him with arms folded. He wore a dark gray uniform with creases that could cut diamonds and a broad-rimmed black hat pulled low over his piercing eyes. Military chevrons on his sleeves denoted the rank of sergeant, but his bearing and demeanor suggested rank closer to a God. A name tag over his right chest read "Sampson". Edric smiled at the literary reference to this massive giant of a man. Clearly, his strength was not from his hair, Edric mused, remembering the story of Sampson and Delilah. Sampson's hard scowl had told Edric that he did not share his amusement.

"I said, stand up, boy!" Sampson yelled louder this time, his voice deepening into a gravelly holler. Edric snapped to his feet and stood at attention. Sampson smiled, flashing a set of pearly white teeth that when contrasted to his dark skin made him look like a tiger flashing his fangs at night. Sampson circled Edric, growing closer to him with each pass. Instinctively, Edric closed his eyes, waiting for the tiger to pounce upon his prey.

"Follow me, boy," Sampson ordered. Edric opened his eyes to catch the end of a satisfied smile. Then, Sampson took off at a brisk march, towards the gate. Edric followed a few steps behind trying to match the quickening pace of the giant in front of him.

As they reached the black wrought iron gate, Sampson came to a halt and Edric followed suit. Unsure of what they were waiting for, Edric used his eyes to search the area, fearful to turn his neck that Sampson might choose to break it! There was a small bronze colored plaque attached to the stone wall on his left. In large gold letters was inscribed, "Shatterly's Obedience and Drill Fraternity." Edric was more interested in the slogan emblazoned underneath it though. "Rebuilding young men through hard work and strict discipline since 1843." Sampson looked over his shoulder at Edric and flashed his teeth again. "Welcome to the Chateau D'If, boy." He let out a forced, sardonic chuckle and added, "Ain't a matter of if you break, just when . . ." A loud click shook Edric and the black gates opened. Sampson moved forward again and Edric followed. Edric looked up at the imposing stone structure in the distance. He couldn't quite get a handle on what it reminded him of. The small windows, set back into the thick stone, made Edric think of a European castle. Yet, the long, symmetrical aspects of the structure and the ivy that grew up its walls had Edric thinking of a historic college. He heard a slow squeal that reached a crescendo as the gates slammed shut behind him. That's when Edric saw the thick iron bars that shadowed each of the windows. Chateau D'If wasn't a castle or a college, it was a dungeon.

He kept it together as they walked to the massive stone structure. Edric even held back his tears when they walked down the sanitized white hallways punctuated by dark stained wooden doors. Edric knew he would be hidden from the world behind one of those foreboding barriers and he shuddered at the thought of it. It was when that wooden door opened that Edric began to feel his grip on his emotions slipping.

Sampson pointed to a neatly made bed with a dark blue wool blanket strangling the mattress. There were two sets of bunk beds in the room. Each had a tall gray locker standing sentinel at the sides. Other than that, the room looked as if it had long ago been abandoned. Sampson's long, dark finger extended out and lingered in the air like the Grim Reaper pointing towards a grave. "That one is yours," he said. "Your class schedule will be delivered later today and your uniform issue will be arranged once your schedule has been processed," Sampson added as he inspected the room, opening the lockers one by one. Edric saw they were all arranged in the same way. There was nothing to suggest their owners had any personality of their own. "Your roommates are in class now. When they return, maybe they will show you how to stay out of trouble." His smile at the word trouble made Edric tremble.

The wooden door clicked closed and Edric was alone. He stood in the center of the room and looked around. It wasn't a cell. It didn't have bars. Try as he may, Edric could not convince himself that this place was not a dungeon. The room was small, probably only ten feet by twelve feet. It felt cramped, despite the bunk beds and small drab lockers. There was no window and that seemed to make it all the drearier. He was surrounded by four off white concrete walls. He might as well have been in the basement of some castle off the coast of France. No one would find him. No one would ever know what happened to him. He was alone, countless miles from anyone who had ever known him.

He sat on the lower bunk, trying to bounce, but it was rigid and gave not one inch. It was solid, like the walls. Solid like the hearts of those who ran this miserable place. Edric felt like he had been encased in stone and buried alive!

He rose and paced the tight confines from wall to wall. It felt more like a cell than a room. Edric's eyes darted around, studying every crater in the concrete blocks that made up his prison. Every moment brought him closer to the inevitable realization; there was no escape.

~

Edric awoke to the sound of mumbling in the hallway. He had no idea how long he had slept. Disoriented and foggy, he could hear the muffled sounds coming closer. He rose, tried to straighten his wrinkled clothes and made his best attempt to stand up straight.

The door swung open and three uniformed boys with close-cropped hair entered. The largest one who had entered first stopped when he saw Edric and the two others ran into him like cars on a freeway. "New kid," the second one observed, moving around the mountainous one in front of him. "Fresh meat, ha!" the last one chuckled as he moved towards Edric. The big one grabbed his arm and shook his head. The joker ignored Edric and moved off to his own locker.

Edric tried to look presentable, but there was little hope of hiding his fatigue. He sat on the bed and watched the three boys as they prepared for bed. His stomach rumbled. He needed little reminder that he had nothing to eat all day. He brought his hand to his belly and pushed on it, hoping to suppress the sound.

"They like to make you starve the first few days," the big one said, not looking at him. "When you get to the cafeteria, they will find reasons to pull you out or toss your food." He turned and pointed his finger at Edric. "It's a mind game man. Don't let them get to you."

Edric shook his head to say he understood, but there was little of what was happening to him that he could comprehend.

"Mr. Warm and Fuzzy over there is Maquet," he said, pointing to the one that looked as if he were a lion, eying Edric like a wounded zebra. "That's Nichols, the class clown. Don't follow his lead, ever," he emphasized with a smile. Then, he reached out his massive hand and introduced himself, "Manente."

Edric shook it, feeling his hand compressed by the powerful grip. "Edric. Edric Davies," he replied.

"Well, let's get you sorted out, shall we?" Manente said, opening Edric's locker.

They spent the next hour discussing how everything needed to look and the things that would get Edric in trouble. The list was long, strange and almost impossible to comply with. Every time Edric felt he had a grip on it, Nichols would chime in with something Manente forgot. The fold of a shirt, the length of a crease, the location of your toothbrush, it all mattered. Which of course led Edric to wonder, "Why does this all matter?"

"It doesn't," Nichols laughed, "but, if you don't want to go see the Commandant every two days, you will do it." Nichols raised his shirt to show a series of massive, dark bruises. "I know him really well," he snorted. "Maquet says this one looks like a map of Italy," he said, his finger tracing around one of the larger bruises on his midsection. Edric didn't see Italy at all. They looked like storm clouds that all came together, darkening as they did.

"Newbie can't see it. No surprise there," Maquet said sarcastically, not lifting his head from his pillow.

"Don't mind him, Davies," Nichols said, tossing his shirt at him. "The D'If sucks. It sucks way worse when you are like Maquet here and you gotta endure this Hell-hole without friends."

"My choice, not yours, clown," Maquet fired back as the shirt impacted and careened around Nichols' face.

A knock at the door had each of them snap to attention. Edric emulated them as Manente granted permission to enter. A uniformed student, older than they were, entered and gave a cursory glance at Nichols. Nichols suppressed all but a hint of his smile. The animosity coming from the elder of the two permeated the room. "Your schedule, boy," he said, handing a sheet of paper to Edric. "Follow it," he ordered and turned to leave. Before he did, he gave another glance at Nichols that suggested whatever was between them was far from over.

"He's still pissed," Manente observed after the door had been closed for several seconds.

"Serves him right, pompous jerk," Nichols responded without a hint of remorse.

"What did you do?" Edric asked.

"He beat him. You don't beat upperclassmen here without paying a price for it," Maquet added.

"Not that you would know," Manente fired back. "He didn't just beat him, he annihilated him. He knocked him out cold in the first round." Manente fist bumped his friend and blew it up, celebrating the victory again.

"Of course, Nichols behaved like a two-year-old and pranced around like he had been crowned world champion. Hence, the visit to the Commandant," Maquet poked the air, popping Nichols bubble a bit.

"Let's take a look at that schedule, Davies," Nichols changed the subject.

Edric handed him the piece of paper. Nichols studied it with Manente looking over his shoulder. Their faces became screwed into odd shapes, an almost synchronism warping as their eyes moved down the sheet. Finally, they both finished and looked at one another. Neither said a word as they handed the schedule back to Edric.

"Is it bad?" Edric asked.

While Manente seemed to search for the right words, Nichols blurted, "Oh, you seriously peed in someone's Cheerios, man."

"Why?" Edric asked, confused.

Manente took the lead this time, "You are not assigned to any class with any of us. You are utterly on your own. They don't do that here, ever. Plus, you have been assigned the Mad Priest for three classes. They mean to bury you."

Edric sat on the bed and studied the schedule. The only name that appeared on his schedule three times was Lt Col. Abraham Feinstein, PhD. He must be the one they called the Mad Priest. "Why?" Edric asked. He was growing tired of that question and the never ending mysteries behind it.

"I don't know, Dude, but the message is clear," Nichols said, hopping into his bed. "They just told every student here that you are poison." He rolled over, turning his back on Edric.

Manente patted him on the shoulder. "Report for uniform issue at 0500. Supply is the building at the top of the hill, #6." He looked at him and tucked his lips into his mouth. Edric thought he might say something more, but Manente just turned and headed to bed.

"Thank you," Edric called to him. He didn't respond. Edric fell back into his bed and stared at the bunk above him. He could hear Maquet's breathing. He was surrounded by three other boys, but Edric felt utterly alone. The room went dark as Manente turned off the last light. There was no window, no moonlight to guide Edric through the darkness. Worse, there was no hope of sunrise. Edric sobbed into his pillow again and for the first time prayed that his father would fight for him, that Mr. Moore or Frank would pay for a lawyer for him and that Meagan would wait for him.

Chapter 11

The Hard Choices

Meagan used her hair as both an offensive weapon and a defensive barrier. Usually, those long brown tresses helped her to get the attention she sought. More often than not, it was a sword that cleaved through the day. A flick of those thick healthy locks of hair, the bounce of a few loose curls and girls would tell her how pretty she was and boys would forget what they were saying. Today she needed a thick and impenetrable wall. Meagan sat with her hands cupped under her chin. Her face was obscured in the darkness her hair provided. Every strand acted as a barrier to the world around her. Though no one could see in, she knew that her hair provided little privacy. It was more of a "go away" signal than what she had really wanted; a place to disappear.

She sniffled and sobbed. Her shoulders bounced as her chest heaved. Rivers of tears ran down her face, her hands, her arms, a small reservoir forming at her elbows. She could surely drown in them in time. This, she could not hide from the world. No amount of hair could shield her grief. There were no ramparts tall enough or thick enough to hide her confusion.

"You okay, Sweetie?" Karen asked loudly, dropping her tray on the table and wrapping her arm around Meagan. Meagan instinctively dropped her head on her friend's shoulder. Even though she knew Karen's concern wasn't genuine, Meagan needed some comfort and she would take whatever was offered. Karen was putting on the show for their peers. The "I'm a supportive friend" role was an expectation that Karen understood came with her social station. Still, she maneuvered to get maximum attention and benefit from it. She could have spoken to Meagan in the morning when they had passed near her locker. Karen could have talked to her in PE class. No. She waited until now. Lunch time provided the largest audience for her to show how good a friend she was to poor heartbroken Meagan. This was an act all too familiar to her. Meagan now regretted how many times she had performed the same show, on the same stage.

Karen asked all the right questions, said all the right things. There were hugs, long and tight. She brushed aside Meagan's hair and told her how beautiful she was. Meagan politely rejected the offers of food and fun as she could not bear much more of the act. When Karen's ponytailed hair smacked Meagan's cheek for the third time she knew something was up. Meagan realized that Karen was performing for someone in particular. She waited and the next time Karen whipped her head around and glanced in the same direction.

Two boys watched the charade intently. She knew both of them well enough. The first was Brett DiVinceo, a freshman who had spent all week in the middle school cafeteria gloating over Edric's disappearance. Meagan knew he was the source of the drug rumors that students had lapped up like thirsty dogs. He had to explain away why Edric had been so much better than him. That was a simple conclusion for him. It could never have been that Edric was just better. The second was Edric's best friend, Frank Macintyre. He had no idea what had happened to Edric either. It had been a week since anyone had heard from him. The teachers said he was no longer enrolled at Mount Collier. That was all they knew or all they would tell. Both she and Frank had called Edric's house only to get voicemail every time.

Meagan had begun to ignore Karen's feigned attempts at comfort. She focused instead on her voyeurs. Brett's face was the direct inverse of Frank's. Where one brooded and frowned, the other smiled and celebrated. Meagan was beginning to understand that she wasn't the only one suffering.

"Hey, Karen," Meagan interrupted her friend's third variation of "you are too good for him," before she could finish it, "I really need to talk to Frank for a sec, okay?"

Karen relented and Meagan headed over to the table where Frank sat and Brett stood triumphantly surrounded by his fair-weather friends. Meagan sneered at Brett and he returned the look full force. She stood in front of Frank and waited for him to acknowledge her. He kept his head down to hide his growing smile. His pained act had made her believe he was as hurt as she was. Their shared pain would be the foundation for a new type of relationship. One in which he planned on helping her forget Edric Davies ever existed.

"Frank," Meagan said, trying to get his attention.

"Hey, Meg."

"You okay?"

"Yeah," Frank made sure his voice was as inauthentic as possible.

"You hear anything different?"

"Nope," he answered.

Meagan waited a moment and then went to leave. "Okay. Bye then."

Frank had been patient. Now, like a coiled snake, he struck. "I was thinking about going to the mall tonight. Kinda drowning my sorrows a bit." He hesitated a second and then added, "You wanna come with?"

Meagan seemed taken aback by the request. Frank immediately began to wonder if he had struck too soon. He watched as she looked over her shoulder towards Karen. She glanced back towards Brett and back again at Karen. She was torn and Frank could see it clearly.

"Sorry. I didn't mean to put you in a spot. Maybe another time," Frank said, holding up his hands in submission.

"No," Meagan said quickly. "No. It's okay."

"I was going to do some of the VR rides and get something to eat. Maybe even a movie," Frank proffered. He watched as Meagan squirmed, knowing she could never afford all of that. After all, nothing stayed secret in Mount Collier, especially messy divorces and financial ruin. "My treat. Say around six?" he added with a devilish smile.

Meagan's shoulders seemed to ease at that. She grinned and accepted his offer, "That should be fun. I'll see you there." Then, without thinking about it, she flicked her hair over her shoulder and looked back at him, smiling as she did. It was the first time she looked forward to something since Edric had disappeared.

~

This was a day Jennifer was dreading. "Jennifer Kelly to see Mr. Germaine," she announced herself as she always did. The old hag kept their dance predictable and gave her the same sneer that usually accompanied her arrival.

"Sit," the secretary ordered. Jennifer stood, like always, just to annoy her.

Germaine quickly ushered her into his office and closed the door. Jennifer sat in the small chair that had once been occupied by Edric. She rocked from side to side, trying to find a comfortable spot on the chair, finally giving up after a few unsuccessful attempts. Germaine studied her intently as he puzzled out whether or not she had really decided to out their relationship. The two glared at each other like stone-faced poker players, neither wanting to show their cards first.

Jennifer suspected that Vincent was behind the disappearance of Edric. She desperately wanted to ask what he had done, but the voice in her head was screaming at her not to. Jennifer understood who Vincent was when they had begun whatever this was. He was powerful, decisive and had a vicious streak that made him dangerous. She had never known anyone like him and the allure was more than she could bear. The first time he kissed her was still fresh in her mind and would be one of the finest memories of her life. He wasn't a high school boy. He was a man who knew just how to treat a lady. Yet, she was under no allusions as to what he would do to protect himself if he felt threatened. She didn't know how it had happened, but she was sure that Edric had confronted him and he had swiftly removed Edric from the board like a knight would sweep away a pawn.

As if he could read her mind, Germaine held up an unmarked envelope. Jennifer gasped and asked, "Is that it?"

Germaine nodded but he didn't hand her the envelope. He put it in his desk drawer instead. Jennifer leaned forward, as if proximity would reveal the contents of the envelope. The desk drawer slammed shut and an angry scowl appeared on Germaine's face. Jennifer knew in that instance that her suspicions were correct. "Oh, Edric," she thought, "Why did you have to do something so stupid?"

"Seems we need to have a talk," Germaine began, every word laced with venom.

Jennifer struggled to control her bladder and tried to put on a brave face. "W . . . why?" she asked, feigning ignorance.

Germaine smiled as her fear fed his arrogance. "You are smarter than that, Jennifer," he replied.

Jennifer did not know what to say, and so, said nothing.

"This is over. We both knew it had to end at some point," Germaine stated coldly. "You understand it was going to end only one way."

It was a statement, not a question. Jennifer nodded. Somewhere deep inside she had known that, but she had hoped for something different. She had allowed herself naïve fantasies that had included marriage and children. Now that the moment had arrived, she couldn't imagine how she had ever thought it would be another way. It made her angry. "You just expect me to stay silent?" Her voice almost stayed strong the entire way, cracking just at the last word.

"Yes," he answered slowly. His voice was calm and self-assured. She wondered how long he had planned for this moment. His fingers tapped at the edge of his desk, just above the drawer where he had stuffed the envelope.

Jennifer felt as if she had been maneuvered into a corner without her even noticing. She was the mouse in his trap, but she was only now just understanding that. She could at least make a grab for the cheese. Her eyes floated down towards his fingers. "If I keep my mouth shut . . ." she said, letting the sentence go unfinished.

"You know that I believe in your application and I would advocate for you to receive the scholarship. If, however, your judgement was to be called into question, then I don't know if I could convince the committee that you were the right candidate."

Jennifer took a long, slow breath. Vincent Germaine held her future in his hands. She could expose their relationship. He would deny it. What evidence did she have? Her mind combed through their time together. She was searching for anything that might tie them together. There was nothing. Not one text. Not a card or note. No pictures. It would be her word against his. Even if people believed her, he would strong-arm or bribe the right person and her reputation would be destroyed. She would disappear like Edric. Worse, she would be left to face her shame. He had planned for this moment from the beginning.

Jennifer rose, her legs shaky and weak. She faced the man she thought she had loved. She stared into his eyes. They were the same eyes she had been so enamored with a short while ago. Now they were cold, calculating, without the warmth she had once found there. There had never been anything real at all. Top of her class, brilliant young mind, and she had been played like a fiddle. It made her feel angry. It made her feel ashamed. It made her feel desperate. She walked to the door and opened it. Turning, Jennifer said, "Thank you for your help and support with the scholarship committee, Mr. Germaine." She walked from the office hoping to never see it or him again.

~

Mr. Moore entered the same door after getting the same phone call. It was the third night in a row and he had hoped he wouldn't have to do this again. In the last few weeks, he had been called to one bar or another more than a dozen times against his will. Yet, here he was. Again.

"Thanks for coming to get him," the bartender muttered from across the empty room.

Mr. Moore wrapped his arm around the lone patron and helped him from his barstool. The man's knees buckled and Moore propped him up, steadying him as they walked. He opened the door and let the darkness inside. The warm night air seemed to wake the man a bit and he stood a bit taller.

"I wish you wouldn't do this," Moore lamented. Before he could answer, the voice of the bartender rang out from inside, "See you tomorrow, Mr. Davies."

Chapter 12

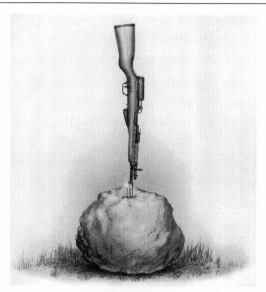

The Meeting

Edric stood at attention in front of the Commandant's desk. He was alone in the office and had been for a long time. He was told to stand here and wait by Sampson, and so he did. Edric had spent the last several weeks in utter despair. He went to his classes because he had to, he mustered with the students because they forced him to. Otherwise, he cried in his bed or slept. He imagined that his visit to the Commandant today would have to do with his attitude. He remembered the bruises on Nichols, but part of him refused to believe the stories.

The door opened and the Commandant walked in and sat at his desk. He did not acknowledge Edric's existence. Slapping a folder on the desk and opening it, the man scanned the documents. Edric heard breathing behind him. Someone else had entered the room with the Commandant and stood at the door. He did not know who was there, but he did sense it probably wasn't good for him.

The Commandant was in his fifties with short cropped hair hiding a receding hairline. He was, like almost all of the staff at Shatterly's, in excellent shape with dense muscle. The man was infinitely confident and just as cold. His dark eyes danced across the file and Edric was able to glance that his name appeared at the top of the paper the man held in his hands. He looked at three other documents before he spoke a word.

"Welcome to Shatterly's Drill and Obedience Academy, Mr. Davies," he said, not looking up from the file. "My apologies that I could not greet you sooner. This job can be very demanding of my time. As this is our first meeting, it is important for us to establish a particular dynamic that will dominate any future meetings we might have."

He nodded his head slightly and Edric felt a stabbing pain alight through his back. He fell to his knees, the pain spreading into his every extremity. Sampson's big hand grabbed him by the shoulder and lifted him back to his feet. Edric wobbled a bit, trying to find his balance, but it was pointless. Sampson's fist slammed into Edric's stomach and he toppled over and collapsed to the ground. The pain was nothing compared to the fact that he could not breathe. Edric's mouth opened and closed like a fish out of water with no hope of oxygen passing through. Edric tried to stretch his legs out, hoping the expansion would allow air to enter his lungs. That proved to be a mistake. Sampson's boot slammed silently into him and he returned to the fetal position still desperate for air.

"That's enough . . . for now," Edric heard the Commandant say.

"Yes, sir," Sampson replied and Edric heard the door open and close behind him.

Apparently, the worst was over. It took too long, but Edric finally took a gasping breath. The air burned his lungs. He forced himself to take another and then another until some semblance of normalcy returned to his breathing. As the shock subsided, Edric began to feel a sudden sense of rage. How dare they do this to him? He wanted them arrested. Edric tried to speak, but could only cough. The effort cost him, agony running through his gut, wrapping around his back.

The click of the Commandant's boots told Edric that the man had stood and was approaching. The shocking pain in his hand let him know that the man had arrived. The boot moved back and forth atop his hand, grinding it into the floor. Edric screamed and swung his other hand around to grab at the man's leg. He wasn't strong enough to do anything.

"Your file from your old school was quite interesting," the Commandant remarked calmly. "Edric Davies is a pathological liar who creates conspiracy theories to convince others that he is a victim. Your record here thus far is not much better. The only teacher who has not complained about you in your first few days is the Mad . . . Professor Feinstein."

The boot heel relented and the Commandant returned to his cushy desk chair. "Get up," he ordered.

Edric rose slowly and stood in front of the man. He sat, stone-faced, waiting for something. Edric was infuriated. "You can't do this to me," Edric said, his sense of righteous indignation growing.

"Every time we meet, regardless of the reason, this will be a part of our conversation," he gestured to the floor where Edric had just been. "We meet once a year, regardless of performance. We will meet far more often if there are issues with your performance." The tone of his voice suggested that he hoped there would be performance issues. "You will not have access to mail, a computer, or the phone until such time as I am satisfied that you can be trusted. Which, will be never. Hence, why I am able to "get away with" meetings like this. If you argue, or utter a single word, I will invite Sergeant Sampson back in to join us."

The Commandant hesitated a moment, waiting to see if Edric would challenge his authority. Edric wanted to. He was also smart enough to understand that it was pointless to do so. Edric stiffened, bit his lip and said nothing.

The Commandant looked down at the folder again and barked, "Dismissed."

Edric limped from the office and dragged himself back to his room. He had managed to do so in a mostly upright fashion. As he passed other students, he stretched his sore body desperate not to show weakness or pain. He had no idea how bad his injuries were. All he could envision was the blur of bruises on Nichols's body. "I'm sorry I doubted you," he thought, struggling not to wince as he walked. He collapsed through the door and onto the bed, writhing in pain.

This was his future. Edric saw an infinite number of days; an endless array of bruises. His roommates tolerated him only when speaking to him was not dangerous for them. He understood it now. Edric knew the price they would pay if they were seen to befriend him. Any hope of communicating with his father or with Meagan and Frank was all but dashed today. Isolation and torture were all that the Chateau D'If would offer him.

Edric waited for dinner that night to obtain what he would need. He had no access to a gun. There was no window high enough for him to propel himself out of. Edric had considered his options and felt the only viable one was a knife. He could steal a steak knife from the cafeteria and bring it back to the room. There, he would end his life.

He loaded his tray with potatoes, beans and a thick piece of chicken. He sat alone as he had every day since arriving at the Chateau D'If. He moved the food around, nibbling on a few bits and pieces. "Some last meal," he mourned. Giving up on it, Edric brought his tray to the trash and dumped the contents. He went to return his plate and silverware to the conveyor. He dropped the plate and fork down, but not the clean knife.

He slid the blade into his sleeve and walked casually from the cafeteria, keeping his pace deliberate. He moved through the hallway hoping that no one would notice the strange way he cupped his hand. Would the knife fall out? Did anyone see him take it? Edric fretted over these and dozens of other questions as he headed back to his room. He had it all to himself for at least an hour longer. More than enough time to do what he had to do.

He sat on the bed and took out his prize. Edric ran the cool knife blade along his arm. He wondered how the cut would feel. Would he be brave enough to cut deep enough or long enough? Would he be strong enough to do it twice? Thoughts of his father ran through his head. Edric wondered which emotion would dominate his father's will, shame or sadness. The thought of his father stayed his hand. Edric dropped the knife on the floor, the handle thudding loudly as it struck. He broke into silent tears and bit his lower lip in frustration. As the drops fell from his eyes he felt overwhelming shame. He could not survive here, that he was certain of. He could not take his own life. That he was less certain of, but he could not do that to his father. Edric was left to cry yet again. The utter hopelessness of his situation turned his quiet tears to quaking sobs. Edric surrendered to them, allowing them to rack his body to the core.

Suddenly, he heard footsteps out in the hall and feared his roommates might be returning early. He wiped his eyes, though he could do nothing about the puffy red eyes. There was a knock at the door. Two loud raps, followed by the announcement, "Professor Abraham Feinstein to see Edric Davies!"

Edric bounded from his bed and hit his head on the top bunk. He let out a muffled ouch, enough for the Professor to hear him through the door.

"Open the door, Davies," he demanded. He had watched Edric's foolishness with the knife in the cafeteria and knew there was a sense of urgency in getting the door opened.

Edric had no idea why the Mad Priest would want to see him, much less why he would do so at his room. When a Professor wanted to see a student, they were summoned to their offices during office hours. They did not trek across campus and pay an idle visit. Edric stumbled to the door and swung it open, standing at attention.

"May I enter?" Professor Feinstein asked with a sarcastic edge in his voice.

"Yes, sir," Edric replied, his confusion growing.

The professor shuffled into the room and his eyes immediately went to the glistening blade on the floor. Feinstein looked at Edric and examined him quickly, assessing all that had transpired. "I was much impressed by you during class today," he said while trying to ignore the evidence all around him.

Edric breathed a sigh of relief that the professor either didn't notice or ignored the knife. "Thank you, sir," he blurted.

Feinstein moved his foot towards the knife and gently nudged it under the bed and out of sight. He seemed infinitely sad, as if the sight of the knife brought him to some place best forgotten. "As old as I am, I need some fresh air to remind me I am still alive," he pronounced. "I would appreciate it if you would walk with me. I believe there are a great many things I could teach you."

Chapter 13

The Tragedy

Mr. Moore entered the office knowing that his mission today would meet with failure. Despite that fact, he was undaunted. He would make the effort today, tomorrow, and every day until he succeeded. He would find out what happened to Edric Davies.

He took a seat in the corner. Despite having no interest whatsoever in the sport Mr. Moore thumbed through a Golf Digest magazine. When the click of the office door garnered his attention, he rose and shook the hand of the man who would tell him no.

"Mr. Moore?" The Superintendent of Schools asked politely. He already knew the answer to who he was meeting with today.

"Thank you for seeing me, Dr. Kelly," Mr. Moore said, shaking the man's hand and smiling at him. Moore worked hard to control his frustration and maintain a friendly demeanor. "I appreciate your time."

"Please, come in. Sit," Dr. Kelly offered him a cushioned chair across from a massive mahogany desk. "How can I help you?" he asked. Mr. Moore seethed with anger as he thought of the dozen emails and twice as many phone calls on the subject he had already sent. Mr. Moore wanted answers.

He adjusted in the chair, sitting forward and interlocking his fingers. "Here goes nothing," he thought. "I would like to know where Edric Davies has been sent."

Dr. Kelly leaned back in his chair and took several breaths before he began the inevitable line of questioning that Mr. Moore had expected. "Are you his parent?"

Mr. Moore answered, "No."

"Are you a legal guardian?"

"No."

"Have you submitted a Freedom of Information Act request with my secretary?"

It was now Moore's turn to sigh. He hesitated before responding, ensuring that his frustration was as well-masked as possible. "I assure you that I have. I have yet to get a response to that inquiry. That is why I am here today."

Dr. Kelly folded his arms. "As you know, I cannot release information about a student to anyone who is not a legal guardian. As to your FOIL request, be patient. Our staff is often quite busy with student information requests."

"How can you make a student disappear?" Moore asked, exacerbated. "He is a good kid and he deserves better!"

The Superintendent never flinched. He never gave a hint of the apprehension he felt. No bead of sweat ever formed on his brow that might suggest he had his own problems to consider. Mr. Moore sought information. Germaine made a living in the information trade and Dr. Kelly was not oblivious to that fact. There were some men that were not worth challenging because they could ruin you with a word. Other men were easily dismissed. Dr. Kelly stood and walked to the door. Opening it, he said, "I'm sorry I couldn't be more help to you."

Moore slammed everything he could on his way out. Despite knowing the outcome before he came, his frustration had gotten the better of him. He slammed the office door, knocked over an inbox from a secretary's desk and kicked a chair as he headed to the door. There was only one other place he could go for information.

He drove to the Davies household knowing full well that he would get no more cooperation than he had received from the Superintendent. Moore was in no mood to be denied today. One way or another, he would compel Edric's father to tell him what had happened to the boy.

He knocked on the door, every time gaining in persistence and volume, but there was no answer. "Mr. Davies, Jack, are you there?" The garage had been shuttered and he was no longer welcome at the bar. Moore had paid his tab twice before realizing that he was allowing the man to go deeper down the hole. The man had suffered and his depression was understandable. Moore tried to be sensitive to that, but Edric needed him now and his father was doing nothing for him. "Davies! Open the door!"

He jiggled the knob and realized the door was unlocked. Moore entered the house. It smelled like stale beer and something foul. Moore navigated his way through the darkness of the living room and the accumulated filth that had been left to pile up on the floor. Bowls of half-eaten food wiggled with life as roaches walked over dirty clothes. Unexpectedly, his eyes caught a pair of boots in the kitchen.

They were odd because the toes faced upward and the heels rested on the floor. Moore moved around the counter and his worst fears were realized. Jack Davies lie on the floor, his face and neck were full of vomit, his eyes open and still, and his face a gaunt white. One more tragedy had befallen Edric Davies, and Mr. Moore had no way of knowing how to even tell him.

Chapter 14

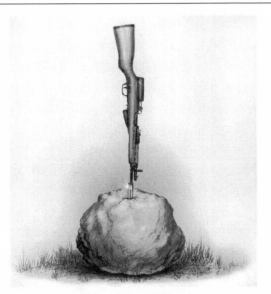

The New Man

Edric Davies awoke feeling like a dark cloud circled over him. He had no idea how his life could get worse, but a sense of deep apprehension seemed to permeate the air around him. His presentation assignment was the causes of the Civil War. Students in Professor Feinstein's class were duly terrified on presentation day. The Mad Priest's class had just three grades all year. The first, a mid-term exam that consisted of three essays written in ninety minutes, usually reduced the class by at least forty-percent. Those that survived the mid-terms were faced with a presentation of at least fifteen minutes that needed to include at least twelve distinct pieces of research, four of which were required to be primary source material, four of the students' choosing and the final four published within the last decade. Edric's presentation today would be supported by twenty-one sources and he was still uncertain whether or not Professor Feinstein would be satisfied. Despite that, Edric had grown very fond of him, and his eccentric personality. Where other students saw a Mad Priest, Edric saw a brilliant and caring man who abhorred people who failed to engage in their own lives.

That had been an apt description for Edric since he first arrived at the Chateau. He had seen it not as a school, but as a prison. He had wallowed in misery, ignoring his classes and surrendering to his despair. So much so that he had almost taken his own life. Then, he had been engaged by Feinstein. The man was passionate about even the simplest things. Edric was in awe of how much energy he could bring, the zeal upon which the man's entire existence was based.

Edric gathered the papers he needed for his presentation and shut and locked the door tight behind him. He had made the mistake of not locking it once before and returned to find the room in shambles. Other students, or maybe even instructors, entered and tossed the room. Edric knew it was done to get at him, but he felt a sense of shame that he allowed it to be done to his roommates. He refused to let them clean up. Manente and Nichols still helped, but Maquet let Edric do the rest. He wasn't going to allow that to happen again.

Navigating the halls of the dorms was something Edric had become used to doing. It was like a gauntlet that he had to run each day. A casual shove here or a trip there. Edric was persona non grata at the school and instructors had encouraged other students to make sure he knew his lowly status. Students took it upon themselves to ensure that he never forgot it. Fighting them was pointless. They were all better trained then he was and their numbers were always greater than one. If Edric could get to class today with just a few pushes and avoid being knocked down, he had a chance at a decent presentation.

He moved down the hallway to the stairs at the end of the corridor. He made two flights before he was noticed by some upperclassmen. They seemed to congeal, forming a shield wall against him. Edric hugged the wall. The boys shifted the phalanx they had created to bar his way. He moved quickly to gain the other side of the stairs, only to have them engulf him and surround him.

"Come on guys," Edric blurted in exacerbation.

They didn't speak to him. None of them ever did. Shatterly's seemed to look down on verbal taunts and trash talk. The school had no such compunction against a good physical thrashing though. Edric felt a fist strike just above the back of his waist. His knees buckled, but he didn't drop. Bent over, he didn't see the guy who grabbed his shoulders and drove his knee into his mid-section. Edric dropped his papers. They seemed to float in the air as elbows and fists, palm strikes and spear hands battered his core. They never hit in the face; that would leave visible evidence of the torture this dungeon encouraged. No, they liked hidden bruises, which only the prisoner could see and feel. One more way that Edric could be surrounded by people and utterly alone at the same time.

He didn't know when he had fallen. Edric had no idea how long he had lay there, curled into a fetal position. He had lost count of the kicks. When he had caught his breath and pulled himself to his knees, Edric tried to gather his papers. They were strewn about the landing. Footprints and tears that made his notes look unkempt seemed the only evidence of what had just happened. It took several minutes of slow, pained effort to locate all of the sheets. Edric was already halfway down the final set of stairs before he had gathered all of his work. He dragged himself out of the door and headed to the building where his class would be held.

~

"Davies, impress us," Professor Feinstein declared to a jittery class that had started with forty-six students and had dwindled to just twenty-two. Students dropped in droves before and immediately after the mid-term exams. Edric had received his mid-term examination back and Feinstein had written in red almost as much as Edric had. He assumed his grade would reflect on all of that commentary. When he turned to the back page to see an A minus, Edric leapt in the air to celebrate. Feinstein chastised him for it, but it was worth it.

As Edric rose and walked to the front of the class, his nerves began to swell. The previous three presentations were shredded by the brilliant professor. Edric was confident in his work, but Feinstein could be a prickly man to satisfy. He breathed deeply and told himself there was nothing that could be done now to change it. Edric reached the dark chestnut lectern and removed his ruffled notes from his folder. He spread them out so that he could reference them, especially the quotes he had chosen to share. Then, he began.

"The causes of the American Civil War are an example of complex simplicity. To a supporter of the Confederacy, the causes are simple, that of states' rights.

To an abolitionist, again, simply, that of slavery. To Lincoln, the preservation of the union. Each in their own way is correct. How can three distinct points of view all be correct? It is because a single thread linked each of those arguments, that of slavery."

Edric paused at the completion of his introduction and saw Feinstein looked satisfied with the beginning. Edric continued, discussing the issue of slavery during the colonial period through the founding of the nation. He quoted Thomas Jefferson, The Declaration of Independence, and the compromise that allowed slavery to continue in the Constitution. He discussed the various compromises that led to a divided nation, half-free and half-slave. Through each, he laced the idea that individual liberties and states' rights dominated southern views of them. When Edric shifted to John Brown's Rebellion, he quoted Fredrick Douglass and then touched on the Dredd Scott decision. Finally, he moved to Lincoln and his election.

"Lincoln was, despite modern views of him, considered a moderate. His platform never called for the end of slavery, though his speeches and writings give clear indication that he hated slavery and felt it must end."

Edric began his conclusion. "General Robert E. Lee disliked secession almost as much as he disliked slavery and still he served the Confederacy. Today, we see him as a man who fought for the very things he disdained. Our contemporary view of the man fails to see through his eyes. He fought for the rights of states to be free of Federal control, to have a voice in their own governance. He, like many southerners, would not see their stance as hypocrisy, rather as a just outcropping of our national history. One in which common men fight against a government that does not represent them. To throw off the yoke of a ruler for which they had no say in electing. Abolitionists' ranks swelled from the publication of *Uncle Tom's Cabin* and they never wavered from their view of what the war stood for. When Lincoln issued the Emancipation Proclamation, he solidified for future generations the idea of the war being fought over slavery. Yet, Lincoln would have endured the continuation of slavery, if it meant the preservation of the union. Slavery was at the center with state's rights and preservation of the union on either side. The Civil War was caused by an inability to compromise on an issue that had seen far too many compromises."

One student coughed into his hand, but the word, "Sucks," could be clearly made out. Another boy in class faked a sneeze that barely hid the word, "Loser" and the rest of them began to laugh. There was one person who clapped for Edric who had never clapped before. His name was Professor Abraham Feinstein.

"An impressive effort, Mr. Davies," he said and the accolades shocked the other students into stunned silence. "I give you this perspective; that of Sam Houston, deposed Governor of Texas, 'You may win southern independence, but I doubt it. The North is determined to preserve this union. They are not a fiery, impulsive people as you are, for they live in colder climates, but when they begin to move in a given direction, they move with the steady momentum and perseverance of a mighty avalanche.' That is what you have done today, Mr. Davies. You have chosen a new direction and no force will be strong enough to stand in your way."

Chapter 15

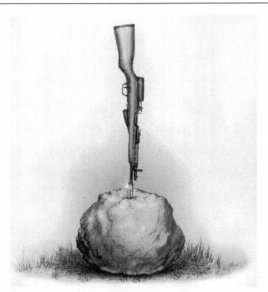

The Epiphany

The next few years were a blur for Edric. Professor Feinstein had taken Edric under his wing and had shown him a world he could never have experienced before coming to Shatterly's. The man's classes were difficult even for dedicated students. He delved into details of history that felt as if he knew more than even he let on. It was as if he were there, living it and taking his students with him. Those who survived the early days of his courses, and they were few, became an elite club, and no student was favored more than Edric.

Feinstein began to shape Edric in his own image. He did more than instruct Edric in history. He selected literature for him to read and spent his evenings discussing the finer points of Dickens, Chaucer,

Machiavelli and Wells. They fought over Hemingway and Hawthorne, argued Marx and Paine. Edric read from Bronte to Sun Tzu, Doyle to Hardy and back. As voracious as he was to learn, Feinstein was an even more energetic instructor.

Edric was stunned by the man's energy as much as he had been by his brilliance. He showed no signs of fatigue as he taught Edric Tang Soo Do Mu Duk Kwan. When Edric had become fluent in the Korean form of karate, Abraham Feinstein began to add Aikido and Jujitsu into their regimen. Contrary to his advanced age, Feinstein was fast and strong. As Edric gained skill, he tried to use his youth, his speed and aggression to gain advantage. Feinstein taught him his most valuable lessons. Edric learned never to underestimate an opponent and to be patient. Feinstein said that in time, your enemy would falter, a lapse of judgement or focus, one minor slip and they would give you a victory. Feinstein taught him the moment the fight really happened. In that split second, victory or defeat was determined.

Edric had grown powerful in the time he had spent at Shatterly's. He had added inches to his height as well as his muscles. Still lean, Edric had added thick dense muscle to every inch of his frame. There was little opportunity to gain body fat and Edric's body reflected that with taut sinew and bulging veins. Feinstein had trained Edric's body into a weapon nearly as powerful as his brain. Edric now walked the halls unmolested, though seemingly forever alone.

After a particularly vigorous sparing match that Edric had gained the upper hand in on a few occasions,

Feinstein had ended the bout with a grappling technique that Edric had never seen before.

"Here I thought you showed me all your secrets, sir," Edric smiled despite his defeat. He was stronger than his teacher, but the man was clearly still smarter.

"You still have a great deal to learn, but you are getting more difficult to beat every day, my boy," Feinstein helped pull Edric to his feet. "Do you have time tonight?"

Every night Dr. Abraham Feinstein asked, Edric said yes, whether he had time or not. "Yes, sir."

"Come then," Feinstein said, and the two of them walked in silence to his office where they would sit and talk as they did quite regularly. The years had brought a strange closeness between them.

As always, Edric waited for Feinstein to begin the conversation. He picked the topic and Edric tailored his questions to drive the discussion in a direction that suited him. It was a form of verbal chess that the two men played together.

"You have read Arthur Conan Doyle's *Sherlock Holmes*?" Feinstein asked.

He had suggested it a month back and Edric understood that the man never suggested anything. He required it through sheer force of will. Edric had begun reading *The Complete Sherlock Holmes* the very next day. "I have, sir."

"Regarding his titular character's powers of observation, do you find them believable?" the professor asked. His Socratic method of peppering students with questions rather than answers was not new to Edric.

"For the most part, yes, Holmes is believable," Edric replied. "With training, study and focus, many of the things he notes can be perceived."

They discussed several particular instances of Holmes's brilliance. Feinstein argued in favor of *A Study in Scarlet* while Edric selected *The Red Headed League* as his favorite.

"Have you considered his methods for your situation?" the Professor asked, casually.

Edric looked curiously at him. "What situation is that, sir?"

"How you came to be here; among the condemned."

Edric had forgotten that he had told the Professor about the day he was sent to Shatterly's. "We discussed that more than a year ago!" Edric thought. The man's mind was a steel trap that missed nothing.

"Cui bono?" Feinstein muttered, clearly frustrated with his favorite student.

Edric, confused, stared and waited for his mentor to elaborate.

"Latin, my boy! You need to learn Latin!" Feinstein's head sank low and he lowered his voice to a whisper, "Never enough time, never enough."

Edric rose and stood at attention in front of Feinstein and formally apologized, "I am sorry, sir. I do not understand."

"The language may be dead, but roughly translated it means, who benefits?" the teacher asked, rising from his desk and circling his student. He waited for the question to register with Edric. Seeing that it did not, he rephrased it. "You had just begun a relationship with a beautiful girl and had become a star player on the basketball team, is that not so?"

Edric nodded, not understanding where Feinstein was going with all of this.

The Professor smacked Edric on the side of the head and let out an exacerbated groan. "Can you really not discern the meaning, boy?"

"I don't understand . . . Are you suggesting that Meagan had something to do with all this?" Edric asked incredulously.

"Bah!" Feinstein yelled in frustration. "Use your head child! Who benefits by making you disappear?"

Edric thought a moment. Suddenly, he felt as if he had been hit in the stomach. "Who benefits?" Edric whispered as Feinstein began to smile.

The epiphany had finally arrived for Edric and Feinstein was happy that it had come, however late it might be.

Edric found himself in the locker room at Mount Collier High. He could hear the words as if they were being spoken now. "My man, don't forget who the star of this team is, okay." Edric seemed to convulse, his body giving a slight shudder of chills, before he spoke again. "Brett," Edric said, looking at Feinstein for his approval. "It was Brett," Edric reinforced the statement.

Feinstein nodded his wrinkled old head and said nothing. He sat down in the spinning chair behind his desk and waited for Edric to continue.

"Brett! He would have wanted me gone!" Edric paced back and forth in the small office, lost in his thoughts. He thought about the freshman; how he was angry at being supplanted by an eighth-grader. "He would be the top player. He would be captain, maybe even get promoted to JV." His fist slammed down on the desk and a tape dispenser popped into the air and crashed down a second later.

"Is that all?" Feinstein asked with a hint of sarcasm, his hands held out in front of him, his bony fingers forming a pyramid.

"No!" Edric exclaimed. Now, he was seated in the cafeteria, across from his friend. "Don't fear, nobody else cares to notice you." Edric remembered the words. He had blown them off then, but now they took on new meaning. "Frank. It was Frank, too." This time, Edric's rage was mixed with genuine hurt. Where Brett had never been his friend, never even pretended to be, Edric thought Frank had been. They had been rivals, sure, but he thought they were friends. They had wanted the same things; good grades, success, escape from the drama of Mount Collier, and Meagan. They had both wanted Meagan. Edric collapsed into the small guest chair that faced Feinstein's desk. "Frank would have benefited the most," Edric lamented.

The Professor waited as Edric's thoughts swirled like waves crashing against the rocks. His hands rubbed harshly at his face and then thumped down onto his legs, venting his emotions. No matter how much they raged, there was no denying the truth. He had been betrayed. Betrayed by his best friend. He seethed with a desire for revenge. Finally, Edric asked the most important question, "But how?"

The Professor had put that together already and suspected that Edric could too. "Well, neither Brett nor Frank had the ability to send you here. Who did?"

Instantaneously, Edric responded. "It was Germaine," though he could not possibly see the connection between the man and the two boys.

Feinstein began to tap his fingers on the desk and asked the most important question again, "How did he benefit?"

Edric's mind sought for the answer. He buried his head in his hands and rubbed his face again. "I was never a threat to . . ." and as Edric said it he realized that he was.

Feinstein saw the look of confusion being replaced by recognition and finally, understanding. "Explain," he said, softening his tone.

"I saw him," Edric said excitedly. "I saw him with her."

"Pronouns, Davies, pronouns," Feinstein chided.

He knew the Professor hated non-specific language. "Jennifer Kelly! I saw him with her!" Edric explained. "I was in the school after a game, and I saw the two of them together in his office."

"Continue," Feinstein ordered.

"He had my phone!" Edric yelled, rising from his seat and flailing his arms. "I received a text, but when he returned it to me, there was no text. Son of a . . ."

"Davies!" Feinstein cut him off.

"My apologies, sir," Edric bowed his head in deference to Feinstein's feelings regarding foul language. "Jennifer was conflicted about what she was doing. I encouraged her to end it. She said she would think about it. I suspected she was going to end it."

"You suspect the text was from her?" He knew the answer already, but wanted his student to finish filling in the story.

"She told me she would let me know as soon as she decided. We had spoken the night before."

"A triumvirate, of sorts," Feinstein suggested. "Three men with power and influence, working together."

Edric smiled at the reference to Roman history and the power vacuum that resulted with the betrayal of Julius Caesar by his friend Brutus. "Well, if you have taught me anything, it is that three powerful men will not share for long without seeking to unseat the others and consolidate power for themselves."

"Quite right. Quite right, you are," Feinstein nodded. "Power cannot be shared by those that seek it. However, you are wrong on this point. Each of these men sought a different prize from you. There is no fear of competition between them. Their victories are complete. Leave them be. Let them have what they have won." He reached into his desk drawer and removed an envelope. He held it between his thumb and forefinger, studying it as if it held the secrets of the universe. Feinstein brought his other hand to his temples and massaged them as if to assuage some unforeseen stress. He put the envelope back in the drawer and stared into Edric's eyes. "I have a treasure far greater to offer you."

Chapter 16

The Games

The cafeteria was electrified. Clanking dishes, dropped forks and nervous banter permeated the air. The coming battle with Citadel Preparatory Academy was the central topic of conversation at every table. The annual games culminated with the two qualifying schools facing off in head-to-head competition that included track and field, wrestling, sparring, fencing and more. Every student in each of the schools was required to participate in at least three events. The schools required the students to be three semester athletes all year in preparation for it. The Academy Games, as they were called, established a pecking order amongst the academies and defined the bragging rights for the coming year. Shatterly's was a clear underdog against the Citadel Preparatory Academy.

That fact only made them hungrier. For Edric, the chance to face and beat students from a rich prep school didn't make him hungry, it made him voracious.

Manente slammed his tray down on the table and dropped his hulking mass onto the chair a moment later. The benches on the far side seemed to rise like an undulating wave in reaction to his arrival.

"What's got your panties in a bunch?" Nichols asked, sarcastically. He was the only one who could get away with speaking to Manente that way.

"Look at it," he muttered, gesturing at his tray. When Manente got depressed, his face sort of sagged, taking on the look of a bulldog that had just lost his bone.

Nichols did exactly as instructed. "I don't see anything out of the ordinary," he grabbed his friend's fork and lifted some mashed potatoes, letting them splatter into the dark gravy surrounding the Salisbury steak. "Still looks like dog food to me."

"How do they expect us to survive on portions like this, much less fuel up for the games?" Manente lamented. Nichols ignored the contrived drama and stabbed the compressed chop meat, lifting it high above the plate. He chomped off the end and chewed as he considered the remainder of the meat.

"Come on!" Manente yelled and grabbed at the fork, but Nichols was faster.

Nichols offered the meat on the fork to Manente and with an overstuffed mouth, mumbled, "If's nop berry gud."

Manente snatched the fork from him and slammed it onto his tray. Gravy splattered onto his shirt. That only added to his frustration and Nichol's amusement. It reminded Edric of something that Manente once said about Nichols. "You can't question the boy's loyalty, but his logic is another thing all together."

Edric, as usual, paid no attention to the antics. Manente and Nichols were good guys and the closest thing Edric could call friends inside the school. They spent the better part of the first year ignoring him in public while privately helping him through the web of problems a new student could face. Slowly, they forgot the need to shun him publicly, and eventually, they were even willing to pay the inevitable price for befriending him.

Nichols was here at Shatterly's because his step-father had sent him. According to Nichols, the man was a right-wing religious nut that had subjected him to floggings, starvation and even exorcisms. When his mother's liver failed, his stepdad shipped him off to military school. The Chateau D'If seemed as good a place as any other to make him disappear.

That was the thing that bonded Edric and Nichols. Both of them were sent here to disappear. The two could not be more different, yet there was a strange loyalty between them; a bond that only pain and loneliness could cement.

Nichols was a perpetual problem child. Rules never applied to him and consequences never deterred his desire for something. Strictly supervised, he was a pleasure to be around and could be kept out of trouble. Leave him to his own devices, and misfortune was sure to follow. He was due to graduate in the spring. That wasn't something a person would wager on however. Nichols was just as likely to be thrown out. One way or another, he would be set loose upon the general population with no supervision. "God help the world," Edric thought.

Manente was a different story. He was the third generation of his family to come through the school. His grandfather, who he dubiously credited with creating the school's nickname, had reached the rank of Captain in the U.S. Army. His father had retired as a Major and Manente was determined to outdo them both. He was a hard charger, more intense in his training than any other student at the school. He was also a really decent guy. Edric hated that he couldn't tell them what he was about to do.

"Jeez, is everyone depressed tonight?" Nichols began to pantomime a whiny baby and then asked in a mock crying voice, "What's bugging you, Davies?" Nichols then folded his arms and sat back, clearly exacerbated. Nobody seemed to want to feign happiness with him today.

Edric had never understood Nichols's boisterous comedy. He knew the guy was depressed at the hand life had dealt him. Where others saw only the class clown, Edric and Manente knew that Nichols suffered deeply. They had endured his tears and his fits of rage that came in the dark recesses of night. They alone saw how the clown act hid a darkness that would inevitably lead to his own ruin. Of all the people that should have understood Nichols, it was Edric. Yet, Edric did not see his own rage at the betrayal he suffered as something that would hurt him. No, Edric was fueled by it, so much so, that he would not know who he was without that hate. He smiled at the thought that soon, he would be able to satiate that hunger.

"I am fine," Edric eventually responded, his smile authentic. The delay apparently made Nichols distrust his words.

"You guys suck!" he yelled and stormed off, leaving Manente to wallow in his mashed potatoes and Edric to ponder what Feinstein had said to him. He recalled their last meeting.

"It is time for you to leave here." That is what Feinstein had said. Edric had initially thought he had meant his office and so had risen to go. "I have an idea on how to get you out," Professor Feinstein added. Edric had looked perplexed, but his mentor did not elaborate. Instead, he shunted him out. "Yes. Yes. Go to sleep. We will talk after the games on Saturday."

Freedom. Was that the treasure the Professor had meant when he said he had something to give him? That would mean he could see his father again, Edric thought, unaware that his dad had been dead for nearly three years now. He dreamed of a reunion that could never be, but the thought of it warmed him to the core.

Edric had not stopped thinking about the conversation. Feinstein had helped to reveal the complex layers of betrayal that had sent him to this place. For more than three years, Edric had suffered here, confused and alone. Now, he at least understood why he was sent to this dungeon. He was supposed to have been buried here along with his enemies' secrets. Maybe they had thought he would have ended his life? Edric reflected on those early days and on how close he had come to fulfilling those desires. No. Edric would have his freedom. Whether it came from Feinstein now, or a few years later, he would have it. Freedom and revenge. That was all Edric cared about now.

The Count of Mount Collier High

The meal went slowly as Edric could not focus on his food. He listened to the din of noise that pervaded the hall. Students were excited for the challenge, if the amount of high fives, fist bumps and back slapping were any indication. Edric would participate only in individual events tomorrow. He had not touched a basketball since he left Mount Collier. He doubted he would ever touch one again. In the coming contests, he may have been the only student who didn't care about the results. Edric knew that Feinstein would want him to give his best effort, so he would, if not for himself, out of respect for his mentor.

He had hoped to catch a moment or two alone with Feinstein that evening, but the Professor never arrived at dinner. Edric had trusted that his plans were progressing nicely; that there were actual plans to free him. The uncertainty was maddening. Edric prayed that his freedom was growing nearer. His inability to confirm that left him anxious. Edric had not felt this nervous since the day he had arrived at the Chateau D'If.

Sleep did not come easily that night. Edric had gone for a long run around campus to clear his mind, but no amount of miles or fresh air could cleanse the thoughts from his head. What was Feinstein doing? How was he going to get him out? Would they scale the wall at midnight? Hide in the trunk of a car? Edric's mind raced faster than his legs. He seemed to be chasing a truth that was always just around the corner. He showered and hit the sack only to toss and turn. Every noise made Edric wait for a quiet knock at his door that never came. When the eerie silence of night dominated, Edric would game out every possible escape plan in his head, inevitably focusing on all of the things that could go wrong.

At dawn, the scratchy trumpeting of the loud speaker blared reveille and the school began to stir. Edric dressed in his PT uniform of black shorts and gray t-shirt emblazoned with Shatterly's logo, a bayoneted rifle sticking out of a stone. As if a student who picks up a rifle at the school shall become King Arthur himself. He slathered on a healthy dose of deodorant and headed off to breakfast.

Feinstein was once again absent from the meal. Edric chose to stick to fruit alone this morning, forgoing the heavier fare of eggs, sausage, bacon and pancakes being offered. He ate slowly, almost in a fog, dragging his heals in hope of seeing the Professor. He hesitated as long as he could and was one of the last students to leave the cafeteria and arrive on the field for the opening ceremonies.

The crowd of students mulled around sticking close to their platoons. Teachers from both academies mingled between the two schools renewing old friendships as much as keeping new enemies at bay. An occasional student would launch a taunt or jeer at the opposing students and the two crowds would press towards one another. The teachers would ease the two sides back only to become lax again and allow the scenario to repeat itself. The back and forth ended only when the crowd was called to attention with the arrival of both school's Commandants. Both school bands began to play and the resulting cacophony brought the platoons to attention, dressing ranks and forming their lines. In moments, the chaos of the crowd became a perfectly arrayed cohesive unit organized into perfect lines and columns.

The speeches were shorter than he had expected, probably because of the humidity. The previous year's droned on for what seemed like an eternity. The crowd cheered over the last lines and the first events began a few moments later. Students and spectators alike were already damp with perspiration as the day began. Edric was not scheduled to compete until the third event which was free sparring. He would also compete in fencing and the eight-hundred meter to finish out the day. He watched Manente wrestle. The guy made short work of any opponent put in front of him. Like a great bear, he would stand tall and then quickly go low, taking out his enemy's legs and with them, any hope of victory.

Edric's first opponent in free sparring was young, inexperienced and too easily beaten. The next two rounds had moderately competent martial artists, but they were in a hurry to win and so they lost. A flurry of poorly aimed blows were easily parried and they left themselves open to Edric's patient attack. The championship round presented Edric with some challenge. The boy was older, bigger than he was and well-trained. He relied on his feet to keep his opponent at bay. Edric figured he didn't like fighting close, so he waited, took a few side-kicks and then came in and finished him with his hands. A palm strike, open-hand sudo, and back-fist ended things in a flurry that even the judges struggled to see. Feinstein would have been proud, but he was still nowhere in sight.

Fencing went well; Edric had won the event easily using the same skills that had brought him to the top of free sparring. He had time now, about an hour before the eight-hundred meter, so he went to the stands to watch some of the field games. He meandered through the other students, looking at the field less often than at the bleachers. Still, there was no Professor Feinstein to be found.

Edric watched restlessly for a while. By the time the first relay began, he knew it was time to make his way back to the field. Edric walked down the stairs and passed a group of Shatterly students in a lively conversation. He would have ignored them, as they had ignored him for over three years, but he heard something. A name.

"What did you just say," Edric demanded.

"The Mad Priest. He collapsed. Last night, in the hallway," the student repeated. "Didn't think anything could kill that guy."

"Is he alive?" Edric asked, desperate for knowledge of his friend and mentor.

The student shrugged his shoulders, "I dunno," and turned to walk away.

Edric grabbed him by the shoulder and whirled him around. "Is he alive?" Edric screamed. The kid looked terrified, unable to utter a word.

"Davies! To the line!" a voice, one of the runners, yelled.

Edric let him go, realizing he could provide no real information. His race would start soon and he could not miss it. It was his last event. He would skip the awards and closing ceremonies, punishment be damned. He had to know if Feinstein was going to be all right.

When the runners approached the starting line, Edric could think of nothing but Professor Feinstein. He took his position, adjusting his feet until they felt firm, his fingers lightly resting on the squishy surface of the track. When the gun sounded Edric darted out of the gate and ran with all the haste he could muster. He never glanced to the side, never listened for the feet of other runners. He just ran towards Feinstein, towards the only person who had truly cared about him since he had been condemned to this place. If it had not been for Feinstein, the Chateau D'If would have consumed him. His thoughts were occupied in this fashion for eight-hundred meters, though they felt like eight-hundred miles. Adrenaline helped Edric to ignore the burn in his muscles, the fatigue in his lungs. His need to see Feinstein propelled him around the track.

He felt the thin line snap as his body passed through it. He had won, by how much, he did not know, nor did he care. The crowd cheered and then fell into a low, confused din as Edric left the field. He did not slow his pace as he came to the edge of the track. He could feel the soft grass replace the spongy material of the track as he headed straight towards the infirmary building, to Feinstein, hoping he would find him alive.

Chapter 17

The Treasure

The infirmary door swung open so quickly that it closed with the ferocity of a taut rubber band. Edric burst into the reception area, his eyes darting in every direction.

"Are you okay, young man?" The receptionist asked, rising slowly from her chair behind the desk.

"Dr. Feinstein, is he here? Is he alive?" Edric peppered the heavy-set woman with questions.

The exertion from getting up left the plump woman somewhat breathless. Edric was unwilling to wait for her to recover. He dashed down the hallway and started throwing open doors. A storage closet, an empty examination room and a bathroom. Edric was frantic.

"Upstairs! Two doors down, on the left," the receptionist called not willing or able to pursue him.

Edric darted up the stairs trying to process every potential outcome of what Feinstein's presence here might mean. He arrived at the door and entered without knocking or slowing down at all.

"Go back out of that door and enter as if you have been taught some manners," the Professor ordered immediately though his voice sounded off, somewhat raspy and weak.

Edric stared at him a moment. He did as he was instructed only after he was satisfied that his mentor lived, "Yes, sir."

Once outside the door, Edric gave two solid raps on the door and announced, "Edric Davies, requesting permission to enter, sir."

Feinstein made him wait two minutes that felt like hours before he granted Edric permission to enter.

Edric entered feeling relieved though exhausted. The sleepless night and stressful day had suddenly hit him. His muscles felt limp with fatigue, his head foggy.

"Sit down, before you fall down," Feinstein ordered.

Edric took a small aluminum framed guest chair from the corner and pulled it close to Feinstein's bedside. The cool metal felt good on his overheated muscles.

The door to the room creaked open and a young nurse popped her head in. "Is everything all right, Dr. Feinstein?" she asked, ensuring that Edric's presence met with his approval.

"Everything is fine, dear. May I have some water for my friend, please?" Feinstein replied and Edric was certain he could hear a slight slur in the man's speech.

"Sir, I . . ." Edric started, but was cut off quickly.

"Did you win?" Feinstein asked with a half-smile, the left side of his face partially paralyzed.

Edric nodded, "I did, sir."

"Let me see them," Feinstein asked.

Edric knew full well what he wanted to see. He didn't have them because he had run off to see him. Amazingly, Feinstein had immediately made Edric regret his choice to charge off and see him. "I don't have them, sir. The ceremonies have not started yet."

"Go get them. Bring them here. I want to see them on you," Feinstein instructed, shuttling him away. "Go!"

Edric left begrudgingly. He walked from the room, jogged out of the building and sprinted back to the fields. He made it just in time for the first medal ceremony, the long jump winner. He had time before they would call his name for the first of three medals. Edric was relieved that Feinstein was alive though his thoughts were of his friend's future and that he would not be in the stands to see Edric receive his medals. They were as much Feinstein's as they were his. An hour ago, they didn't matter to him. Now, those medals would stand as proof of all the Professor had taught him. He looked forward to sharing them with him.

Edric returned to the infirmary. This time he could walk at a much slower pace. He wore three medals around his neck, the only student in the school to win all three of their events. His hand rested gently on his chest as he tried to stop the awards from clanking together. He knocked hard and Feinstein called him in before he even had a chance to make his formal request for entry.

"Congratulations," Feinstein called out, beaming with pride.

Edric carefully removed the medals from his neck and laid each of them on his mentor's chest.

"They are yours," Edric said. He meant to make them a gift. The man had given him so much and there was nothing he could offer in return. Three years of watchful care, a treasure trove of knowledge and skill and Edric could offer a few medals in return.

"Bah! You earned them. Keep them. Your father will be proud of you. Remember me every time you look at them," Feinstein went from impatience to remorse.

His words hit Edric in the gut. He had not considered that his freedom, when it came, would mean an end to his relationship with Feinstein. He would trade one father for another now, but it didn't lessen the hurt.

"Hand me that folder, please," Feinstein tried to gesture to a manila folder resting on a tray table, but his muscles were failing him.

Edric moved quickly to grab it and laid it on Feinstein's chest, exchanging it for the medals.

"Open it," he ordered.

Edric did so. He laid out the papers on the tray table that stood next to the bed.

Feinstein struggled to grab the first one. "These are your release forms," Feinstein explained, the sheet shaking in his hand. "Do not get too excited just yet, my boy," he added quickly as he watched the glow in Edric's eyes alight. "There is work to be done first." Feinstein paused a moment to collect his strength. "You will need to put this on Arlene's desk inside the Command Information Center. It needs to go in her dismissal folder," Feinstein instructed, tapping the paper left on the tray table.

Arlene was the admissions secretary. She made a great showing of being tough and all business, but underneath, she was sweet and caring.

"Yes, sir." Edric replied, hesitating to challenge his mentor's plan, despite the diminished mental capacity. Feinstein looked so feeble and old lying in the bed. Edric had known the man was aged, but his energy and skill had never allowed that reality to set in.

"I know students are not allowed in the CIC. You will have to find a way. I am certain you will be able to do this," Feinstein's voice was weak. Edric grabbed a container of orange juice off the tray table and offered him the straw. Feinstein shook his head as vigorously as he could muster. "No. There is very little time and I have a great deal to tell you. Sit, Son."

Edric was perceptive enough to notice the choice of words. It wasn't boy this time, but son. He smiled, despite his concerns, and did as he was told, waiting for Feinstein to begin.

"Once Arlene processes the form, it will go out to the instructors. You will need three signatures from your teachers to approve your dismissal from the school. I have arranged with the nurse to have a few visitors. With the information I have at my disposal regarding their indiscretions, I should be able to convince two of them to sign."

Edric didn't know what to say. He would be free! He had dreamed of that moment for over three years; had hoped this was what Feinstein was planning. "Thank you, sir," Edric said, reaching out his hand to Feinstein. The old man gripped it weakly and grinned appreciatively.

"Edric, once you are free, there is something you must do."

"Anything, sir. Anything you ask."

Feinstein pulled his hand free of Edric's and pointed across the room. Edric looked to see Feinstein's jacket hung on the door. He went and retrieved it, resting it on top of the professor. His mentor reached into the inside pocket and removed an envelope. He brought it to his lips and gently kissed it before handing it to Edric.

"I give you the gift of a new life," Feinstein said proudly. "Open it."

Edric slid his finger under the fold and gently ripped along the top of the envelope. He drew out the contents. Wrapped in a single sheet of bright white paper was a Social Security card, a birth certificate, a bank statement from Mount Collier Savings and Loan as well as a letter addressed to a man named Marc. "Who's Marc?" Edric asked, confused.

"He is you and you are he," Feinstein said, obviously proud of his work. "When you leave here, you can be a new man. You do not need to return to your old life."

Edric looked dumbfounded. "Why?" he asked, shocked by what he was suggesting. "Why would I want a new life? I want my freedom. I want my revenge. I want justice!" Edric was shocked to hear himself yelling at his teacher and friend.

"No," Feinstein whispered. "You can put all of that behind you. Marc Cunningham is you now and Marc is a wealthy young man. He is wealthier than any man you or I have ever known. When we spoke last, I told you that I had a treasure to give you."

"What do you mean?" Edric demanded, his thirst for vengeance getting the better of him.

"I found the treasure," Feinstein admitted. "I located it almost twenty years ago."

"The Treasure of Lima?" Edric was incredulous.

"Keating and Gissler had been fools," The professor nodded. Edric had recognized the names from their conversations. They were two of the earlier and more famous treasure hunters to have failed in their attempts to find the stolen Spanish loot. "They focused on the Bays. Chatham and Wafer Bays were logical assumptions for a person who didn't want to hide something! Thompson had stolen the greatest treasure in history. He would not have brought the Spanish to it. Yet, he would not want to be marooned far from it if there was hope of escape." Feinstein recounted his thought process as if it were the simplest and most logical of deductions. Edric felt like a hapless Dr. Watson to the professor's brilliant Detective Holmes. "It wasn't on Cocos Island. That had been a distraction. A place for Thompson and the first mate to run and hide. No, it was hidden in a cave on Isla Manuelita. They could have swam to it, if they could survive the hammerheads, that is." He paused, taking several shallow breaths. The recounting of the story seemed to have exhausted him. "I have spent the better part of my life selling it off to private collectors, away from the prying eyes of the Costa Rican government." His pride gave way to sorrow and regret before he finished. "It was to be a retirement gift to my wife for tolerating this life of mine."

As Feinstein reflected on his wife and her loss, so too did Edric. Dr. Feinstein had spoken lovingly of her deep into the evening on many occasions. Her loss was a wound that had never healed. Edric understood in those moments how much Feinstein had loved her. She was an archeologist; he was a historian, a match made in Heaven. He knew how much her death had changed him and wondered who the man had been when she was alive. How much he would have loved to have known that man, Edric thought.

"After she passed, I had no use for it anymore," Feinstein said, his voice laced with the sadness of knowing that his own life was waning. "I spent many a night with the muzzle of a gun in my mouth," Feinstein admitted. "I could not live without her, but I lacked the courage to end things. I feared I might not be reunited with her."

Edric finally understood what the professor had seen in him. They were wounded souls. Both bright and determined; both black holes of pain and sorrow. Edric represented Feinstein's second chance at life. Clearly, Feinstein had not given up all hope.

Young Edric's life was only just rising. Though his was soon to set, Feinstein could ensure a bright, beautiful life for his student. "It is yours now," his voice swelling with hope and something deeper, "I bequeath it to you, my heir." His voice filled with pride and tears began to stream from his eyes. "To a man I would be proud to call my son. To you, Edric."

Chapter 18

The Last Day

His heals clicked loudly as he hurried down the empty hallway of the infirmary. Edric had stopped by Feinstein's office and collected some creature comforts for his mentor. He brought his folio and fancy inkwell pen that his wife had bought him, his collected works of Walt Whitman and, most importantly, the photograph that had rested at the corner of his desk. Edric now knew where the photo had been taken and what the two of them had been up to when it was taken. It was hard for him to imagine the excitement the married couple must have felt as they discovered the largest lost treasure ever recovered in history. That thought was quickly replaced by the idea that they had never been able to share in the joy of it.

Edric knocked on Feinstein's door and announced his presence. There was no answer. Edric hesitated at first to enter, then thought something might be wrong and burst through the door. The professor was asleep in his bed, his chest gently rising and falling in rhythm. Edric put the picture from his office on the small table next to the hospital bed and rested the folio, pen, and poetry collection next to it. He quietly pulled the guest chair over to the bed and sat. He planned to patiently wait for the man to wake from his slumber.

After a time, Edric picked up the book of poetry by Walt Whitman and began to read. He read the poem, "Friend," but as was often the case, he didn't fully grasp the meaning of much of it. He knew at least that Whitman was talking about the value of friendship. He read "Whispers of Heavenly Death" and was utterly confused. Edric went to the table of contents and found the one poem he knew and understood. "O Captain My Captain" was one Feinstein had taught them in class.

"You could broaden your horizons. You are capable of understanding more than one poem," Feinstein said, his voice strained and weak as he awoke.

"I will try, sir," Edric promised, though he doubted his skill in the area of poetry would ever improve.

Feinstein glanced at the photo on the table and gave a half smile. "Thank you," he murmured.

Edric saw water clouding his eyes. "I did it," Edric pronounced proudly, trying to distract the man.

"How?" Feinstein asked.

Edric sat back in the chair and put his hands behind his head. "I took Carl's keys from his cleaning cart yesterday afternoon, after he finished his rounds. I waited until dark, slipped into the office and put it in the inbox on her desk. It was easy," Edric bragged.

Feinstein shook his head a bit, as if to nod in agreement. "If only my efforts were as speedy as your own," he lamented. His eyes tracked towards the tray table and Edric looked at it. There was a single signature on it. Nowhere near enough to secure his freedom. As if he could read the emotion on his student's face Feinstein said, "With time, we will succeed."

Edric quickly faked a smile. "You just get better and we will worry about all this later," though he worried about it every waking second.

"Would you read to me?" Feinstein asked.

"Of course, sir," Edric replied and sat up in the seat.

"*Good-Bye My Fancy*," please," Feinstein requested.

Edric thumbed the pages until he came to the requested poem. He cleared his throat and began to read.

"Good-bye my Fancy!
Farewell dear mate, dear love!
I'm going away, I know not where,
Or to what fortune, or whether I may ever see you again,
So Good-bye my Fancy.

Now for my last--let me look back a moment;
The slower fainter ticking of the clock is in me,
Exit, nightfall, and soon the heart-thud stopping.

Long have we lived, joy'd, caress'd together;
Delightful!--now separation--Good-bye my Fancy.

Yet let me not be too hasty,

Long indeed have we lived, slept, filter'd, become
really blended into one;
Then if we die we die together, (yes, we'll remain
one,)
If we go anywhere we'll go together to meet what
happens . . ."

A strange gurgling sound had distracted Edric. He
glanced up and saw that Abraham Feinstein was in the
fits of a second stroke. Edric tossed the book aside and
frantically looked around the room as if there might be
something he could use to stop this from happening. He
tried to yell for the nurse, but his voice croaked in his
throat. Edric watched, powerless to stop it. Feinstein
tried to speak, but it was so slurred that Edric could
understand nothing of it. He held his hand. The old
man's grip slackened. Edric realized that he was dying.

Edric looked into the eyes of the man who had been
a second father to him. What could he do? What could
he offer the man at the moment of death? He had nothing
but his love and respect to give. So, he gave them.

"O Captain my Captain!" Edric began. "Our fearful
trip is done, The ship has weathered every rack, the prize
we sought is won." Edric could not recite the whole
poem, but he had favorite parts. He skipped to them,
battling back tears. "O Captain my captain! Rise up and
hear the bells; Rise up – for you the flag is flung for you
the bugle trills, for you bouquets and ribboned wreaths . .
." Edric's voice trailed off as he watched the life drain
from his teacher's eyes. They remained open and glassy,
like a window into oblivion. Edric brought his hands to
the man's face. He winced, fought through his fear and
then closed Feinstein's eyes for the final time. "It is

some dream that on the deck, You've fallen cold and dead," Edric whispered through his tears.

Edric did not know how long he had laid his head on Feinstein's still chest before he heard the sounds. He rose and realized that he had rained tears enough to form a small lake where he had rested. "Nurse!" he yelled, trying to gain the attention of the feet shuffling outside the door. She entered slowly, as if the world had not just ended. Without a word, she checked for a pulse and listened for a heartbeat. Satisfied that Abraham Feinstein was gone, she looked at Edric and tucked her lip in, shaking her head. It was her wordless effort at sympathy or a frustrated pout over the work that needed to be done, Edric could not tell.

She left and Edric was alone with him. He stared at the stiff frame that lie in the bed. Where once there was energy, brilliance, there was now still silence. Suddenly, the silence struck Edric as something even worse. The professor had not signed his release! Resting on the tray was the document with a single signature. He had time enough to convince only one other instructor to sign it. Now, Edric was condemned to a fate worse than death. He would have to face the Chateau D'If alone. He picked up the paper and stared at it. If it had two signatures it would have been the greatest treasure in the world. Edric crumpled it into a tight ball, his knuckles going white with rage. It was nothing more than garbage now. He tossed it into the trash and sunk down into the chair.

"Why?" Edric asked aloud. "Why couldn't you wait? Just a few more days. That was all we needed!" For the first time, Edric felt angry at his friend and mentor. "God, I was so close. I miss my dad," Edric mourned, tears and anger blending into an emotional cocktail of painful proportions. "I cannot do this alone!"

The door opened again and the nurse entered with two men close behind her. "You should leave," she said.

"I would like to stay with him," Edric sniffled. It came out more like a demand than he had intended it to.

"Suit yourself," she said. She nodded to the two men. They both checked his vitals and seemed satisfied that he wasn't going to sit up anytime soon. The bigger one unfurled a bag while the smaller one rolled Feinstein's frame up on his shoulder. His partner tucked the bag underneath him. Then they rolled the professor the opposite way and he was neatly tucked in the bag. The zipper squealed and stopped abruptly when Feinstein was no longer in view.

The men went to unlock the wheels on the gurney but the nurse stopped them. "Oh, no you don't. Paperwork first. You boys can take him to the coroner's and the crematory when the I's are dotted and the T's are crossed." It seemed the smaller one was going to argue but thought better of it.

They left the room. Edric stared at the black bag resting on the bed. The one which neatly concealed his friend so that no one had to see death. A bag that would make him invisible. The idea hit him so hard he nearly collapsed. He had to act quickly.

Edric ran to the bed and unzipped the bag. At first he was overzealous and pulled quickly, but as the sound grew, he slowed his pace to muffle it. He tucked the bag down to the sides of Feinstein's body and moved behind him. He grabbed the man under the arms and pulled him upwards. Carefully, Edric tugged him free of the bag and off of the bed. Feinstein's heels struck the ground with a thud and Edric felt certain he would be caught. He hesitated, waiting for the sounds of footsteps coming towards him. When he was satisfied with the silence, he dragged his friend's body across the floor towards the bathroom. He sat the professor on the floor. Gently, he kissed the man's forehead. "Thank you, my friend," Edric whispered. "You have saved my life one more time."

Edric rose and gently shut the door to the bathroom. He walked over to the gurney and shimmied into the bag. Darkness enveloped him. A thought suddenly occurred to him; he realized that his uniform might give him away. Edric scurried out of the bag and went back in the bathroom. He stripped to his underwear. He folded the uniform neatly and laid it on the sink more from habit than need. He removed the envelope Feinstein had given him and tucked it in his underwear. He gave one final glance at Abraham Feinstein, who rested upon the floor, his body half propped against the wall. "I will never forget you," Edric said, double tapping the envelope against his body. He returned to the pitch black of the bag.

He had no idea how long he hid inside the bag. Edric had assumed they would be back quickly, but it felt like hours before he heard anything moving outside the room.

Muffled voices began to reach his ears. Edric could hear two men speaking as they walked down the long corridor. They were coming for him now. His heart pounded and he imagined the vinyl material of the black bag that covered him undulating with the beat of his own terror. They would discover him, alive and attempting escape. He would fight, he told himself. He would use their shock to his advantage and knock them aside and run. Run! He would run as far and as fast as he could to freedom. What would happen after that, he could not say.

"So, how late did you stay?" one man asked the other as the door opened.

The other responded, "We left after Them Bones finished their set. That band is awesome. The lead singer rocks! I just couldn't stay after they were done. That other band the bar hired is like listening to a dog get hit by a car."

"Come on, Oil and Water isn't that bad," the first protested.

"Man, you have no taste or no hearing," the second chided and laughed as he said it.

"Well, my wife always says I'm deaf and I have been told I have no taste!" the first man replied, laughing at himself as Edric felt the gurney wheels unlock and begin to slide out of the room. He tried to slow his breath but his heart would not slow. Blood pulsed rapidly through his veins and Edric expected to hear the men question the supposed corpse they transported at any moment.

The two men continued their banter, discussing Them Bones and the songs they sang, their quality and how they should have greater recognition. They laughed as they joked about their wives, other bar patrons and the follow up band. Edric felt the gurney come to an abrupt halt and then found himself lifted into the air. Suddenly, he felt the whole thing slam into something and a gasp escaped his lips.

"Did you hear that?" one asked.

"What?"

"I don't know. It was like a breath or something."

Edric tensed his muscles. There was no time to chide himself for the mistake now. A single breath would cost him his freedom.

"Yeah, no worries," the other man responded. "Sometimes, when you shuffle corpses around they make funny noises. I even had one sit up on me once," he chuckled and slammed the door closed. Edric breathed a sigh of relief and then felt the road begin to pass underneath him. He was on his way to the crematory!

Chapter 19

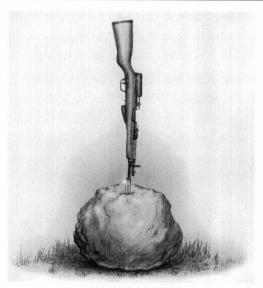

The Escape

The noise of the roadway settled into a steady drone. Edric could hear voices in the distance, obscured by the vehicle's interior. His heart pounded and his breath quickened. The heat of the body bag became oppressive. He opened it, tearing at the zipper, desperate for fresh air. He gasped, drinking in the salvation that only oxygen could bring.

He had not thought this through. In his haste to escape, Edric had allowed himself to fall down a path that he could not predict the destination. He had time now. How much time he would have was anyone's guess. He needed a plan and he needed it quickly.

They would stop sooner or later. The rear door would swing open and the men would bring him into a building. The coroner would discover the switch and Edric would be arrested and sent back to Shatterly's. He would stand in front of the Commandant and face his sneer. Sampson would beat him to within an inch of his life. Edric's body would be a message to every other student to never attempt such a stunt ever again. Edric could feel the blows against his body as surely as he was being beaten that very moment.

"I am never going back to the Chateau D'If," Edric swore to himself. He figured that his best moment to strike was when they opened the door. The element of surprise would be in his favor. The two men were larger than he was, but he was trained, honed as a weapon. Moreover, Edric needed only to shock them enough to make his escape. He hoped that they would not try to subdue him, but he was determined to fight them if he was forced to do so. How far he would have to go in that fight was something he refused to think about.

He laid the plan out in his head. Edric would hold the bag closed from the inside. The door would open. He would allow the men to pull the gurney from the vehicle. When it was clear, Edric would pop out of the body bag, knocking one of them off their feet. He would flee in that direction. Somehow, he would have to get his bearings, find a place to run and hide. That was impossible to plan. He would have to adapt to whatever conditions presented themselves. He had planned all that he could. The rest would have to play itself out. Sun Tzu, the master strategist and author of *The Art of War* would be proud. He hoped Abraham Feinstein would have been, too.

The vehicle came to a stop. Edric heard the doors creak open and close, first one, then the other. He could make out the shuffle of footsteps alongside the car. Edric took a deep breath and tightened the bag around his head again. Beads of sweat rolled into one, flowing like a stream down Edric's body. He was suffocating! He would die in this bag and no one would be the wiser. He tried to fight against his fears. He focused on his breathing; tight shallow breaths, controlled and steady.

The moment had come. He felt the tug of the gurney as he was pulled out of the car. The wheels grumbled and one of the men huffed loudly as he strained. "Perfect!" Edric thought, as the sound of the man's voice gave him a better sense of where his target was located. The wheels of the gurney barely touched the ground before Edric struck.

He threw the bag wide open and used his palm to strike underneath the chin of the man to his right. Edric heard the man's teeth clatter just as his hand impacted the lower jaw. The man crumpled to the ground, stunned by the pain of the sudden attack. Edric quickly wiggled himself out of the bag and stood up on the gurney. He tried to hop off of it, but the smaller of the two men had recovered from his shock at seeing the dead rise. He grabbed at Edric's legs, knocking him off balance and sending him into the concrete floor of the loading dock. Edric winced in pain as his shoulder collided with the ground. The rest of his body had been shielded by the impact. Edric gave a silent thanks for landing on the larger man's unconscious frame.

Edric tried to push himself up, but the smaller man leapt over the gurney and tackled him before he regained his feet. He quickly reversed the man's hold on him, using his palm to turn the man's chin while wrapping his arm around his opponent's elbow. Edric rapidly pinned the man to the ground. He buried his elbow into the man's throat and stifled any sound. He fought harder, trying to push Edric off of him, but he had no training and even less skill.

"Please, don't make me kill you," Edric whispered. Edric eased the pressure off of the man's neck, but only slightly. In turn, the man stopped struggling. The two had seemed to come to some sort of arrangement.

"If I let you up, will you stay quiet?" Edric asked.

The man tried to nod and Edric took that to mean he would cooperate. He took his elbow off of his throat and sat up, remaining on top of the man. Edric struck him hard against the temple and watched the man's eyes roll back in his head as he slipped into unconsciousness.

"I'm sorry," Edric whispered, shocked by his own ferocity. He rose to his feet and tried to get his bearings.

The scream was unexpected. A blood curdling, God awful scream of terror cut through the air. Edric turned to see a woman, probably in her early twenties, standing on the far side of the loading dock with her hand to her mouth. A door swung open and Edric didn't wait to see what came out of it. He ran as fast as his legs would take him.

The brick facades whirled past him. His legs carried him quickly past stunned onlookers. Edric felt the cool air across his body and suddenly remembered that he was in his underwear. He would not be able to blend in. He needed a place to disappear. His head darted from side to side as he ran, looking for an alley or park, anywhere he could find cover for a moment. He needed time to think, to assess his situation and formulate a plan. He couldn't do that running in his skivvies.

His bare feet ached. The first sirens began to reach his ears. It would not take long for the police to triangulate his location. There was no time to think about the pain. Edric made several turns, trying to find streets that were unoccupied. Whether it was conscious or unconscious decision making, he kept choosing streets that looked run down. The worse they appeared, the more attractive they were to him. He could hide amongst them. People would be less shocked or at the least, less interested in him.

He found an alleyway behind some abandoned buildings. He made a few more turns and realized that he had not seen anyone around for several minutes. He slowed his pace. Now that he had stopped running, Edric felt the exhaustion wash over him. The adrenaline spent, Edric wanted nothing more than to collapse into sleep.

Edric was utterly spent. Today, he had lost his only friend in the world. He had discarded that friend's body, hiding it, so that he might escape the Chateau D'If. He had hidden, naked and afraid, inside a body bag while men took him to a crematory oven. Then, he had brutalized those poor souls so that he could be free. Now, he was alone, afraid and cold. "Not my best day," he thought.

The wind bit at him. Every gust acted to remind him of his exposed skin. His mind turned to seeking cover. Edric needed someplace to hide from the cool air and the authorities who pursued him. The alley offered just one realistic spot for someone to hide; the dumpster. He looked in and it was his nose, not his eyes that said no. Instead, Edric gathered a few empty boxes and stacked them behind the large green dumpster. He would use these to block the wind. So long as the breeze could be blocked, Edric could handle the temperature. The smell was bad behind the dumpster, though nowhere near as bad as the interior. His fatigue and fear were worse than cold, smelly air. He bunkered down behind the dumpster, bringing his legs tight to his chest. He wrapped his arms around them and tucked his chin into his chest. Here he would spend the night and tomorrow morning would bring the worries of the future.

Almost without thought, Edric's hand reached towards his underwear, fearing he had lost the envelope. He felt it there and took a deep, relieved breath. He took it out and looked longingly at it. As he sat, Edric finally had time to process the loss of his friend, Abraham Feinstein. When the tears began, Edric immediately felt ashamed. Feinstein would have chastised him for this moment of weakness and Edric knew that. But, he wasn't here to chide him or castigate him. He wasn't here to teach him or lift him up. He was gone and Edric felt alone in the world.

Chapter 20

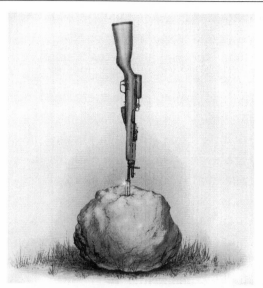

The Rescue

Edric awoke confused and cold. He had dozed off, for how long he did not know. It was darker than he remembered and his eyes needed time to adjust. His first thought was of the envelope clutched in his hand. He fought with his fingers as they creaked open and proved to his eyes that they had not failed in keeping it safe. His limbs felt numb and strange sounds pummeled his eardrums. Edric yawned and took in a deep breath, only to discover that the scents that surrounded him were far worse than any temperature or sound could be. He gagged on the mix of stale urine and garbage that permeated his mouth and lungs. He realized that he couldn't clear the stench and had to begrudgingly deal with it. While he fought with his lungs to accept what air he could offer, he rubbed his arms and chest for warmth. As the blood began to flow, Edric needed only to address the odd thumping sound in his head. He shook it, rubbed his ears and forehead, but the sound continued. In fact, it seemed to grow clearer. Edric's senses were beginning to clear and he recognized the sound as familiar. Someone was being beaten and Edric could clearly identify the thud of impact and the sudden expulsion of air that often followed getting hit.

"We don't want no Jews in this neighborhood."

Edric peered around the edge of the dumpster that had concealed him. His eyes shunned the light coming from a passing car. As his eyes adjusted he could make out three men of varied size standing over a fourth who lie in a fetal position on the pavement. The largest of the three reared back and sent a kick into the man's gut and the sounds that had awoken Edric repeated once more.

Edric faced a choice that to him amounted to no choice at all. He could flee, leaving the man to his fate, and securing his own freedom or he could intervene, potentially saving the poor fellow and condemning himself to a return to the Chateau D'If. So, Edric did the only thing he could. He tucked the envelope into a metal joint in the back of the dumpster and gave it one last look, praying that it would remain safe. He then rose to his feet and revealed himself.

"Gentlemen, may I enjoin you to cease and desist your assault on that fellow so that I might converse with you." The three thugs turned almost in unison, staring blankly towards Edric. He stood before them in only his underwear. That seemed to further confuse his opponents. Here was a naked teen that had spoken as if he had spent a lifetime with his nose in a book. His body told a different story. It was thin, well-muscled, sinewy and fearsome. Edric's muscles tensed as the three men glared at him. They were razor sharp weapons and he had every confidence in them. He worried more about his nerve than his abilities.

"I would ask you to disperse, but I suspect you would ignore that request," Edric said nonchalantly, reflecting more confidence than he felt. "The Mad Priest would be proud," he thought as he waited for them to make their move. He watched their eyes, just as he had been trained. The eyes would tell him who was a threat, who would run. The big one, light skinned and hairy was overconfident and aggressive. Edric watched his eyes grow wide with anticipation. The one to his right was the next largest. He seemed hesitant. Edric could read his eyes as they tried to process the strange events of the last few seconds. Why was a naked man who spoke so formally challenging them? This one was the intellectual of the group, Edric supposed. The third one, the smallest of the gang looked hungrily toward the big one, awaiting a decision. That told Edric everything he needed to know. Hobble the giant and the smart one will withdraw. The little one had the most to prove and therefore would be the most aggressive.

"Get out a' my alley, you nut job," the pale giant ordered with a chuckle at the end. He had evidently decided Edric was an insane homeless man. The runt of the litter joined in with laughter and a similar rejoinder, before returning to their victim.

"I want it noted that I asked politely. When you are begging for your life, you must remember that I tried, but you were simply incorrigible," Edric said as he took a step forward and settled into a fighting position. His knees were bent slightly and his hands up, open handed, ready for defense.

"Kill this idiot," the giant ordered as he pushed the runt forward.

"You gonna cry before I end you, boy," he threatened as he settled in front of Edric. The runt's legs were stiff and his fists were tight and low. He was used to fighting people who were scared or weak. He had no training and even less talent in a fight. Edric smiled and let him throw the first punch. He dodged it without parrying it. He allowed three more wild swings before he executed the first and only block. Edric slipped into a back stance and used his right forearm to block the runt's punch. He felt his arm slam into his opponent and moved rapidly to control the arm. Instantly, his hand slipped into position and took the meaty portion of the man's hand. Edric shuttled the hand upward as he bent the wrist and jammed it into position. In a single second the runt had lost the ability to fight. Edric turned his opponent away from him. The man's wrist bent and his arm straightened in a desperate attempt to stop the wrist from breaking. Edric forced him to the ground, holding his wrist down and turned so that any fight would result in untold damage to both wrist and elbow joints. He screamed as Edric placed his knee at the man's elbow and applied just enough pressure to let him know what might happen if he cared to resist further. The screams of the little one garnered the attention of the giant and the intellectual.

Edric waited until they were both looking right at him before he applied additional force. The elbow gave way and the runt's tibia shattered as Edric's knee forced it forward. A small portion of the bone protruded from the skin as the runt screamed out in pain and then succumbed to it, collapsing unconscious onto the ground. Edric smiled at the intellectual and waited for him to make his decision. It didn't take long at all before he ran.

That left the giant to deal with. The man on the ground had inched his way back from his attackers and had propped himself against the brick façade of the alley. From what Edric could ascertain, the man didn't look too badly injured, but if he didn't remove the giant there would be no telling how much further his injuries would go.

"You gunna pay for that," the giant said, tossing his head towards the lump of human that was the unconscious runt. Edric watched as the giant circled towards him. Edric began to match his movement. Keeping his body sideways, Edric gave the giant the smallest possible target. He watched the eyes and allowed his peripheral vision to take in the subtle movements of his opponent. When the giant came forward, Edric knew exactly what he had planned.

Edric stepped to his left and chambered his right leg into a side-kick position. He struck out at the giant's left knee with lightning speed, blasting through the side of it and sending the giant to the ground. The crunch of his knee was quickly followed by a blood curdling scream that was cut short as Edric used his open right hand to strike at the giant's throat with a chop. It was over in less than two seconds.

Edric walked towards the victim and offered him his hand. For the first time, Edric realized that he was fairly close in age to the man who was probably only in his late twenties. Less than a decade separated the two. Still, he was disheveled from the attack and struggling to breathe.

"Try not to speak. If you need an ambulance, nod your head," Edric said, dropping to one knee in front of him.

The man shook his head and held up his hand as if to say, "Wait," and so Edric did.

"Than . . ." he choked a bit before being able to finish the thought, "Thank you."

Edric bowed his head slightly, saying nothing in response. The man moved to his knee and prepared to stand. Edric rose and again offered his hand. This time, the man took the help.

"Appreciate the assistance," he said, still coughing and struggling for breath.

As Edric hauled him upwards, the man groaned and held his side. "Sir, are you certain you do not need an ambulance?" Edric asked again.

"Name is Jacob," he squeaked out, "and no, I'll be fine, thanks to you. More excitement than an accountant should have in a day, much less a lifetime."

Edric stepped back and allowed Jacob to steady himself and take his first step. It was wobbly, but enough to ensure Edric that he would be all right.

Jacob stared at Edric and his nudity suddenly struck both of them. "Looks like I might be able to return the favor," he said, removing his jacket and handing it to Edric. He hesitated a moment before accepting it.

Jacob smiled at him and said, "Why don't you help me home and we can find you some clothes to wear?"

Edric nodded and took Jacob gently under the arm. He leaned him against the brick, and with his eyes, wordlessly asked if he was all right. "I'm okay, really," Jacob assured him.

"I just need to retrieve something before we go," Edric said allowing his hands to drift from the man tentatively, as if he might collapse at any moment. When Edric felt confident that Jacob could stand on his own, he moved to retrieve the precious envelope that Feinstein had entrusted to him. He had been dead less than twenty-four hours and Edric had not quite accepted that fact yet. Now, however, was not the time to grieve. He grabbed the envelope and burrowed it away in his underwear.

"What's your name, kid?" Jacob asked as he returned.

Edric hesitated for a moment. He thought of his last moments with Professor Feinstein and then gave him the only name he could. "Marc. Marc Cunningham."

Chapter 21

The New Friend

Jacob's brain felt as bruised and battered as his body. All the way to his apartment, he had been pondering this young man who had saved his life. Granted that was just three blocks, but when you had just got the snot kicked out of you, that trip took quite a long time. At the tender age of twenty-nine, Jacob could not recall a more surreal day. Marc Cunningham was more easily explained away as a dream than could be defined as reality.

"Do you like pizza?" Jacob asked, as they reached a few doors away from his apartment building. They were the first words that had been said since they left the crumpled bodies of his attackers in the alley. He considered calling the cops, but didn't know how to explain away the enigma that was Marc. Curiosity, as always, was getting the better of him. Jacob had considered buckets of statements and whole bushels of questions, but couldn't quite find the one to jump-start the conversation. His mother said food is always the best start to a conversation and so he went with it.

"Of course," Marc replied.

"Good," Jacob smiled, "I'll have it delivered. I don't really think either of us is fit for dining out right about now."

They continued to walk in silence. Jacob had been assessing his would-be savior and had settled on a likely scenario. Marc was young, in excellent physical shape, clearly well trained and calm in a fight. That led Jacob to think martial artist. A short, cropped haircut and polite manners suggested he was well cared for and educated. His walk was steady, a thirty inch step complete with a heel that drove and clicked into the pavement. That made Marc a military man, Jacob would bet money on it.

There were no military bases for a hundred miles or more. The nearest one he could think of was a Marine Corps base that was two-hundred twenty miles to the south. Jacob thought of his father and the terminology that had been part of his everyday vocabulary. His father had never left the Marine Corps far behind. In his house a wall was a bulkhead, a bathroom was a head, and aye-aye, always meant a thing would get done.

They climbed the stairs to the third floor apartment. Jacob winced a few times and regretted not taking the elevator before he had finished the first flight. "I'm gonna rest on this bulkhead," he said, leaning on the wall. He watched Marc's face intently, trying to see how he reacted to the word. "No sign of anything yet," he thought.

"You afraid of dogs?" Jacob asked before he turned the key to the apartment.

"No," Marc replied calmly.

"Good. Monster! Daddy's home!" Jacob yelled as he pushed the door open. A massive, broad chested yellow lab barreled down the hallway towards them. He leaped in the air and launched himself into his master's arms. After a copious amount of licking, Jacob said, "This is Monster. As you can see, he is friendly."

Marc bent down and gave the dog a scratch under the chin and behind the ear, only to have the dog present his behind for scratching. Marc obliged and Jacob began pushing them into the apartment. "Come on Monster, let the guy in. Some guard dog you are," he chided.

Jacob threw down his keys on the table and pointed down the hallway, not giving up his attempts to learn about his guest. "The head is the first door on the right, if you need to use it," he said. Marc gave no sign of the classic comradery that Marines share with one another. Jacob had witnessed numerous chance encounters where his father would recognize a fellow Marine and an instant friendship existed. No, Marc wasn't a Marine, he decided. He was something else.

Jacob dialed the phone and called to Marc, "What do you want on your pizza?"

"Meat of some variety, if that is agreeable," Marc poked his head out of the bathroom to answer, while Monster was waiting at the door for him to come back out.

"My kinda guy," Jacob responded, pointing a finger at him. "Large meat-lovers, a two-liter of Pepsi and let me get an order of breadsticks with cheese too. Oh, and extra sauce. Thanks!"

Jacob hung up the phone and headed into the bedroom. He rummaged through some drawers and found clean shorts, a t-shirt and socks for his guest. He stacked them on the bathroom sink, only to find Marc staring at his reflection. "You okay, man?" he asked. He still suspected military, though now Jacob thought he might have a PTSD victim in his apartment. Marc was probably a veteran of one of the Middle Eastern conflicts. So many of those guys came home and became homeless, incapable of matriculating back into civilian society. Jacob had read about the enormous numbers of suicides, the homelessness, and joblessness.

Marc turned towards Jacob and thrust out his hand. "Thank you. This is very kind of you," he said, looking down at the clothes. "I promise, I will repay you."

Jacob shook his hand and laughed, "You saved my butt out there tonight. I think dinner and some clothes are the least I could do." He hesitated a moment and then added, "I think, maybe I can do more, if you let me." He let the statement float for a moment, hoping that Marc would reach for the life-preserver instead of choosing to drown. Jacob had watched his father succumb to those demons. If he could save someone from the same fate, he was going to try.

Marc did not respond, but he didn't argue or run away. Jacob took that as an important first step in accepting help. Soldiers were the ultimate alpha males. Accepting handouts, assistance and admitting weakness never came easy to them. Jacob treaded lightly, as if he was coxing a timid animal, always cognizant that he could scare him away.

After a healthy dose of aspirin they headed to the living room. "Sit," Jacob offered as they entered the somewhat spartan living room. "Mi casa, es su casa," he added flopping down onto an old recliner and offering the couch to Marc. Monster climbed into Jacob's lap, making the man almost disappear from view.

They chatted about small stuff, movies, television shows and sports. Marc was evasive in his answers, but no matter how coy or non-specific he was, Jacob got the sense that the young man in front of him had serious gaps in his pop culture knowledge. It was clear that Marc had not been to a movie in several years. He also had no interest or access to a television. The man had sports knowledge, though not of any professional teams, only the rules and strategy behind it. It was as if he had been on a deserted island for a few years, hidden away from society. Jacob realized that he might be wrong about him. There was a growing sense of dread inside him. Had he invited an escaped convict into his home?

The pizza came and both men ate voraciously. Marc sat, straight backed in the chair and ate quickly, though with careful manners while Jacob tossed bits of pizza for Monster to catch. When the food was near gone, Marc finally dealt with the elephant in the room.

"I was a student at Shatterly's Obedience and Drill Fraternity. Not of my own choosing, mind you," he began. "I am certain you were curious about my appearance. I felt you deserved an explanation."

"Thank you. I was," Jacob replied, relieved.

"You have already been very kind, but I wonder if I could impose on you for a favor?" Marc asked, offering the last slice to Jacob.

"No thanks," Jacob politely declined and quickly realized how his words might have caused confusion. "The slice, I mean, not the favor," Jacob blurted. "Oh, damn, I can't get this out right. What do you need?" he said, exacerbated.

Marc smiled at the awkwardness of his new friend. "I left the school without permission. Potentially, they will be looking for me . . ."

"You can stay with me," Jacob interjected.

"I am in your debt. I would ask something else of you though, if you are willing?"

Jacob waited, not sure how far down the rabbit hole he was willing to go.

"I have not been able to contact my father for almost four years. No visitors were allowed on campus, not that he knew where I was, and I was not allowed off campus or access to electronics." Marc paused a moment, then his words became a mournful lament, "I wrote him letters sometimes, but they wouldn't let me send them."

Jacob's jaw nearly fell off at the statement. "Why?" he asked in stunned disbelief.

"I was sent to the Chateau D'If to disappear. They would not allow me any contact with the outside world."

Jacob was awed by how controlled the young man in front of him could be regarding all of this. "You want me to contact him?" Jacob offered.

"Please," Marc said, for the first time showing some hint of emotion. "I fear that if I seek him out, I may be discovered."

"Call him," Jacob said excitedly.

"I cannot. I do not want anything that could be traced."

Jacob got up and went into the kitchen. He grabbed a pen and paper and asked, "What's his name and address?"

"His name is Davies. Jack Davies," Marc replied and gave him the street address.

"Well, Marc Cunningham," Jacob said, stressing the name to insinuate he knew it wasn't real, "am I going to tell him his son Marc misses him?"

Marc hesitated, "Don't tell him a name. Just that his son wants to see him."

"Suit yourself, kid," Jacob said, deciding not to push the issue. "Sorry, I know you aren't a kid," Jacob corrected himself despite his instinct that the young man before him needed as much help as he had given Jacob earlier.

Marc slept fitfully that night. Jacob had offered his bed, but Marc had politely refused and slept on the couch. His dreams were filled with hope and dread. He was free, but for how long? He awoke to the smell of bacon and eggs as his host continued to show him kindness the likes of which he had not seen since disappearing behind those stone walls. The two men ate as Jacob queried his guest about his days at the school.

"I took the day off. I'm going to find your father today," Jacob told him as they cleared the dishes. "It's about a three and a half hour drive from here. Stay put. Catch up on some of the shows you missed the last couple of years. Feed and water Monster for me. I'll be back late, hopefully with your dad in tow."

Marc opened his mouth to speak, but Jacob held up his hand to silence him. Gently, Jacob put the same hand on Marc's shoulder. "I figured I owed you one."

Marc felt like crying, cheering, or hugging him. The emotions became a log jam, and none reached the surface. Marc stood in stunned silence.

Jacob collected his car keys and headed for the door. He turned and asked one final question, "What can I tell him to convince him I'm not a crazy person?"

Marc seemed to ponder a wealth of things that he might say. Then, he settled on one. "Tell him, I left the Honey Nut Cheerios out for him."

"That'll do," Jacob said, smiling. "You need anything before I go?"

"I want to repay you. Is there a Mount Collier Savings and Loan branch anywhere nearby?" Marc asked, fingering the envelope in the pocket of his borrowed shorts.

"Three blocks down to the left. I won't accept a penny, though."

~

Marc sat at the desk in front of the skeptical woman. She, in her perfectly fitted pantsuit and designer glasses, he in a loose fitting t-shirt and shorts that would fall down if it were not for the belt that almost wrapped twice around him. It was no wonder that she checked the documents twice and then had the bank manager review them as well.

"Everything looks to be in order Mr. Cunningham," she said, handing back the identifying papers. "The bank would like you to meet with our financial planner to discuss how best to allocate your rather large fortune. Would that be something you would be interested in?"

She handed him the updated bank statement he had requested. It detailed over three dozen accounts of various types. The most important figure sat at the bottom of the ninth page. Marc smiled at the number of digits and the volume of commas needed to separate them. He would be able to care for his father and exact his vengeance without ever thinking about money.

"Would you like to visit the safe-deposit box now, sir?" the woman asked shivering at the thought that she might offend such a wealthy client.

"What?" Marc thought, shocked! He had come to one of the branches, the closest he could find. Never did he think it might be the branch that Feinstein had set up his accounts in. Where he deposited his secrets. It made sense though. It was probably the closest branch to Shatterly's. "Please," Marc replied. He rose from his seat to follow her having no idea what to expect.

They gave him a private room to wait. Shortly, the woman returned with a guard carrying the safe-deposit box. He placed it on the table in front of Marc and left.

"Please let me know if there is anything you need," the woman said and then gave him his privacy.

Marc stared at the long box for a while before he opened it. He did not know what it would contain. Would it be full of Professor Feinstein's memories? Treasure? He wanted to know. He didn't want to know. Marc opened the metal lid of the box.

He took out a small felt bag that was far heavier than he expected. A dark brown journal was the only remaining item. He removed that as well and closed the lid. First, he spilled out the bag. His initial thoughts had been confirmed. Several large gems each shimmered in their own unique color, mixed with old gold coins. "The Treasure of Lima, I suppose," he thought. Marc held a massive diamond between his thumb and forefinger for a moment and then deposited it into his pocket. He bagged the other coins and gems and returned them to the safe-deposit box. He took the journal with him as he left.

"Thank you for your time and your diligent efforts to secure my accounts," Marc said as he passed the woman on his way out. "I would like to pick up the debit card tomorrow. Will that be possible?"

"Of course, Mr. Cunningham." she replied and went immediately to her desk, presumably to make sure it was done for him when he returned.

Marc walked back to Jacob's apartment with a massive diamond, five-thousand dollars in cash and access to hundreds of millions more. "Thank you, Professor Feinstein," he whispered, squeezing the journal in his hand.

He walked up the stairs to the apartment and found the door was open. It had only been a few hours. Could Jacob have returned with his father so soon, he wondered. "Dad!" he yelled, looking to and fro.

He stood, stone faced. Jacob's countenance told Marc all he needed to know. "I'm sorry. Your father died two years ago."

Marc collapsed to his knees. A massive chasm of emptiness had just opened within him. That crater seemed to demand to be plugged and all he had to fill it with was his tears.

Chapter 22

The Reconnaissance Mission

Several months later

The restaurant was slow tonight. It was quiet most nights, only picking up on the weekends when people were looking to escape the hum-drum existence of everyday life. There was an endearing elderly couple that came in every Wednesday and lingered for a few hours. They drank as many sodas and ate as much bread as they could endure and they tipped sparingly. Other than that single table, there were the two regulars at the bar. Old friends that treated each other as if they had both kicked each other's puppies. They seemed to hate each other, except when the other wasn't around. Only then would they rave to anyone who might listen about the wonderful qualities of their dear friend.

Chris had been waiting tables here at Pinocchio's for over two years now. The place wasn't posh, or stylish, or en vogue. It didn't attract the wealthy clientele of Mount

Collier. What it did attract was the working class in search of great food. Matt, the owner and chef, was a good man who had given Chris a chance when he needed it most. Chris had become a devotee of sorts, modeling himself after the man, ever conscious of impressing him. Whenever a guest entered Pinocchio's, Chris would always greet them pleasantly, just as he did now to the man who came through the door.

"Hello. Welcome to Pinocchio's. Are you joining us for dinner, or would you like a seat at the bar?" Chris gestured to both locations. His voice changed slightly as he mentioned the bar and it seemed to indicate his preference was a table in the dining area.

The new guest was a young man built hard and athletic. His hair was shoulder length, jet black and looked as if it had been ironed straight. His clothes mirrored the man; black, perfectly neat, not a wrinkle to be seen. He carried a brown leather satchel with him. His jaw was square and powerful, but he smiled politely, "Dinner. Please."

Chris sat the man at the window overlooking the main road into town. The view was the most pleasant one the restaurant had to offer and Chris made a habit of seating new guests here. Since the town was nestled in the valley south of the mountain, the restaurant looked down on it, rather than the town doing the same. The view was a source of irony to Chris. The elite of Mount Collier wouldn't be caught dead here, after all.

"Can I offer you something to drink while you wait for the rest of your party?"

"Water with lemon, thank you."

Chris returned to the table with the drink, watching as the young man stared down at the town. He placed the water on the table. "Great view, isn't it?"

"The illusion of serenity," the patron observed, not taking his eyes from the window.

"Hah!" Chris blurted, unable to hide his disdain for the town and the stranger's feelings towards it.

The guest turned to him and smiled. "I did say, illusion."

"You're not from around here, are you?" Chris observed.

"No. I have no friends . . ." he said and then quickly added, ". . . here."

"Just passing through then?"

He hesitated and took a deep breath in before responding, "Just long enough to take care of some business."

"Will anyone be joining you tonight?" Chris asked, not wanting to get too deep in conversation.

"No. I am alone."

Chris took his order and checked on the old couple. He returned with bread and salad and did not reappear until the main course was ready. He delivered a heaping pile of homemade linguini covered in jumbo shrimp and a sauce that quite literally sweetened the air around the table.

"Can I do anything else for you?" Chris asked, refilling the man's water as he bathed in the aroma of the meal.

"Maybe," the man in black replied.

Chris waited for the request without response. He probably assumed the patron would have some trivial and easy to fill need.

"Did you know a boy named Edric Davies?" the man in black asked.

Chris felt like someone had just dropped a 45 pound plate on his chest. He stepped back, shuddering at the name. His shock was clearly evident to his guest, but he was utterly unable to hide it.

"I assume by your reaction that the answer is "yes," correct?"

Chris nodded his head, his mouth agape.

"Would you please join me for a few minutes? I have some questions you may be able to help me with."

Chris sat across from him. His mind raced, wondering who this young man was, what he had to do with Edric Davies and worse, what he might want.

"Who . . . who are you?"

"A friend of Edric's; from the Chateau," he replied.

Chris was obviously confused, so the stranger elaborated.

"Shatterly's Obedience and Drill Fraternity. We call it the Chateau D'If," the strange patron continued. "He asked me to deliver some gifts to friends of his before he died."

"Oh my God," Chris said, stunned that Edric Davies was dead. He knew he had a hand in what had happened to him. That was a guilt he had carried a long while now. He was different now, better. He would have made different choices today, but the news he had just received closed down any hope of undoing a past wrong. There would be no redemption.

"I am sorry. Was Edric a friend of yours as well?" the young man asked, looking taken aback.

Chris suddenly realized he had tears streaming down his face and tried to pull himself together. He wondered if he was crying for Edric or for himself and that made him feel all the more selfish. He took some napkins from the silver dispenser on the table and dabbed at his eyes. "I'm sorry. I am just shocked by the news. I . . ." Chris couldn't control his feelings before finishing and succumbed to tears once more. The stranger was respectful and allowed Chris the time he needed to compose himself.

"What happened to him?" Chris asked, sniffling.

The man in black took a fork full of his meal and savored it before he swallowed hard. "Edric was sent to the Chateau almost four years ago now. He struggled to fit in. Never certain why he was even there to begin with, he spent his days trying to understand. I think it may have driven him mad. He killed himself, alone in his room just a few months ago."

As Chris struggled to digest all that he had heard, the young man ate steadily in silence, watching him intently. Unaware, the stranger seemed to be studying his reactions. He rubbed his hands on his face and pitched forward, then backwards in his seat. There was nowhere to run and Chris had to endure the pains of processing all of this.

"I believe your other table needs you," the stranger pointed as the elderly man held up his empty glass.

"Thank you," Chris replied and hopped to his work. He returned quickly and sat down again. "I'm very sorry to hear about Edric," his voice creaked.

They sat in silence for a few minutes, each collecting and arranging their thoughts. The man neared completion of his food before he spoke again. When he did, it was the question Chris had dreaded. "So, were the two of you friends," he queried again.

Chris sat back in the booth and crossed his arms. His answer was slow in coming. When it did, it reflected the man he wanted to be, not the boy he was. "No. Edric was my friend, but I am ashamed to admit that I was not his."

Chapter 23

The Story

The stranger waited at the table until Chris had finished busing the remnants of the dishes from the elderly couple's abandoned table. The restaurant was now empty, except for the two of them.

"I don't know your name," Chris stated as he sat across from the stranger.

"Stephan," The stranger offered with no elaboration.

"So, you met Edric at school?" Chris asked, knowing the answer, but not having a clue where to begin his own story.

"If you could call it that," Stephan chortled.

"What do you mean?" Chris wondered aloud.

Stephan leaned forward with a serious glean in his eye. When he spoke, there was venom in his voice, "Is it a school when children are beaten? Is it a school when boys are denied the ability to see or even communicate with their families? Edric was not in a school. He was in a dungeon!"

"I'm sorry," Chris said, not knowing what else he could say or do.

The two sat in silence for several long moments. Stephan sat as stone faced and silent as a granite statue. Chris was the one to finally break it. "He didn't deserve it. He was a nice kid."

Again, time stalled. Chris watched Stephan move the remaining food on his plate from one side to another. It had grown cold with time. "Can I warm that for you?"

"Thank you, but no," Stephan replied. "I have no appetite anymore." He shoved the plate away and the ceramic warbled against the wood.

"Did you graduate?" Chris asked, trying to understand the presence of the stranger here today.

"Yes," Stephan said, "I join the Navy in a few days. Hopefully, sail the world for a few years." Quickly, he changed the subject back to Edric. "Why was Edric sent to the Chateau D'If?"

Chris huffed, "It's complicated."

"I have time. Please, explain it," Stephan asked, but it felt to Chris like an order.

"He made people jealous," Chris said, making what was complicated utterly simple.

The epiphany struck the stranger like a boulder had crashed into his chest. "Was it really that simple?" he thought. Though he knew the answer, he asked, "Who?"

"Brett DiVinceo, for one," Chris began. "He was a freshman when Edric was in eighth grade. They played basketball on the freshman team together. The star player, this kid, Jason, hurt his knee in the homecoming game. Edric came into the game, rallied the team and won it for us. He was amazing," Chris smiled at the memory. "Anyway, Brett wasn't one to play second best. He started rumors that Edric was on steroids and dealing drugs."

"Is that why Edric was expelled and sent away?" the stranger asked.

"No," he shook his head, "Brett was just a part of it. He wasn't smart enough to set up Edric. That was Frank Macintyre." Chris thought he saw the stranger shudder at the name. He nodded and continued, "He was Edric's best friend. Supposed to have been, anyway."

"Why would he have betrayed him?" Stephan prodded.

"Over a girl," Chris said, as if it were obvious, "Meagan Dumas." This time, he was certain the stranger had heard the name before. "He told you about her?"

"I know of her," he replied, each word as icy as the last.

Chris continued, as he released the guilt that had shamed him for nearly four years. Recounting the story had become cathartic, freeing him in a way. "She and Edric were finally dating. The girl had liked him for a while. He just never had the courage to ask her out. Frank was a spoiled rich kid who wanted anything Edric had. He wanted Meagan," Chris added, a hint of menace in his voice.

"I see," Stephan nodded.

"Frank was the one that wrote the letter to Mr. Germaine," Chris said. "He was the assistant principal. When they found the drugs in his locker, Edric just disappeared. Nobody knew what had happened to him."

"Someone knew," the stranger added without bothering to hide his anger. "What happened after?"

"They all seemed to get what they wanted, honestly," Chris admitted. "With Edric gone and Jason's injury, Brett became team captain. Frank didn't wait long before he snapped up Meagan."

"And now? What of them?" the stranger asked, hungrily.

"Brett is still in school. He had to retake a bunch of classes. Still doesn't take them very seriously though. His father is rich. Owns half the town. He has been ill lately, with ulcers, I think. Brett figures he will just wait him out until he dies and inherit the fortune. He says school is something he does to keep busy until his dad dies."

"What of Frank?"

"He's still rich, still smart, and still miserable," Chris described him with obvious disdain.

"You don't like him very much, do you?" Stephan queried.

"He has more money than God, a beautiful girlfriend and the brains to do just about anything he wants. What does he do with all of that? Wallows in his own misery and tries to ruin other people's lives so they can be just as unhappy as he is!"

"So, Meagan is still his girlfriend?"

Chris chuckled at that, "Oh, yeah! She is like one of his little possessions. He parades her around, buys her stuff and she tolerates whatever he says or does to her."

"What about the assistant principal? Is he still at the school too?"

"Yeah. He runs it now. Probably be the superintendent in a few years."

"Earlier, you said that you had not been a friend to Edric. What did you mean?"

Chris squirmed uncomfortably in his seat, "I sort of encouraged them at first. I made fun of them. Two rich kids who were supposed to have it all. Then, here comes this poor kid who has all the attention, all the respect and the girl." He sighed and continued, "I was enjoying it, you know? When Edric disappeared, I was scared. Germaine was ruthless. I had no real proof of what they had done. I just kinda stayed silent. Edric suffered because I was scared to speak up." Chris spoke with shame and sorrow and then all of it seemed to collapse on top of him, "He died because of me."

He hung his head in shame for some time, sobbing. The stranger said nothing as he watched the waiter's body heave and shudder. When he finally raised his head, Chris watched as the stranger pondered all that he told him. Stephan seemed to churn the information over and over, waiting for some fresh understanding to surface. "I'm sorry for your friend," Chris said again, knowing that he could not undo his part in the crime that had been done to Edric.

Stephan rose and straightened his clothing. "Thank you for your time this evening," he said, pointing to the bag sitting on the chair beside him. "Seems to me that Edric did not have any other friends." He began to walk away. "Keep that for yourself," the stranger called back and walked out the door. Chris stared at the man with a baffled look.

After he had left, Chris switched his seat to the one the stranger had occupied. He pulled open the brown leather satchel and nearly fainted at the sight of its contents. There, in the bag, were neat stacks of one-hundred dollar bills, maybe fifty thousand dollars' worth. Enough to change a young man's life.

Chapter 24

The Gift

The next morning two men entered Moore's Lumber looking to make a purchase. The shelves were stocked only one or two items deep. It was a place that worked hard to look well-travelled, but underneath was struggling to survive.

They were greeted warmly by the cashier, "Good morning, gentlemen." It was Julie. She had grown into a beautiful young woman.

"Good morning," Jacob replied. "Is there someone we could speak to about scheduling a delivery for contractors?"

The woman looked stunned, "Sure! I'll get the owner for you." Julie picked up the phone and paged her father.

After a few minutes, a man came slowly from the back of the store. Mr. Moore had aged in the years since Edric had disappeared. What hair he had left was now gray. His stomach protruded beyond an overworked belt and he walked hunched over like a man whose back had been broken by time and struggle. "How may I help you, gentlemen?"

"My friend here is building a home," he motioned to young man at his side, solidly built with long black hair. "and he does not speak English." The young man nodded, but said nothing, clearly more interested in his surroundings than the business at hand. Jacob continued, "We would like to open an account for our contractors to draw upon for deliveries."

"Of course! Of course! Let me get the paperwork for you. What kind of credit line are you looking for?" Mr. Moore asked as he shuffled towards a square set of counters at the center of the store. He rummaged through some drawers until he finally found what he was looking for. Clearly, it had been some time since anyone had opened a new account here.

"Just fill out here, here, and everything up to this line for me and then we will get you all set up," Mr. Moore said, excited energy in his voice.

Jacob began to fill out the paperwork. He had specific instructions from his employer on what address was to be built first. He filled in the address of 515 Naohilles Road. It had been his father's house. When he reached the line regarding bank credit, he filled in the account information for a man named Stephan Marin, roughly translated, Steven the sailor. "Sir, my employer wanted to ensure that there would be no delay in the start of his credit," Jacob added as he handed the man a check, "so he wanted to fund the account now."

Mr. Moore took the check and looked at the amount. He was stunned. The check was in the amount of five-hundred thousand dollars. "There is no need for this, sir." He handed back the check, "The account will clear by tomorrow and we will charge the account only for the purchases made.

Jacob looked at his employer for a moment trying to gain the man's attention. When he did, they walked a few steps away and spoke in low tones. Jacob returned to the desk when the conversation was complete and left the check on the counter in front of Mr. Moore. "My employer will be doing a great deal of construction in the area. This check will only scratch the surface of the amount he intends on spending with you." Without another word the two men exited as quickly as they had come.

Moore's Lumber had the busiest summer season of their entire existence. They delivered enough lumber and supplies to build two dozen houses, but they only delivered to two addresses.

Marc Cunningham, under the guise of Stephan Marin, closely supervised the construction of both homes. Each, in their own way, would be used to repay a debt. One would be the base from which he would function. It would act as his home for the time he would spend in Mount Collier. But, 515 Naohilles Road, the place where Edric Davies was raised could not be that for him. Instead, he would ensure that something good would happen there again. The address would bring joy again, as it had once in the past.

When he was ready, Marc traveled along an old, familiar path. He went to the back gate of Moore's Lumber and found that hard times had not changed the man's ways. He was still generous and trusting. Marc hesitated a moment and gently caressed the bag under his arm before pushing through the gate. He took the key that was left on the top molding of the back door and unlocked the store. Marc stood and smiled at the place. The shelves were fully stocked, the walls freshly painted. Mr. Moore could feel proud of it once more.

Marc climbed the stairs to the office and entered. He removed a jar from the bag he carried and placed it on the large wooden desk. He repositioned it several times before he felt satisfied. He left following the same path he had come in by.

Mr. Moore and his daughter opened the store early on Monday morning. Lately, coming to work was something he enjoyed again. He could come to his desk and see orders that needed filling rather than bills that needed paying. If things kept up, just a little longer, he would be able to send Julie to college again. He wouldn't need her here, working for free. The years she sacrificed, fighting to keep the family business afloat would not be in vain. Pangs of guilt shot through Mr. Moore as he considered all she could have done with that time. Tuition money, room and board, he would be able to pay it all. The thought that he could repay his daughter for her love and loyalty, her hard work and sacrifice drove him harder and harder every day. She deserved it.

The store was quiet. The sun was rising outside and its rays spilled in through the windows, filling the store with an array of color.

"Love those rainbows," Julie said as she walked back and forth through them.

Mr. Moore smiled at his daughter. He would miss her, but he couldn't wait to make her happy. "I'll be upstairs. Call me before you unlock the doors."

He made his way to the back of the store and up the stairs. He unlocked the office and flicked on the lights. That's when he saw that his office had been broken into. They had left something behind.

There, sitting on his desk was a large plastic jar, a piece of paper taped to it. He walked to the desk and picked it up, smiling at it. He had seen it long ago, when his daughter had been happier, sillier than she was today. It was labeled "Julie's Dowry."

"Julie!" he called down the stairs. "Julie! Come up here!" He reached his hand in the jar and removed the contents. There was a rolled document and a small black felt box. He unrolled the document and saw that it was a deed. He immediately recognized the address, 515 Naohilles Road. Stunned, he saw that the deed was in his name. He went for the box, hoping that it would explain something. Laid within the box was a set of house keys and a massive diamond ring.

"What is it, Dad?" Julie asked as she came into the office.

He sat, white-faced and pointed at the jar.

"Where did that come from?" Julie asked.

"I thought you did it!" her father said exacerbated.

"I haven't been up here. I didn't put this on your desk," Julie said, confused.

"Look," her father pointed at the contents spread across his desk.

Julie read the deed. She picked up the ring and then the jar. She looked inside and noticed that there was something written on the inside of the paper. "My undying gratitude, Stephan Marin."

"What does it all mean?" she asked.

"I don't know," her father said. "I don't know."

~

Jacob sat at the massive ornate oak desk that Marc had imported from France. He was fielding his fifth phone call from Mr. Moore this afternoon. "No, sir, Stephan Marin does not speak English and so does not take phone calls," he repeated, as patiently as possible. Jacob traced the intricate scrollwork on the edge of the desk with his forefinger as he listened to Mr. Moore plead his case. "Sir, my employer refuses to take calls directly and he is currently traveling and unavailable to meet with you." Jacob began to tap a pen on the desk as he continued the delicate dance around Mr. Moore's questions, "No, my employer does not know anyone by the name of Davies." Tap-tap-tap-tap, the speed and intensity picked up. "Yes, I will express both you and your daughter's gratitude. You have my word on it."

Jacob hung up and let out an enormous sigh. He slunk back into his puffy rolling chair and stared intently at Marc for several long minutes. Monster sat at his feet, snoring lazily. The two had become fast friends since they first met. That day felt like a lifetime ago.

Marc had told Jacob the story of what had happened to him the same night Jacob had been forced to bring him the heartbreaking news of his father's death. Marc shared the stunning accusations, the devious trap, his years at Shatterly's, and how Feinstein helped him to escape. It was that same night that Jacob had agreed to help him in any way he could. Little had he known how deep he would become involved. That was before Jacob knew about the treasure; before he knew about the plan. Still, Jacob had faith that there was a good man at the heart of that plan.

"You did a wonderful thing, you know," Jacob said, finally breaking the silence.

"I balanced his kindness as best I could with an act of simple generosity," Marc replied, not looking up from his book.

"Ha!" Jacob snorted, jolting Monster awake. "Simple generosity? Is that what we are calling that? All this?" He gestured to the library, the vast mansion they lived in now.

Marc soothed Monster with a few gentle pats on the head. "I call it balance," he explained, "and there are a few other sets of scales that need to be dealt with."

Chapter 25

The Return

The arrival of Marc Cunningham at Mount Collier High was a carefully orchestrated affair. Registration required numerous forged documents beyond those that Abraham Feinstein had given him. Though Marc had grown used to the creation of identities, this one was beyond his ability. Gone was the long hair of Stephan Marin. He had returned to the short crop that he had grown accustomed to over the last few years. He knew that a haircut wasn't enough to generate a new persona. Not one to be deterred, he reached out to the only person he knew who could help. Nichols had provided school records and fictitious parental identities that Marc had needed to complete the ruse. Marc didn't want to know what other types of businesses his old comrade was involved in since being expelled from Shatterly's. He was just glad to have the help.

Standing before the entryway again, Marc was feeling more than a little overwhelmed. Nostalgia came from every direction, through every little thing. This place, this path to the door, was where Edric Davies had disembarked from the bus. It was the same place that he had seen Frank cheer for him. Marc walked forward. He retraced the steps he took that fateful day. He imagined the crowd. He could hear the noise. Marc closed his eyes and could hear a name being chanted, "Edric! Edric!" A few steps more and then he stopped abruptly. "Right here. This is where she was," he thought, trying to shake the moment from his mind. He felt Meagan crashing into him, her arms wrapping around him as they did that day. No! It wasn't real. Memories. Just memories. His fists clenched and Marc had to refocus. He shook the shadows from his mind and walked on. He wasn't that person anymore.

Marc entered through the large glass double doors. He looked left, nostalgically. Part of him wanted to turn left and head down the hallway towards the middle school section. That was the past. There was no going back, no recovering what had been stolen from him. He looked at the large electronic bulletin board. Really, it was a big screen television for school propaganda. It cycled through a predetermined set of videos with each providing information to new students and a sense that everyone would have equal opportunity here at Mount Collier. He watched it for a moment, two attractive young girls discussing their experiences participating in a science program. The principal entered the room a few moments later and put his arms around them, proclaiming how proud he was of the two girls. It was Vincent Germaine, pompous smile and all. Marc grimaced, feeling a swell of animosity rise within him. He turned right, his heartbeat cresting as he walked towards the high school section and away from the man who had helped destroy his life.

Marc deliberately constructed his class schedule to avoid anyone who might have once known him well. As with all things at Mount Collier High, classes were stratified by class. Wealth determined everything here. Unlike his experiences at the middle school, Marc would attend only the most elite classes now.

In theory, every class was open to all students. For example, students could register for studio art, ceramics, or Classical European Masters. Studio art had no additional requirements, while ceramics required a supplies fee of three-hundred dollars. Meanwhile, Classical European Masters had a study abroad requirement, where every student had to attend a mandatory field trip to Italy during the spring recess to the tune of over five-thousand dollars.

Every department, be it math or social studies, had established a social wall, tall and thickly built, to ensure that the elite classes did not have to sully themselves with those poorer than they. As Marc combed through the course selection guide, he made it a point to register for classes with the highest required fees. This would guarantee him anonymity from most of Edric's classmates and access to those he sought to destroy.

His first period class was technology and innovation. It was a classic example of a class that wasn't really a class. All registered participants had to have the newest Ipad, a five-hundred dollar professional software evaluation fee, along with their own transportation to downtown, where students would intern at technology companies. There was no real internships and the class was more of a design your own app, if you want. Otherwise, the fee to register meant you got an A.

The hallway was quiet. Marc had deliberately planned to be late. He made his entrance, ensuring maximum visibility.

"Excuse me," he said apologetically, peering his head through the door and leaving the remainder of his body obscured by the door. "Is this Technology and Innovation?"

The teacher nodded and waved his hand for him to enter. Marc opened the door and stepped in. He wore a collared shirt, tie and slacks trimmed out with expensive leather shoes and belt. His entire ensemble was carefully chosen to create a splash. He would be overdressed for school, ensuring that he would be talked about. His clothes were from the finest Italian and Spanish designers, ensuring he would be talked about by the right circles.

He repeated a similar procedure for the next two periods, Twenty-first Century Math and Classical European Masters. It was in that class he found his first target, though an unexpected one at that.

"You going to rent the same villa as last year?" a student asked loudly from the back of the room as the teacher went through her classroom expectations.

"That a dig at me or something?" Brett DiVinceo replied, threateningly. He was still here! As arrogant as Marc remembered him, though bigger and more brutish than he imagined. Brett should have graduated last spring. Clearly, he didn't make it. Marc smiled. He could now take down the triumvirate together, just as they had done to him.

Marc took a seat three desks away from him. Close enough to hear the conversation, not so close as to look like he was paying attention to it. He felt his heart pounding, protruding from his shirt. Marc didn't hear the girl introduce herself the first time.

"I'm Kayla. Welcome to Mount Collier," she repeated. "You're new here?" She was a beautiful blonde; tall and athletic, with perfect skin.

He reached his hand out to her. "Marc Cunningham. Yes, I am new here," he replied.

They shook hands as Marc watched her take in his attire. It had the desired effect of impressing her while making her wonder about the formality.

"Pardon my appearance. My staff has not had an opportunity to unpack my things just yet," he said, the suggestion of immense wealth obviously implied.

"Where did you move into?" Kayla asked, not so coyly digging for information.

"My parents just built a place on Hilltop," Marc said nonchalantly, knowing that there was only one new construction in town.

"Oh!" Kayla said and then tried to cover her shock, "I've seen that house."

"It's smaller than I am used to, but it means we don't have to rent that awful suite when we go skiing this season," Marc explained as if it were a mere trifle. He watched her eyes widen. The house he had built with Mr. Moore's lumber was easily three times the size and five times the grandeur of anything this town had to offer. In a town full of extravagance and overblown wealth, Marc's house dwarfed them all.

Marc understood what Kayla would become for him. She would be his ambassador of gossip. She would be tasked with spreading a mix of truth and fiction about his enormous wealth. He decided to double down and give her something more to talk about. "Who is that gentleman there? I heard him discussing a villa in Italy when I came in," Marc queried, using the formal speech patterns that he had learned to hide behind.

"That's Brett. My boyfriend. He is pretty much the most popular guy in school, though some days I don't know why. Probably why he worked so hard to make sure he could come back for an extra year," she spewed sarcastically, then added, "His family is super rich."

"Kayla, it has been a pleasure meeting you. I will be throwing a gala at my home next week; a sort of get to know everyone event. I do hope the two of you will come," Marc said, shifting his attention to the teacher.

"I would love to come to a party on the Hilltop," Kayla said. Her excitement had caught the unwanted attention of the teacher. A stern look did nothing to dampen her spirits.

Marc's final period before lunch was the one he had anticipated most. It was his history course, Strategy and Tactics of Twentieth Century Wars. There was a time when the subject matter would have been enough for him to look forward to it. Today, he knew there would be a student in that class that he had not seen in a long time. He arrived early for that class.

Frank Macintyre strolled into the class a minute late and sat towards the front. The teacher, a rotund man with a green jacket and tweed elbows smiled warmly at him. Marc noted the relationship; how much the history department loved its favorite student. So much was about to change in Frank's life. "It is sad that no one has the decency to let you know what is coming," Marc thought as he stared at the back of his head.

Mr. Arthur cleared his throat and straightened his ugly green jacket, "The President of the United States has ordered a drone strike against a U.S. citizen in the middle of an Afghan terror camp." That statement seemed to get everyone's attention. He followed it up with a question, "Did the President act within his Constitutional authority?"

Marc raised his hand quickly, as did Frank and another girl. Mr. Arthur took the opportunity to study his new student and called on Marc, "Mr. Cunningham, correct?"

Marc nodded and then answered, "No." He silently hoped he would get the chance to elaborate on his response.

"Would you care to explain why?" Mr. Arthur prodded.

Marc fought to hide the smile that he could feel growing across his face as Frank turned to face him. Frank would evaluate him; assess him to see if he was a threat. Marc decided to be just that. He took a shallow breath and answered, "As Commander-in-chief, he has the authority to direct military forces. He does not, however, have the right to order the execution of an American citizen who has not had the benefit of a trial by his peers." He watched as the girl on the other side of the room nearly dislocated her shoulder as she reached her hand high into the air, desperate for attention. He finished his thought before Mr. Arthur could call on her, "Like many presidents before him, he has exceeded his Constitutional authority because he believes the situation requires it."

"Be bold and let history be the judge," Frank added without being called on. The girl's hand plummeted to her desk with a frustrated thud.

"Indeed," Marc said, giving a slight nod of agreement to Frank. The trap was set and Frank had just made the first oblivious steps towards his own end.

At lunch, Kayla graciously invited Marc to their table. Brett noted the new guy with typical alpha male behavior. Initially, Marc received a grunt and a handshake meant to break every bone in his fingers. Brett pawed and molested Kayla the entire period as if he had an incessant need to rub his scent on her like a cat on a piece of furniture. He was as complicated as a twelve piece puzzle that a three year old might put together. Marc ensured that he remained physically non-threatening and showed no interest in Kayla whatsoever. Soon, Brett, the star player he claimed to be, would not see him as a danger to the status quo and drop his guard. When that happened, Marc would walk right in and destroy him. He would never see it coming.

Chapter 26

The Party

The tents were arrayed in a long line on the back lawn. Tables, chairs and a dance floor slowly filled the space where grass once stood. Staff spread table clothes and decorated with fresh cut flowers. Lilacs, on Marc's orders, were added to every centerpiece. Rented china and silverware glimmered in the sunlight while ice carvings of Greek Gods and Goddesses were displayed and angled just so.

Caterers were scurrying through the house, setting up stations for food and drinks. Pasta stations, carving stations, and butlered service, seemed to pop up in every spare space. Marc also played to the expected crowd of young people. There was to be an ice cream bar with over thirty flavors, including a shake maker. The house filled with the aroma of freshly baked bread and sumptuous baked goods.

The band could be heard doing their sound tests and the gentlemen in charge of the fireworks had nearly completed his setup. Marc's instructions had been specific. Jacob was to throw a party that would project wealth and youth. "Make the Vanderbilts jealous," Marc had said, referencing the Gilded Age family famous for their excess. He then went on to list every detail he wanted. Jacob's job was simple. He needed to make sure that it all happened. The one thing he had going for him was that money was simply no object. Marc never asked how much something cost to arrange. He simply wanted it done.

The greatest struggle Jacob had was in dealing with Nichols, Marc's friend from a previous life as he was described. The boy was constantly seeking thrills, focused on his own pleasure. He was more than happy to distract the staff or anyone who passed by in the hopes that they would join in the fun. Jacob found him funny, but royally difficult to deal with. Where Marc was serious and focused, Nichols was a clown who thought nothing of consequences.

It was Jacob's job to ensure that Nichols and Brett met at the party. He was also tasked by Marc to drop hints that Nichols booked bets and was Marc's own bookie. Jacob supposed that was to suggest that Nichols could handle big money transactions discreetly. Jacob doubted Nichols could do anything without someone noticing. Still, Marc trusted him, so Jacob would have to.

Marc greeted each guest as they arrived and then shuffled them off into the house or out into the back gardens and to the tents. They were distractions, mere camouflage that he would use to study his enemies. He was formal, almost stiff as he invited them in. He reminded Jacob of an eighteenth century aristocrat. Marc was both courteous and respectful, but cool and aloof. Charming and dangerous at the same time, Marc projected confidence, but not arrogance.

"This is Brett DiVinceo," Marc whispered to Jacob as two people entered into the foyer and climbed the ornate marble stairs.

"Thank you for coming!" Marc said cordially as he held his arms in the air.

"Wow, this place is amazing," Brett said, stepping in front of Kayla and sticking out his hand.

Marc shook his hand and put the other on his shoulder. "My parents think they are railroad tycoons from another age," Marc replied, downplaying his singular role in the creation of the opulent home. "Kayla, you look incredible," he said, still holding Brett's grip. "Please, come in. Enjoy yourself."

Brett and Kayla moved into the house, ogling every detail of it. Jacob waited until they had walked deep enough into the house not to be noticed and then followed them. Marc remained, continuing to greet others as they entered.

"Are you Brett DiVinceo?" Jacob asked, approaching the couple from behind.

"Yeah," Brett replied, inconvenience obvious in his reply. "Who are you?"

"An old friend of Marc's family. Sort of a personal assistant to Mr. Cunningham," Jacob demurred. "He has spoken very highly of you," he added. "You must be Kayla," Jacob said, offering her a warm smile.

"Thanks," Brett said awkwardly, not knowing how to take this man that had approached him.

"I am sorry," Jacob proffered. "Mr. Cunningham wanted to make sure that certain of his guests understood that they were important to him. You are among that very small group. I am at your service," Jacob bowed slightly.

If Brett's ego could be seen, it would have filled the room to bursting. "Cool. That's cool," he said. "You got beer?" he asked.

Jacob smiled and said, "Follow me, please."

"Ah, Mr. Nichols," Jacob said as he entered the study, where a bar and waiter were stationed. "This is Mr. Cunningham's good friend, Brett DiVinceo and his girlfriend, Kate, was it?"

"Kayla," she corrected him.

"My apologies," Jacob offered. Marc had told him to forget her name on purpose. Anything to inflate Brett's sense that he was the most important person in the room.

"Nichols handles all of Mr. Cunningham's fun," Jacob explained. "He arranges the vacations, the entertainment and the gambling ventures."

"Really?" Brett said, intrigued. He took a beer from the counter of the bar and downed a long swig. "So, you take some pretty large wagers I bet," Brett asked.

"I'll leave you two to get acquainted," Jacob said, leaving the room. He was astounded as to how right Marc was. "Feed Brett's ego and he will be blind to everything happening around him," Marc had said. Now, the next step was up to Nichols. Get him betting. Get him losing and going deeper and deeper in debt. That was Marc's plan. Jacob didn't know what would happen after that, but he was certain Marc did.

"I was hoping you would make it," Marc said excitedly as Frank came in the door.

"Wouldn't miss it," Frank replied trying not to be overwhelmed by the enormity of the house.

"You came alone?" Marc asked quizzically.

"She'll be along later. She had to work," he said the last word, work, as if it were degrading.

"Well then, all the better for me," Marc smiled. "I think I have a collection you would find very interesting. May I show you?"

"Let's see it," Frank replied and the two headed down the hallway.

Marc brought Frank into a dark paneled room with sixteen foot ceilings. The molding in the room alone had to cost close to a million dollars. The room was filled with books with fancy inlaid spines, tapestries and statues made of every conceivable material. "My father and I built this together with the help of a good friend," Marc explained, a hint of sorrow seeping through the façade. The statement was at least partially true.

"Are those real?" Frank asked, pointing to a shimmering sabre and flintlock weapon.

"French. Napoleonic Era," Marc answered. "You have a good eye." Marc allowed Frank to explore the room, following two steps behind. He did not attempt to explain the collection, simply letting it speak for itself.

When he was done, Frank rubbed his chin and exclaimed, "Wow!"

"I am happy that you were impressed," Marc said satisfied. "Of all the people I have met in this town, you were the only one I thought might appreciate this room."

"How did you . . ." Frank began.

There was a knock at the door.

"Yes," Marc responded.

Jacob entered the room and asked, "Could I have a word with you in private, sir?"

Marc squashed the idea, "No need. We are among friends." He looked directly at Frank as he said the words.

"There is a problem with the show . . ." Jacob seemed to be hesitant to say it, "The fireworks display you have planned, sir."

"What is it?"

"They are claiming that they have not been fully paid. They intend on leaving if they are not paid immediately. I'm sorry. This is my fault, sir," Jacob bowed his head.

"How much do they require?" Marc asked showing not a hint of frustration or concern.

"Twelve-thousand dollars," Jacob informed.

"Use some of the money in the drawer. Be sure to replenish it by tomorrow though," Marc dismissed him.

"My apologies. You were saying?" Marc asked, but Frank was lost in thought as he watched Jacob count out the required sum and return a much larger amount to the drawer.

Marc suppressed a grin, "My family likes to keep enough cash on hand for emergencies. Shall we join the party?" Marc asked ushering him to the door.

The party was an enormous success. His guests were duly impressed. His plans had been set in motion. Despite that, Marc was frustrated that she had not come. He had wanted to see her, to look into her eyes. Would she recognize him? Would she see the boy that once was under the man he had become? He thought he would have to wait for another day for answers.

"Marc!" He heard a voice cry out. It was Frank. "Marc! Come meet my girlfriend."

His stomach dropped. Marc took a deep breath and tried to prepare himself for the moment he had been waiting for.

Marc reached out his hand in formal greeting to the young lady. She returned the gesture, offering to shake his hand, but neither hand met. Marc looked upon that hand and lost all his nerve. Stretched across her wrist, was the silly bracelet he had bought her the night they had gone out together. Marc recognized the small silver charm in the shape of a heart. The red elastic band had aged to a sun-burnt pink and her wrist had stark tan lines where the bracelet had rested. Marc stared at her hand while she stared into his eyes. That moment, a fleeting few seconds that might have been something like recognition, was interrupted when Brett came slamming into Marc, throwing his arm over his shoulder.

"What's up, buddy?" he yelled louder than was required. Brett clearly wanted everyone at the party to know he had a new friend.

"Hello again, Brett," Marc responded, offering up a fist bump. No sooner than it had been reciprocated, Marc reached into his pocket and drew out his phone. "Excuse me, I have to take care of some things," Marc proffered and began to walk away.

Meagan's eyes rested on him, he was certain of it. Marc could not see them, but he felt the penetration of their gaze, nevertheless. He could hear the conversational banter of the other students around him; Brett's obnoxious teasing, Frank's arrogant musings, but Meagan's voice was utterly silent. It was as if there were no words for what she was experiencing in that moment.

"She is here," Marc reported the moment he found Jacob.

Jacob knew who his friend was talking about. "Where?" he asked.

"Downstairs, in the entryway, under the grand staircase," Marc said nervously.

Jacob scurried to the railing and looked down on the growing crowd gathering in the house. He had never seen Marc nervous before. "Which one?" he asked.

"Purple dress, silver necklace and earrings, and long brown hair worn over her shoulder," Marc described her.

"Could you give me a few more details?" Jacob asked sarcastically before announcing loudly, "I see her!"

"Find out everything you can," Marc instructed and disappeared into a bedroom.

Chapter 27

The Descent

"I have news," Jacob announced as he paced into the expansive back yard.

Marc smiled and tossed the tennis ball high in the air. Monster took off and scampered across the lawn, oblivious to where the ball would land. "What have you discovered?" Marc asked, wiping his hands on his pants.

"You asked me, among other things, to look into Mr. Winston, a custodian who worked at the school," Jacob began, a hint of exacerbation in his voice. Monster returned with the ball and dropped it between the men. Jacob bent down and fired the ball straight down the tree lined path on the edge of the property. "He retired three years ago."

"Where is he now?" Marc asked, assuming Jacob knew more than he was letting on.

"He moved to New Port Richey, Florida," Jacob continued. Monster barreled past the two men, unable to adjust his speed in time to stop. He made several circles around them and dropped the ball a few feet away from them, nudging it with his nose.

Marc picked up the ball and made a fast motion, then tucked it behind his back. Marc flipped the ball to Jacob and showed his empty hands to the confused dog. Monster curiously searched around them to no avail. Hurriedly, Jacob rifled the ball past the dog and sent both bouncing away.

"I have been calling around for several days, trying to locate him," Jacob said, frustrated.

"I take it you found him, otherwise you would not have brought the subject up with me now," Marc said, encouraging his friend to get to the point.

"I couldn't get in touch with him or his wife," Jacob edged nearer to the heart of it, "so I went another direction." Here, his voice saddened. "I started looking at the obituaries."

Monster returned, circled and dropped, ever further away.

"I'm sorry," Jacob added.

"Does he have any family?" Marc inquired, turning towards Monster and walking towards the ball.

Jacob scrunched up his face, "I figured you would ask that. No. He had no children."

Marc tossed the ball one final time. "You did well, my friend," he said, patting his arm. "I was too late," Marc lamented and walked away.

"It isn't your fault," Jacob said, but Marc could not or would not hear him. "Not your fault . . ." Jacob whispered, knowing that his friend was desperate for balance. This was one that was out of his reach now.

~

"Wanna bet?" Brett taunted Frank as they sat in the cafeteria.

"Please! I'm done taking bets from you," Frank exclaimed.

"What?" Brett said wounded. "I'm good for the money. You know that."

"I'm not waiting any longer. You can wait for your father to die. I've got other customers."

"Oh, come on!" Brett pleaded, "It's the Knights versus the Cavaliers! The Cavs are giving three points! I could make a fortune on this one."

"Or lose one," Frank observed as he gathered his books and left Brett and his lunch tray behind. "Find some other idiot to take your bet. How about you try fantasy football online?"

Brett sulked over his chicken patty sandwich and French fries. He hated fantasy sports. He liked the old school feel of betting the game's outcome. It was an all or nothing roll of the dice, live or die, just as he liked it.

"May I join you?" a voice from behind asked.

Brett was about to tell them to go away until he saw who it was. "Marc! Yeah, man, sit down."

"Rough day?" Marc asked, already aware of what was bothering Brett.

"Nah, I'm good," Brett lied.

"Well, if there is anything I can do to help . . ." Marc suggested, letting the last word linger in the air. He waited, letting the thought sink into Brett's thick skull. "Make the connection, you moron," Marc thought. It took longer than he had anticipated, but Brett's slow synapses finally came through in the end.

"Hey, could you put in a good word for me with your friend, Nichols?" Brett's face seemed to alight as the idea struck him.

"Of course. Why?" Marc asked feigning ignorance.

"I want to place a bet on the Cavs game tonight."

"I'll call him and tell him to expect your call. Let me give you his number," Marc offered graciously as he maneuvered Brett deeper into the trap.

~

Over the next few weeks Brett lost twice as much as he won. Every bet was a sure thing, until it wasn't. Each loss led Brett to riskier and riskier bets, hoping to recover his loses. Nichols took each bet, no matter how red Brett's ledger was. He knew Marc would cover the growing debt. Brett, however, had no one to go to for help. His father stubbornly clung to both his wallet and his life. Frank refused to extend him any further credit. His luck had simply gone sour. He remained hopeful as always. Brett needed one big score to turn it all around.

Nichols informed Marc of each bet made. Wherever possible, Marc maneuvered what pieces he could influence with money or information to ensure that Brett's loses would pile up.

"Nichols called," Jacob informed Marc as he entered the dark paneled room that they used as a library. "He said Brett placed a large bet on Friday night's game."

Marc immediately took his phone from his pocket and dialed. A voice on the other end picked up and Marc said, "Nichols? I have another job for you." There was a few seconds of banter and then Marc gave the details. "I want you to make sure that Tanner Wood doesn't make it to the game on Friday night."

Jacob shot Marc a look, but didn't interrupt.

"No. There is no need to hurt him, if that can be avoided," Marc continued.

Jacob slammed the book down on the end-table and glared at Marc.

"Do what you need to do. Just make sure he doesn't make the game," Marc finished with Nichols and ended the call.

"What the hell was that about?" Jacob immediately blared.

"It doesn't concern you," Marc brushed his friend's concerns aside and walked towards the door of the library.

Jacob stood blocking the doorway between the library and the entry foyer. "Like Hell it doesn't!"

Marc tried to move past him. He refused to budge.

"I agreed to help you. I owed you that much. But, I am not going to let you do this. Whatever this is," Jacob waved his hands as if to encompass the whole house, the town and maybe beyond.

"This is vengeance!" Marc screamed at him.

"Oh, come on!" Jacob retorted, "You told me you were innocent! Sent to that place, betrayed by friends. I said I would help balance the scales, not make new ones for other people to rock on! What you are doing right now, isn't right. You don't care about that kid! The only thing you care about is your vengeance. He is innocent and doesn't mean a thing to you; just a means to an end."

Marc seemed to take a step back, as if someone kicked him in the gut. He fell into a chair and sunk down, bringing his hand to his head. Jacob awaited his reply while still standing sentinel at the doorway.

"Machiavelli would be proud," Marc murmured.

"What?" Jacob asked, unable to hear him.

Marc looked up and met his friend's angry gaze, "I said Machiavelli would be proud."

"Yeah, he would be," Jacob snapped back at him.

"Thank you, my friend," Marc said earnestly. "I cannot become the very thing I hate."

Jacob stood at the door not knowing what to say. He watched as Marc made another phone call.

"Make sure the boy is unharmed. I don't care what it costs. He comes to no harm," Marc abruptly ended the call.

Jacob stared at the enigma before him. This mysterious man that he had been saved by, had befriended and given his loyalty and trust, despite the many unknowns. He remembered looking up from the concrete and seeing Marc reaching his hand out to help him up. Since then, they had shared meals, laughs, and more. Jacob had grown used to sparring with Marc, both physically and mentally. He knew what his friend wanted, and supported much of it. Jacob also understood that without someone to guide his conscience, Marc ran the risk of becoming something that neither man would be proud of. Jacob didn't know if all of this was worth his friend's soul. "Why can't you give this up?" he asked in frustration.

Marc looked at him. It was a cold, blank stare, as if he were seeing straight through to his soul. He simply asked, "Could you?"

Chapter 28

The Dubious Pair

"No!" Brett exclaimed. "No! No! No! This isn't happening to me," he kept saying as if he could will the opposite to be true. Tanner Wood wasn't at the game. The Indians were without their star cornerback. For those that bet football or play fantasy sports, they know it is all about matchups; how each player measures up against those on the opponent's squad. Without Tanner Wood on the defense, the Mount Collier Spartans were lighting up the Indians. Where it should have been impossible to pass the ball, the Spartans were gaining hundreds of yards and making it look easy.

Make no mistake; Brett did not care about either team. It was the bet he made; a sure-fire wager that guaranteed to pay dividends. This was the one that was going to cover all of the others he had lost recently. It was a string of bad luck, nothing more. Tonight, that string extended by one. Brett had no idea how he was going to get out from under the mountain of debt he had built. The crowd was going wild. Students chanted "Spar-tans, Spar-tans," while the band struck up the fight song. The mood was pure jubilation, minus one, of course.

"Let's go," Brett demanded.

Kayla, decked out in blue and gold, was in no mood to go, "I want to stay. It's gonna be awesome!"

"I'm leaving," Brett replied and stormed down the blue and gold trimmed aluminum stands, shoving students out of the way as he descended.

Marc Cunningham watched intently as Brett scurried towards his car. He heard the peel of rubber as Brett's hundred-thousand dollar Lexus left the lot and sped away. He was running away from his troubles. Marc Cunningham was going to ensure that those problems had only just begun. He took out his phone and called Jacob. "The Spartans won by fourteen. Have Nichols call in the debt first thing in the morning. Make sure he collects the vig, too," Marc ended the call before Jacob could reply.

The vig is a gambler's term that denotes the amount of money the bookie makes on a bet. Brett had not paid his previous five. Nichols would normally have stopped accepting bets from a person like that. Instead, Marc asked him to allow Brett to go deeper and deeper in debt. Marc could easily cover any losses Nichols might endure. Now that the gallows were constructed, it was time to put the noose around Brett's neck and see if he would jump.

"Kayla," Marc called loudly several times to get her attention.

The two met half-way and smiled awkwardly at one another.

"Brett left, I see," Marc observed.

"He was upset," Kayla said.

"On a night like tonight? A big win, a beautiful girl at his side, what is there to be upset about?" the compliment hit just the right note.

"He has a temper," Kayla admitted, then timidly asked, "Are you staying for the bonfire?"

"Of course. Do you need a ride home afterwards? My driver would be happy to take you anywhere you need to go."

"That would be great," Kayla replied happily.

"One catch, though; you'll have to be seen with me," Marc said, offering his arm to her.

Kayla smiled and slid her arm through his.

~

Two days later, Brett didn't notice the danger he was in before it was too late. Had he been paying attention he could have turned away, banked or swerved, rather than walking inexorably towards trouble. Nichols, the bookie who Marc Cunningham had introduced him to, was leaning against the driver's side door of Brett's Lexus.

"You are a hard guy to track down," Nichols said without a hint of emotion. When Brett did not respond, Nichols added, "You lose your phone or something?"

Brett held out his arms, palms to the sky, "Sorry man. Been busy." Nichols would not be the first or the last person he blew off.

"Busy gathering twenty-five large, right?" Nichols asked, this time a clear edge in his voice.

Brett thought of the twenty-five thousand dollars he owed. His luck had gone sour. His father hadn't died yet. No inheritance was coming soon. "Sorry my friend, I don't have it," he admitted.

"Not my problem," Nichols spit at him. "You made the bet. You cover the bet."

"I can't," Brett said, stepping towards the car door.

"You will," Nichols ordered, raising himself off the car and standing tall.

Brett scoffed. "Whose gonna make me?" he asked, puffing out his broad muscular chest.

Nichols moved away from Brett's fancy car. He smiled wickedly as he did so. He reached to his side and slowly lifted his shirt at the waist. A large black handled knife was tucked at his side. "Be careful," Nichols suggested smugly, "You're playing in the big leagues now." He tapped the handle of the knife twice before letting his shirt fall. "Twenty-six large by next Friday," Nichols said, stressing the six so that Brett understood the cost associated with late payments. "That, or we start taking pieces of you instead."

Brett watched Nichols walk away. He waited several minutes before cursing boldly into the empty air. He kicked the tires in frustration a few times before unlocking the car and getting in. Unexpectedly, he noticed something on the passenger seat. He had not left anything there. Brett grabbed the small piece of paper and read the handwritten note.

"We can get to you whenever and wherever we want. Don't forget that."

Brett crumpled the note, trying to crush the fear he felt in his hands. He floored the gas and pealed out of the parking lot, a loud squeal obscuring the pounding of his heart.

~

Two days later, Brett had been unable to find a way out of his predicament. He was forced to turn to the only person he could.

"There is a way out of this," Frank suggested.

"How?" Brett asked, "You don't have the cash to cover it."

Frank scowled at the thought. "Even if I did, why would I cover your debt?" he wondered.

Brett returned the dirty look, "Don't forget what we did together. Don't forget what I know."

Frank stood and leaned in close to Brett's ear. "Don't threaten me you muscle-bound moron!" Frank whispered. "If I go down, you go down."

Frank went to turn and leave, but Brett grabbed his arm. "Wait. Tell me your idea," he said in a conciliatory tone. "Please tell me you thought of a way to knock my dad off."

"No," Frank replied, but sat again and faced Brett. "We pay him with his own money," he suggested, smiling from ear to ear.

"How do we do that?" Brett asked.

"We know where he lives. We know he keeps huge sums of cash in the house. His parents are away. You go there, rob the jerk and pay him with his own money."

"What's in it for you?" Brett wondered.

"Other than knocking that smug idiot down a peg or two? Oh, and you paying your debts. All of your debts. I figure two grand would cover me."

"Two large for doing nothing," Brett exclaimed.

"Are you going to plan this?" Frank asked with a raised eyebrow.

Brett considered the offer for a moment before he replied. "I'm in."

Chapter 29

The Trap

Brett and Frank had more in common than either young man would care to admit. Marc had been observing them for weeks now, learning all that he could of them. Physically, they were opposites. Brett was imposing, broad shouldered, tall and thickly muscled, every bit the athlete he proclaimed to be. Frank was medium build, medium height; seemingly average in every way. His advantage was hidden behind a pair of keen brown eyes. Frank was brilliant and he was smart enough to realize that fact. Brett was dimwitted, though he didn't see himself that way. Marc knew Frank's thought's on that subject; Stupid people never do. Both guys, despite their obvious differences, treated their girlfriends horribly. To them, the girls were like old worn out toys that they had not gotten around to disposing of yet. Sure they played with them from time to time and had fond memories of days gone by, but they wouldn't miss them if they disappeared.

Kayla and Meagan were not friends. As near as Marc could see, the two girls never even interacted. He had never seen them speak to one another, never even glance at one another. Their common experiences did not bring them together, but rather drove them to stay as far from one another as they could. As if looking into a mirror would force them to face who they were; what they allowed others to use them for.

Kayla often sat alone in the cafeteria if Brett was off bragging to his friends. Most boys wouldn't dare to befriend her and Kayla found that she didn't get along well with other girls.

"Penny for your thoughts?" Marc asked as he sat across from her.

"I think you can afford a bit more," she replied sarcastically.

Marc laughed and begrudgingly agreed with her assessment. "Too true. How much will this cost me then?"

"Your juice," she demanded with raised eyebrows as she stared at the fruit punch.

"Deal," Marc agreed and went to hand the bottle to her. "Start talking," he demanded, getting his fair share of the bargain.

"It's Brett," Kayla admitted. It was always Brett.

"Anything I can help with?" Marc offered.

"No," Kayla said. "Unless, you know what he is up to tonight."

"No idea," Marc admitted, shrugging his shoulders. "Why don't you just ask him?"

"I did. He won't tell me," Kayla said defending herself. "He doesn't have a game. There is no practice. I know he isn't spending time with his family."

"Are you worried that he is cheating?" Marc asked.

"Nah. I think he and Frank are up to something."

Marc closed his eyes. It was little longer than a blink, but just enough to steady himself. "Well, if the two of them want to waste the night away plotting and planning, why not join me?"

Kayla gave him a confused look.

"A group of us were going to the movies, then maybe to the paintball place. Come with us," Marc offered. "My treat," he added with a smile, ensuring she had no excuse to say no.

~

"It will be tonight," Marc promised, standing in the kitchen, whisking a bowl of raw eggs vigorously.

"How can you be sure," Jacob asked incredulously, "and why don't you hire someone to do that?"

"Elementary, my dear Watson," Marc smiled.

"Oh, here we go again," Jacob settled into the chair waiting on Marc to explain the logic.

"First, I like to cook," Marc dealt with the latter question first.

"Are you any good at it?" Jacob's tone suggested he already knew the answer.

Marc scoffed at the question and chose not to respond. "Eliminate the impossible, whatever remains, however improbable, must be the truth," Marc quoted Holmes. "Kayla told me that he and Frank are up to something. He won't tell her what his plans are for tonight."

"So how does that equal a break-in?" Jacob asked exacerbated.

Marc poured the eggs into a frying pan. "Brett is a simple animal. He wasn't the brains behind what was done to me. We have made him desperate for cash. We have driven him into the arms of Frank. Frank knows where I hide the cash in the library. It presents an opportunity for both. Brett could pay his debts; Frank could attack his new rival without revealing himself as an enemy."

"You are ruining them," Jacob remarked.

"That is the plan," Marc agreed.

"I meant the eggs! You are burning them," Jacob added, shaking his head.

~

Marc made sure to tell Kayla that they would be leaving late tonight. Then, in a calculated maneuver, he had Jacob drive him to the house three hours earlier.

"I am so sorry. I was mistaken," Marc lied to her.

"It's okay. I appreciate you picking me up," Kayla said, salivating over her imminent ride in a limousine.

They spent the evening with friends watching a sci-fi adventure flick and then sprinting in and out of defensive structures and pelting one another with paintballs. Kayla was relaxed, enjoying the freedom of being away from Brett. Marc hoped to extend that freedom for her, regardless of whether she thought she wanted it or not.

"Do you mind if we stop at my house first on the way home?" Marc asked casually.

"Sure," Kayla responded.

When they got to the mansion, Kayla was again awed by the monstrous size of the place. "Aren't you the least bit scared, being here alone, I mean?"

"No. I have Jacob and Monster," Marc replied as he stepped over the sleeping dog near the entryway.

"He does seem really aggressive," she joked.

The two sat in the living room and chatted. Kayla forgot that it was only supposed to be a quick stop, getting more comfortable by the moment. She was attracted to him, Marc was certain of that. Yet she seemed to move one step forward and two steps back in that regard. Marc knew why. She lived in fear of Brett. If tonight went as he expected it to, she would be free of him as he would be too.

As if on que, suddenly, there was a pulsing noise in the room, like an alarm clock, but more urgent.

"Excuse me a moment," Marc said as he popped off the couch.

"What are you? Batman? Is that like the Batphone? Is the wall going to open up to a hidden cave?" Kayla asked, tucking her legs under her, a sultry tone in her voice.

"I am no hero," Marc dismissed her. "However, I must ask you to stay in this room," he added, a hint of concern seeping through.

"Is everything okay?" she asked.

"The sound is a house alarm. I do not want you to be alarmed, but someone is in the house," Marc said quietly. "Call the police and lock the door behind me," Marc ordered.

"Marc!" Kayla said, half-whispered and half-yelled. As the shock of what was happening settled in, Kayla ran to the door and turned the lock. Then, she dialed 911.

Marc moved swiftly and silently towards the library. He knew who was in the house. He knew exactly where Frank would have sent him. The room had four windows, but only one door. Brett would have entered the house through the service area. Frank knew it would be unlocked.

The door to the library was open and Marc could see the circle of Brett's flashlight dancing around the room. Marc kept close to the edge of the room, skirting the walls. He was only a few feet from Brett before he spoke, "Hello, old friend."

Brett leaped in fear and swore. His flashlight made a tight circle as it dropped to the desk and rolled around.

"I want you to know, I have waited a long time to do this," Marc said, stepping into the light.

Brett's look of confusion and fear fed Marc's adrenaline rush.

Marc lifted his knee and thrust his foot forward, landing a front kick directly into Brett's chest. The air whooshed as the oxygen left him and Brett collapsed to the floor. He moaned, his hands holding the spot where Marc had connected. Marc walked casually over to Brett's head and looked down at him.

"You are tougher than I thought," Marc observed and then drove his heel into his face, knocking him out cold. "Edric Davies sends his regards."

~

"Oh my God!" Kayla exclaimed, over and over again. She watched two burly deputy sheriffs walk past her as she peered over Marc's shoulder.

"You are safe now," Marc proffered confidently. "He is in the library, officers." Marc watched the two men move in. He offered Kayla a seat on a long settee, moving cushions to make her comfortable.

"Thank you," she said, taking his hand and sitting down. "I've never been so scared in my entire life."

"I will have Jacob take you home just as soon as this is all over," Marc promised.

Kayla hugged him and he felt her begin to sob. Her night was about to get far worse.

The police walked the groggy intruder out of the library. His hands were cuffed and his face was already swelling from the blow Marc had landed. None of that mattered to Kayla. "Brett!" she screamed and leaped to her feet.

"You know this man?" One of the deputies asked.

"He's my boyfriend," she explained. The deputy looked quizzically at her for a moment and then gave a knowing smirk as he glanced at Marc. Kayla suddenly felt dirty. "It's not what you think," she added, wondering why she had come tonight in the first place. Had she hoped to replace one man for another? Kayla collapsed back onto the sofa and cried feeling like a toy that had become loose at the joints and worn at the edges.

Chapter 30

The Memory of the Heart

The wealthy of Newport, Rhode Island during the Gilded Age would have been proud of the excess on display in Mount Collier. They styled themselves as the new American aristocracy, building homes ever larger and more ornate. They threw lavish parties, always with the intent of outdoing the previous host's efforts. To fail to do so meant that your party would be compared to the previous endeavor and found wanting. For Frank, that was something that simply wasn't an option.

"Where the Hell is the band?" Frank slammed the door for the third time.

"I will call them again," Sherry, the party planner offered.

"Find them! I want them set up before guests arrive," Frank ordered.

His mother watched from the hallway as her son gave yet another tongue lashing to the party planner. She understood the pressure he was under. She had graduated from Mount Collier, had been through the social gauntlet and had survived it with guile and cunning. Frank had inherited those qualities from her. He was intelligent, decisive and unafraid to do what was required, regardless of the cost. "Do you need me for anything before I go?" she asked.

"Can you increase the IQ of these fools?" Frank asked, loud enough for several of the party staff to hear.

"Guests will not arrive for another two hours. You have time," his mother said, trying to ease her son's concerns.

"I know that Mother," he hissed. "But, if you don't stay on top of these people, then nothing gets done."

"Your father and I will be at the club," she replied, ignoring the venom in his voice. "We'll be home late. Don't forget to put on your costume." She kissed his cheek and left him to manage things.

The first guests arrived to a fanfare of horns. Frank had decided to throw a costume party. Guests were encouraged to dress as seventeenth century aristocrats. Soon the house was filled with fancy collars, poofy dresses with large crinoline and fancy umbrellas and expensive up-do hairstyles. Frank knew he could not compete with the amount of money Marc threw at his party. Instead, he went for a style that would give his guests the sense of wealth and elitism that only an aristocrat could be comfortable with.

Meagan arrived among the early guests. She wore a rented gown, pink with white trim. She adorned it with costume jewelry and a small white parasol umbrella. She fidgeted nervously as Frank looked her up and down, a piece of her brown hair slipping out of the complicated curled bun.

"Check on the caterers for me, would you? They should be coming out with appetizers," Frank dismissed her without further comment. There would be no compliments. No, "You look pretty," or "Wow! That dress looks great on you." Meagan did as she was told. She always did as she was told. Ever since her parents divorced, money had been tight. Meagan fought to remain in the upper strata of the social circle. She had to work at the mall two or three days a week and spend more and more of her college savings to keep up. Frank helped sometimes, spending money on her to impress his friends or to ensure she didn't embarrass him. She paid for that in other ways though. His constant disrespect, his violent mood swings, had become a part of her everyday world.

Meagan circulated through the party. She watched her peers behave as if they were the most important people in the world. As if they did something for the world other than spend their parents' money and make condescending remarks. Meagan smiled at all the right people, laughed at all the right jokes and felt emptier and emptier inside as she did.

The house was beautiful. Frank's parents had spent lavishly to decorate it. There were numerous paintings, mostly watercolors that perfectly complimented the color schemes of each room. Each piece of furniture was the right size and shape for the room, as if it were custom made to be in just that spot. It seemed as each item had been carefully selected, molded and shaped to the will of the Macintyre family so that it reflected only what they wanted someone to see. Nothing in the house showed the volatile arguments, the passive-aggressive assaults, and the back stabbing that was common among the family.

Meagan stood against the wall and twirled her parasol over her shoulder. Guests past her without noticing her. She blended into the décor. Was there ever a time she wasn't just window dressing? She wondered. Just when she thought she might fade into the wall, she saw a ghost.

She saw a boy, who could not be. Meagan's eyes locked onto a man who had disappeared; onto a man who was rumored to be dead. She found herself staring at the facial features. They had grown older, had thickened, but she could swear they were those of the boy she knew. He was chatting amiably with a few people when he saw her staring at him. That was when she became certain.

Marc's eyes lingered on her for a moment before he turned away. He knew she was staring at him; studying him. He was not ready yet for her to know. He was not certain yet that she didn't deserve his justice. Conflicting emotion swirled in him and he had to excuse himself from the conversation. Marc moved towards the back of the house. Meagan followed.

He navigated his way through the house and the gauntlet of socialites, looking to ingratiate themselves with the newest and wealthiest arrival to Mount Collier. Marc used his phone as a shield, giving the screen his full attention and generating an excuse to not notice or hear those that called out to him. Soon, he was moving quickly, bobbing and weaving his way towards the back door. It didn't matter; she was still gaining on him.

Meagan followed Marc Cunningham as he fled the room. She watched him dart around the big crinoline skirts like a football player avoiding tacklers. Where he was slowed by people who sought his attention, Meagan was ignored. She was gaining on him and intended on finding out if she was right.

They had met before for only the briefest of moments. She never saw him; never really looked at him until now. There had been something off about that first meeting. A part of her must have known, though she could not discern it. Now, as she pursued him out into the back yard, she was growing more and more certain.

"Edric!" She yelled, desperate for him to stop. He did not. She thought she saw his shoulders shudder. Maybe it was her imagination. "Edric!" she called again, but he kept walking. "Marc!" she finally conceded.

"Hello," he turned and greeted her, no hint of recognition in his eyes or his tone.

Maybe she was wrong. Was she seeing ghosts? Was depression taunting her with impossible dreams?

"You are Frank's girlfriend? Meagan, correct?" Marc confirmed.

She nodded, suddenly feeling the sting of being called Frank's girlfriend.

"What can I do for you?" Marc asked nonchalantly.

"Tell me the truth," Meagan blurted, overwhelmed with need.

"The truth of what?" Marc asked, feigning confusion.

"Tell me if this is true?" Meagan asked, holding up her wrist. The small silver heart dangled from the frayed band.

Marc hesitated. Then, he stepped towards her and gently took her hand. "It is beautiful," he remarked, studying it. "Is it a gift from Frank?" he asked.

"No," Meagan asserted quickly.

"I don't understand?" Marc said, maintaining a controlled demeanor. "What truth are you asking about?"

Meagan withdrew her hand. Could she be wrong, she wondered.

"Do you have a girlfriend?" Meagan queried, changing her approach.

Marc was slow to respond, "Once."

"You have not forgotten her?" Meagan asked sweetly.

Marc heard the softness of her voice, the concern it held, as if it were swaddled in a baby's blanket. "I could never forget her." That at least was true.

"I assure you that she could not have forgotten you," Meagan responded quickly.

"You are wrong there," Marc chided her while turning his back.

Meagan slipped her hand on his shoulder. Her fingers gently rose, cresting, then coming to rest just at the nape of his neck. Marc took a deep breath, as a waft of her perfume reached his senses.

"I've been wrong about too many things to count, but I am not wrong about this," Meagan whispered. Marc could feel her hand tighten on him through his shirt. She wanted him to turn around, but he was resisting.

She would not be denied. Meagan instead maneuvered herself in front of him. Marc tried to avoid her eyes, tried to look down, but Meagan moved close to him. She rested her chin on his chest and looked up into his eyes. Marc looked down a cliff, desperately wanted to dive into the pristine blue ocean below. It would free him. All he need do was jump.

"She did not forget," Meagan said as her eyes closed and her lips pushed up towards his.

"Meagan!" the voice cut through the cool night air. Frank had come seeking her and had found them together.

The two separated, both stepping back from the other, so that there was now too much distance between them. Nearly six feet of space separated the two and Frank looked queerly at them as he rounded the corner of the house.

"I was looking for you," Frank said sternly, wrapping his arm around her neck and shoulder as if she were a possession he was claiming as his own.

"I must go. Thank you for tonight," Marc said as he walked backwards, making his exit. A gust of wind picked up and seemed to push the two young men apart. They stared at one another, long years of hatred acted as ballast for Marc, slowing their separation. He reminded himself that it was not yet time. Even nature herself would not deny Marc Cunningham his vengeance.

Chapter 31

The Sell-out

The cell smelled. Brett had been in some pretty foul locker rooms, but this place stunk. There was a pungent odor of stale urine, mixed with some of the most offensive body odor Brett had ever come across. Add to that cocktail a stomach full of vomit and the air in this jail was almost impossible to breath.

"You puke again, you better get to that toilet," said a drunk man who was lying in the corner with his hat over his head.

On any other day, Brett would have pummeled a person for a comment like that. Then again, on any other day, it wouldn't have been his vomit strewn across the concrete floor of a jail cell. "I'm sorry," he said, slowly rocking back and forth on his haunches, his nerves getting the best of him.

"Shut up already," the man said as he tried to return to his hangover induced nap. They had spent the last eight hours with one another and that had been the lengthiest conversation of the day.

A loud buzzer went off and the man groaned. Brett could hear the tap of solid heeled shoes coming towards them. His stomach lurched and Brett retched uncontrollably. Luckily, there was nothing left to bring up and the worst of it was the big gasp of involuntary air he took in.

"Brett DiVinceo?" a Deputy asked, looking at a clipboard instead of Brett.

He wiped his chin and responded, "Yes," then quickly added, "Sir."

"Your lawyer is here. Follow me." The Deputy pressed a button on the wall and the thick barred door unlocked. Brett stepped out and felt as if he had suddenly returned to earth from an alien planet. The air was cleaner, fresher; lighter, too. Things were not so bleak.

Brett found himself in a small room with his father's lawyer, an old, frail man named Sanders. He handled all his father's business and was paid extremely well for his services. The man was thick in every way. A thick belly protruded over his belt. Thick glasses clung to a thick nose. Even his voice was thick with phlegm.

"Good morning. Sit down, son," Sanders ordered immediately. He was setting a clear tone for who was in charge.

Brett did as he was instructed.

"Your father . . ." Sanders began.

"Couldn't make it, but he sent you," Brett finished as if he had heard this a thousand times.

"Do you understand the charges against you?" Sanders asked, ignoring the spoiled, petulant child routine. His fancy gold pen scanned down a piece of paper on the table between them.

"Yes, but . . ." Brett replied, but was sharply cut off.

"Have you told the police anything?" Sanders voice grew sterner, if that were possible.

"No. They didn't ask me anything," Brett mumbled.

"You are eighteen, correct?" Sanders continued.

Brett only nodded, but it was enough.

"In a few moments, you are going to be interviewed by a detective. I will be with you the entire time. Answer only the questions I tell you to answer. If I advise you not to answer, then don't. Do you understand me?"

Brett looked at Sanders expensive suit. He was perfectly put together. Probably a nerd in school, Brett thought. He was being ordered around by a kid who probably got stuffed in lockers or dunked in garbage cans. Brett's life would turn on this pencil-necked fossil.

"Do you understand me?" Sanders repeated.

"Yeah, I got it," Brett snapped back.

~

"Would you mind telling me why you were inside the Cunningham's home last night?" The detective asked.

"I would advise you not to answer that," Sanders said flatly.

"I was going to rob them," Brett admitted, ignoring the lawyer.

Sanders flung his gold pen into the air and it pinged against the metal table, echoing through the small room.

"You were going to rob them, is that your statement?" the detective confirmed.

"Yeah," Brett said. "I go to school with their kid, Marc. He introduced me to a bookie that has been robbing me blind. So . . ." he trailed off.

"Could I have a moment alone with my client?" Sanders chimed in.

The detective nodded, but Brett ignored him. "So, I was going to steal the money to pay off his bookie from him. I wasn't going to hurt anyone."

"How is this bookie stealing from you?" the Detective queried.

"He keeps taking higher and higher bets even though I keep losing," Brett explained.

"How did you gain entrance into the house?"

"Frank Macintyre gave me the key. He is buddy-buddy with Marc," Brett smiled as he added that last part.

"Frank Macintyre?" The detective asked, seeking confirmation.

"Yeah. He was my bookie, but he stopped taking bets from me a while back," Brett continued. "These guys have no patience."

"Heck of a high school," the detective muttered. "Does the administration do anything there?"

"Oh, Germaine knows about it all," Brett admitted. "Here's how it works; Germaine lets Frank run gambling and drugs in the school. Frank scopes out girls in need of favors that only a school administrator can give; grade changes, college application stuff. He feeds Germaine the names, helps him keep the affairs quiet."

"What do you get out of all this?" the detective asked.

"I get to do and say pretty much whatever I want because I know about it all," Brett said. "That's gotta be worth something, right?"

"Okay. I have everything I need," the detective said. "Thank you for your cooperation. We will take it into consideration." He hastily left the room.

"See, he'll offer me a deal now. I'll turn State's evidence or something," Brett bragged proudly as he folded his arms behind his head. A short lifetime wasted watching television police dramas made Brett think he understood the law.

"I'll go pay your bail," Sanders said, shaking his head in disgust.

~

The detective exited into the hallway with his notes. "Hey," he called to a deputy on duty. "Get me the recording of this last interview. Kid is probably innocent and his father is the rich and famous type. I don't want it falling into the wrong hands, you know?"

"Sure thing, Detective Collins. I'll leave it on your desk."

"Thanks," Detective Collins replied and then seemed to think of a better idea. "Actually, just leave it in my inbox on the door. I have an important phone call to make."

"Will do."

Detective Collins had to look up the number he needed on his computer. He dialed it and had to fight his way through the automated menu of "press one for" this and "press six for" that. He was stalled momentarily by a secretary before he finally heard the voice he was looking for.

"Vincent Germaine speaking."

Detective Collins leaned back in his chair, "It's Collins. You are in serious trouble. No worries though.

I think I can help you . . ." Collins looked at the photograph of his family on the desk, "for a price."

Chapter 32

The Unravelling

Vincent Germaine had lost his leverage. Still, it had saved him from disaster. What was having leverage for if not for a situation such as this, he thought.

Collins would destroy the recording; even make the charges against Brett disappear. Germaine understood the price. They would meet clandestinely; exchange thumb drives with scandalous data, pretending those were the only copies. There were backups to the backups of course. Neither men were dumb enough to surrender that sort of influence.

Germaine understood that he wasn't dealing with an idiot teenager. No, Collins had proven a worthy adversary. The balance of power had shifted in their relationship. That was something Germaine had to come to terms with. Yesterday, he lived in a world where only he had access to a nuclear weapon of information. Today, he faced an adversary that could do as much damage to him as he could to them. His social studies teachers would call a situation such as this mutually assured destruction. He simply called it a temporary setback.

"I want to see Frank Macintyre," Germaine ordered, storming into his office without so much as a good morning.

The old hag was unfazed. "I'll call him during homeroom," his secretary replied.

"Now!" Germaine screamed. "I want him in this office yesterday! Do you understand me?"

Mrs. Harris shuddered in her seat. "Yes," she muttered, and then added, "Sir," almost from instinct. Old fingers, frail and thin, picked up the phone and dialed into the classroom. No answer. She let the phone ring for an eternity. "I'll try again in a minute," Mrs. Harris said, more a question than a statement.

"Fine," Germaine barked as he walked into his office and slammed the door behind him.

Mrs. Harris picked up the phone and dialed again.

It was three periods later before Frank meandered into Germaine's office.

"He's here," Mrs. Harris announced, allowing Frank through and quickly shutting the door behind him.

Germaine waited to hear her footsteps fade before he spoke. "You took your time," he began, not hiding his animosity.

Frank lifted the silver ball on one side of Newton's cradle and let it go. It slammed into the others and they bounced back and forth, tapping in time. Germaine watched the desk toy for a moment and then grabbed it to stop the balls. A look of disdain cut across his face.

"What's got you so angry?" Frank asked, more arrogant than concerned.

Germaine sat back and folded his arms. "Have you seen Brett recently?" he asked, his eyebrow raised.

Frank had not. He figured Brett had found the cash and had wanted to delay giving him his share. Worse, maybe he had decided to wager it somewhere, trying to make money off it before he was forced to give it to Frank. If Germaine was asking about him though, it was because there was trouble. "No," Frank said, not volunteering any information.

"That's strange, don't you think?" Germaine observed.

"Not really," Frank blew it off. "We aren't exactly best friends."

"So, you have no idea why he would have been arrested the other night?" Germaine watched Frank's face intently. Try as he might, Frank could not hide the concern on his face. Germaine knew the young man had never worried about anyone but himself. Frank was involved in this. He was the driving force behind Brett breaking into the Cunningham kid's house. Those subtle facial movements told Germaine all he needed to know. Frank's involvement explained why Brett decided to spill his guts and rat on the both of them. "Don't bother lying to me," Germaine added, "I already know."

Frank squirmed in the seat, faux leather squeaking with every move. "What did he say?" Frank asked, trying to assess the damage.

"He told them everything," Germaine responded quickly.

Frank's stomach lurched. Brett knew enough to send both of them to prison. He rubbed his head, trying to think of a way out. "What do we do?" he asked. He could think of no way to put the genie back in the bottle. It was out and the mischief that would be done was beyond his control.

"It's under control, for now," Germaine informed him.

Frank felt his spirit lift. "How?" he asked, shocked.

"The investigating detective is a friend of mine," Germaine explained.

"Collins!" Frank exclaimed.

"Yes," Germaine assented, the last letter of the word strung out. Clearly, he thought that the young man in front of him knew too much for his own good.

"Anyone who cared to pay attention knew he was your dog," Frank said defensively. "What did you have on him?"

"None of your concern," Germaine brushed the request aside. "He will dispose of the charges for us as well as the tape."

Frank nodded his head, impressed by whatever hold Germaine had over the Detective Collins. It had to be powerful for the man to be willing to tamper with evidence. Frank's brain calculated a hundred different scenarios, but they all ended the same way. "That leaves us to deal with Brett, then?"

"Us?" Germaine's question was laced with sarcasm. "Us?" he asked again. "There was no us. There is no us. This is your mess. You fix it." Germaine demanded.

"He is our problem, like it or not," Frank bemoaned. "If you don't help, you risk exposure, just like me." Frank began to spin a pen on the principal's desk. "Who has more to lose?" Frank suggested.

Germaine seemed to ponder that for a moment before he responded. "He has to be silenced," he said finally.

"There is only one way to guarantee that," Frank agreed. The two sat across from one another and let the finality of that thought sink in. Brett DiVinceo had to die.

Chapter 33

The Repeat Performance

"Anything yet?" Marc asked for the fifth time as he paced the wide hallway.

"Nothing. Everything is quiet," Jacob admitted, sharing his friend's confusion.

"I do *not* understand it," Marc stopped long enough to shake his head and wave his hands before he began to pace again.

"He was released to his parent's attorney. I thought he posted bail," Jacob explained again, as if saying it out loud would help the two of them to sort out the problem. "Nothing has appeared in the police blotter, not even the arrest. There has been no indication that Germaine or Frank have been or will be arrested. I'm sorry."

"He has someone inside the department!" Marc exclaimed. "How could I have been so stupid?" Marc shook his head, castigating himself. He started to slap his head with his palm, over and over. "What was his name? Connors? Compton? Collins! It was Collins!"

Jacob stared dumbfounded. "Who is Collins?" he asked.

"The deputy that Germaine used to arrest me. Germaine has some hold on him," Marc shouted, his hand fist pumping in the air.

"Are you suggesting the police buried this whole thing?" Jacob queried doubtfully.

"Maybe Collins would trade Brett's confession for whatever Germaine has on him? Maybe, Collins is in so deep he feels he has to help him? Whatever it is, Collins is the reason, I am sure of it." Marc's response left no room for doubt.

"I'll call the department and ask for a Detective Collins," Jacob said, reaching into his pocket for his phone.

"Wait!" Marc reached towards him to stop him. "Just find out if he works there still. If he does, we will have to come at this a whole new way."

Jacob dialed the phone and asked to speak to the man. He was put through to Detective Collins' voice mail. Jacob hung up and nodded to Marc, "He still works for the department."

Marc stood and ruminated on that for moment. "I didn't want to do this," Marc fretted, "I'm going to need you to find someone for me."

~

"Do you have it?" Germaine asked impatiently.

"I have it," Frank replied petulantly.

"Let me see it," he demanded.

Frank took two small bags from his pocket. They were filled with a horrifically addictive powder; heroin.

He flashed them in his palm and then stuffed them back into his pocket. "I'll leave a few hundred dollars he paid me with too. The bills will have his prints on them," he explained.

Germaine pursed his lips. "Thorough. Well thought out," he remarked.

Frank seemed impatient, "Well?"

The principal handed him a small slip of paper. "Here is the locker combination," he began, "Put the stuff in the locker. I'll take care of the cameras. Make sure you are not seen."

Frank yanked the paper from the man's hand. "You know, we've done this before?" he observed.

"Well aware," Germaine responded sarcastically. "Just do your job."

~

The next morning the school went into lock down during history class. It was just a drill, no cause for alarm. Teachers taught as normal. The only thing that changed was that students were not allowed in the hallway. Everyone knew why, but Marc wasn't about to admit that.

"Why is this happening?" Marc asked, injected a bit of concern into his tone. He watched Frank intently, studying every muscle in his face as he asked.

"Drug sweep," Frank said flippantly, staring at a map of the Invasion of Normandy. "Brilliant deception, don't you think?" he asked.

Marc ignored the question and looked out the door and into the hallway.

"Relax," Frank said. "Unless, you know, you need to worry?"

"No," Marc replied, shaking his head fervently.

Frank refocused on the map and the text below it. "Eisenhower worked hard to make sure the Germans were looking at Calais, not at Normandy. Then, once the landing occurred, the paratroopers created havoc in the rear. Germans thought the landing was a feint. Unfortunately for the Nazis, it was the real thing. Brilliant, really," he spoke in awe of it.

Marc watched as Frank got lost in the moment. The two loved history. It was the initial glue that had brought them together a lifetime ago. Marc saw history as a study of human behavior. A laboratory used to study why people acted as they did. A predictor of future behavior. Sort of a magic eight ball that would offer guidance. Frank saw history as bold moves, gambits, and failed opportunities. The story of great men who were great because they acted when others feared to. To him, rules did not matter, only results. He was the ultimate student of Machiavelli.

The current assignment was an analysis of history's greatest battlefield maneuvers: the Trojan horse, Austerlitz, Trafalgar and more. It was right up Frank's alley. He was mesmerized.

"Do you think they are after someone?" Marc queried.

"Of course," Frank muttered, slight annoyance beginning to show.

"Wow!" Marc exclaimed.

"Happens all the time," Frank explained as if he were speaking to a small child, "One day they are here, the next day they are gone."

Marc struggled to maintain control. He could feel his face flushing with anger. It made him wonder just how many lives they had ruined. How many people had been pawns in their games? "Speaking of disappearing, have you seen Brett lately? My friend Nichols has been asking about him," Marc asked, trying desperately to hide his emotions.

"Doubt we'll be seeing him anytime soon," Frank remarked, smugly.

That was the problem with the bold men Frank loved to emulate, Marc thought. Far too many of them needed credit for their actions. Almost all of them continued to push until they met an enemy they could not master. Usually, it was an enemy they should have seen coming, but they were too arrogant to believe in their own vulnerability. Frank would get his wish. Marc would help him to become just like them.

Chapter 34

The Graduation

Marc waited in the shadows. He had grown used to living in the darkness, but today was particularly frustrating for him. He glanced out of the tinted windows of the limousine, impatiently checking the time on his phone. His view was the same; that of the daunting stone walls of Shatterly's Drill and Obedience Fraternity. In all his days imprisoned at the institution he never dreamed of a day that he would want to return. Yet, that day had come. But he couldn't. Nervously, Marc had flipped open every compartment, explored every button that the fancy car had to offer. Nothing could keep his mind occupied. When the door finally opened, Marc still managed a smiled.

"Thank you," Marc said, offering his friend a cold bottle of water as he sat across from him. "I could not do this without you."

Jacob took the bottle of water and drank half of it down. "Sometimes, that's what scares me," he replied, wiping the sweat from his brow.

"How did they treat him?" Marc asked nervously.

"It's small, but respectful," Jacob said, handing Marc his phone.

Marc flipped through the photographs quickly, like an alcoholic offered his first drink of the day. They were of a graduation ceremony. Shots of long lines of military students, dressed in identical uniforms, parading in front of visiting relatives. Others pictures were of individual students or buildings. Some were of open fields or trees and a few of a small cemetery. Marc smiled brightly at some, giggled like a young boy at others, and almost came to tears at a few. Then, he went back through them more slowly a second time, soaking in every pixel, with a steady, controlled hand. He stopped at a picture of a small headstone inside a wrought iron fenced cemetery. "He was important to me," Marc admitted, sadness overtaking him.

"I know," Jacob said, putting his hand on his shoulder. "I did exactly as you asked me to."

"Thank you," Marc said again.

"The lilacs are at the base of the headstone and I buried the coin just underneath them," Jacob confirmed his instructions were followed.

"I would have liked to have gone myself," Marc lamented.

"Too risky," Jacob said quickly.

"I know," Marc admitted. "Thank you."

"You said that already," Jacob said as they pulled away.

Marc watched the dark stone wall disappear behind them. He never thought he would yearn to go behind those walls. "Professor Feinstein, thank you," Marc whispered, hoping that somehow, somewhere the Mad Priest could hear him.

They drove in silence for miles. Jacob had known him long enough to understand when to give him space. Marc would break the silence when he was ready. "Manente graduated today," Marc said. "He has honored his family." Marc always spoke formally, Jacob observed. He assumed that was a byproduct of military education. Having met Nichols, Jacob now understood that Marc's pattern of speech was due more to Professor Feinstein than Shatterly's.

"Do you want me to . . ." Jacob asked, but was cut off before he could finish.

"No," Marc said quickly. "I would never want to put him in the position where he would have to lie."

Jacob ignored that, considering all of the times he had lied for Marc. Instead, he changed the topic to one of his most recent lies.

"I contacted the university as you requested," Jacob shifted.

"Did they accept our offer?" Marc queried.

"A fifteen million dollar endowment! Once they realized we were serious, they fell over one another to meet with me," Jacob laughed at the question.

"They will allow us to review the applicants? To interview them?"

"Yes. That wasn't a concern for them," Jacob replied. "Are you sure this is the easiest way to find her?" he questioned.

"She will apply," Marc said confidently. "I know her too well."

~

They arrived back at the mansion and were greeted with the fanfare of European royalty by Monster. He scampered to them, then ran from them in the hopes they would give chase. He wasn't alone though. Nichols sauntered out of the door shortly after Monster. As pleasant as it was to be greeted by his dog, it was as unpleasant to be greeted by Marc's.

"This dog is a pain in the . . ." Nichols started, but Marc brought him to heel.

"I have a job for you," Marc cut him off, showing no interest in his opinion of Monster.

"You always do, boss. You always do," Nichols nodded towards Jacob as if he were a player in a game that Nichols had just defeated.

"I want you to follow Brett DiVinceo for me," Marc began, "When you cannot be on him, have someone else do it. I want eyes on him at all times."

"Done," Nichols said brashly, then seemed to realize that he might have missed something. "Why?"

"Frank Macintyre. Any time he is in Brett's presence, I want you to video it and send it to me," Marc explained.

"You expecting something?" Nichols asked.

"As a matter of fact, yes," Marc conceded. "Get to it."

Chapter 35

The Applicant

Jacob sat and stared at the application. He knew this one was a waste of time, just like the two dozen others he had interviewed. The applicant, number twenty-five, was a tall, athletic African-American girl. She simply didn't fit the description. The young woman shifted in her seat nervously. She had no idea that she had become caught up in an intricate web of deceit and intrigue, bent on destroying a single man that she had never met.

Jacob gave her a forced smile and harrumphed. "What is your name?" Jacob asked barely hiding his disinterest.

"Sarah Gent, sir," she replied brightly.

Her application was stellar. Sarah was a brilliant student, hard-working and utterly capable. Jacob would be furious with the entire process if he had not already known that Marc fully intended on funding scholarships for all of the candidates. The winner, if one would dare describe it as that, was predetermined. Sarah didn't have a chance at that. At least the consolation prize was a full ride through the university doctoral program. That at least would make her time worthwhile.

"You have an impressive resume," Jacob observed. "If you were to receive the fellowship, what do you intend on doing with your studies?" he asked robotically.

Sarah launched into a brilliant, idealistic speech about all of her plans. She would go to med school. Then, she would specialize in surgical orthopedics. Her plan was to spend some time abroad in the Middle East and help reconstruct people in war torn areas.

She was the most deserving candidate Jacob had seen yet. When she had finished, Jacob thanked her and dismissed her as he had all the others. "Thank you for your time. As soon as a winner has been selected, we will inform all of the candidates via mail."

Number twenty-six entered as her predecessor left. It was hour number nine and Jacob was more than done with the charade. He wanted to crawl into bed and forget that he would have to do this again tomorrow. He unsuccessfully stifled a yawn and could feel his eyes watering as if the agony of these useless interviews had finally brought him to tears.

Twenty-six stood in front of the desk and held out her application. Jacob couldn't even bother to feign a smile. He snatched it from her hands. "Sit, please," he ordered. Rubbing his eyes, he began to read the document. Suddenly, he wasn't tired anymore.

It was the name. She had applied, just as Marc had predicted. Finally, right in front of him was the girl he was searching for. Jacob felt energized. He felt nervous.

Marc had warned him that any hint of what he needed her for might send her sprinting the other direction.

"Please, tell me about yourself," Jacob asked.

The young woman did as they all had done. She described her excellent qualifications, her history of success, and what she planned to do with the money and her education if she was lucky enough to win. Jacob found that last part more than a little amusing.

"I believe you are just the type of candidate my employer is looking for," Jacob informed her, rising from the desk and stretching infinitely into the sky. "When could you be available to meet him?"

"I'll make myself available," the young lady said excitedly.

"Well then," Jacob smiled, "Please pack for a warm climate for at least two days. Meet me in the lobby of the administration building. I will arrange a car to take us to the airport. He has a private jet waiting for us." Jacob had no idea which of them was more excited. She may have been on cloud nine over the fellowship, but he had finally found who he was looking for.

Chapter 36

The Moment

Frank had to admit that he was impressed. Brett had avoided him for over a week. He had tried all the usual places; the practice fields, the locker room, the weight room, but Brett was nowhere to be found. When Frank inquired after him, the answers were a mix of, "Haven't seen him," or "You just missed him." It was growing frustrating, to say the least. He gave up texting him after two days and calling him after the third. Frank felt like an overeager girlfriend, desperate for affection. Frank decided the only way to get to him was to go to the one place Brett couldn't avoid; his house.

The place was the oldest mansion on what was affectionately called, the Row. It was a long, meandering road that basked in the cooling shade of Mount Collier. It was long considered the prime real estate of the area. Brett's family had bought the estate decades ago and had spent that time restoring it to the classical elegance of the early twentieth century. The place looked like a Greek palace on the outside and J.P. Morgan's library on the inside. Frank had been to only one party there, thrown not by Brett, but by his parents. It was a tightly controlled event with much of the house securely off limits to guests. Even the wealthy of Mount Collier could not be trusted with DiVinceo treasures.

Brett was alone in his ability to remain in the upper strata of the social circle without throwing exorbitant parties that mirrored the most ridiculous Hollywood teen movies. Where every other person was expected to reciprocate at the least, and outdo the previous host as a precursor to success, Brett was simply immune to that expectation. His family was viewed much like the items that filled the house. They were fragile.

"How's your dad?" the ladies would ask, softly, as if they were holding a rare vase from the Ming Dynasty in their hands. Brett would put on a somber face and answer, "He's struggling," and then quickly add, "He's a fighter though. Tough as nails that guy is," as if that spirit was a family trait that had not fallen far from the tree. Frank knew Brett hated his father and not so patiently waited for the day the man kicked the bucket. Brett knew exactly how to manipulate the crowd though. He got sympathy, a free pass on parties and instant forgiveness for any emotional outburst. "You would have a hard time too, if you went through what he has to deal with," his apologizers would say.

His father was brilliant, wealthy, and hardworking. He also suffered a series of stomach related ailments that even the best doctors had failed to nail down. "Are you poisoning him?" Frank had asked Brett once. "No. You know how?" Brett had responded, sarcastically seeking advice. Despite that denial, Frank had always suspected that Brett had tried and failed to take the man's life and his money.

In contrast, Frank lived up the mountain, where the new money looked down on the old. This was a town that no matter how much one had, it wasn't enough or it wasn't the right stuff. Living in Mount Collier was like being a human black hole of need and want. The older families may not have been the wealthiest in town anymore, but they had their names. They appeared on banks, elementary schools, parks and even street signs. The names of the old families were so entrenched here that no amount of new money could scrub them away. To the neoveau riche, they were like port wine stains on a white couch that no one could clean; eyesores that reminded them of some past indiscretion.

That was what he was here to correct. Brett was a mistake; an oaf, too stupid to understand when to keep his mouth shut. Frank should never have involved himself so deeply with a jock, much less a fifth year senior and all around lay about. Brett seemed to be extending his stay in school so long as his father survived. Frank supposed that his plan was to stay a student until he could transition into an indolent heir. If it wasn't for running his mouth to the police, Brett's plan might just have succeeded.

The sun had just begun to tickle the tops of the trees when Frank watched the front gate creak open, a steady electronically guided pace. He slunk down in the driver's seat. Frank's instincts told him to hide, despite the tint of the windows. With shoulders low like a cat about to pounce, he watched intently as Brett's head emerged from inside the fence.

Brett looked left and right, his neck snapping to and fro like some nervous gazelle peering out of the tall grass. When he was satisfied the coast was clear, Brett closed the gate behind him and started jogging down the road.

There were two directions Brett could go for his jog. One would bring him to a steep mountain trail. The town had an annual charity fun run through it. Frank had never seen the path before, but he knew it would be difficult to follow Brett if he chose that option. However, if Brett chose the opposite way, he would descend deeper into the valley. There, he would follow a long straight concrete trail that had once been the town railroad before it had become useless and expendable. As long as it was empty, it would be the perfect place for a final, quiet discussion.

Frank started the ignition and lifted his foot from the brake, allowing the car to roll. He waited and watched as Brett turned toward the valley. Frank tapped the brake. He waited a few moments before releasing the pent up energy of the car and allowing it to creep to the stop sign. Peering downward, Frank watched as Brett rounded a tree and disappeared down the path. He pulled forward and drove into the small parking lot. Frank checked his pocket again, the feeling giving him a sense of consolation. He headed confidently down the path to intercept Brett.

A pickup truck passed by the parking lot. Frank bent over, pretending to stretch and the driver moved past. If Frank had not feigned the need to prepare for a run, he might have recognized the driver.

Nichols muttered a curse under his breath as he pulled two blocks away and parked his truck on the side of the road. He dashed quickly, running down the side of the street, branches lashing at him. He needed to get into position. "Tonight's the night, boys," he muttered aloud into the rapidly cooling evening air.

Nichols moved carefully through the brush, keeping Frank a good distance in front of him. He walked leisurely, not like a man who was intent on doing another harm. Nichols wasn't complaining about that. It made his job that much easier. They moved at a snail's pace for almost a half an hour.

The thumping of footsteps coming towards them made both men tense. In tandem, they both craned their necks and searched the horizon for movement. As if pantomiming one another, they both saw movement and retreated into the shadows like a turtle would his shell. Two hands fluttered for their respective pockets in preparation for what was about to happen.

Brett was a few feet away from them when Frank stepped out into the open. Nichols immediately started filming from his hideout.

"You've been avoiding me," Frank remarked.

Brett was breathing deeply, bringing his heart rate down. "Nothing to talk about," Brett huffed.

"Ha!" Frank exclaimed. "Nothing to talk about huh?" Frank asked sarcastically.

Brett did not respond. He tried to move past Frank, but his path was blocked.

"You talked," Frank accused him.

"You think I care that you go down for all of it," Brett replied brashly.

"Isn't just me, you know," Frank added. He needed Brett to talk. He needed to know what Germaine and his cop friend might have on him; to assess the danger.

"Who? Germaine? I told the cops all about him too. They know it all now. The drugs, the girls. All of it," Brett admitted. "I traded the two of you for me. Seemed fair."

Frank watched Brett arrogantly brush aside the damage he had done. It infuriated him. Frank reached into the sweatshirt and caressed the handgun through his thin glove. He felt the small bundles he carried. He would plant them on Brett when it was done. It would look like a drug deal gone bad.

"All of it?" Frank wondered aloud.

"What? Davies? Is that what you are wondering?" Brett chuckled. "Nah. I kept what we did to myself."

"Good," Frank said, taking the gun from his pocket and aiming it at Brett's chest.

Brett's face barely had time to register shock before the first round left the chamber and slammed into his chest. The tiny bit of metal tore through his shirt, his skin and his organs. It ricocheted off his vertebrae, bouncing around and shredding his insides.

A second muzzle flash lit the coming dusk. The bullet hit high on the chest, just above his heart. One of Brett's ribs shattered, sending shards of bone through the top of his heart. Two seconds. Pop. Pop. Brett was dead by Frank's hand.

Frank stood above the body and studied his work. He had wondered if he were capable of doing it. Brett helped with that. His disregard for Frank's future made killing him so much easier. His adrenaline was pumping and Frank had to move fast now. He took the bags of heroin from his pocket and sprinkled them around Brett as if he were salting a steak. Then, he walked briskly to the parking lot.

Frank sat in the car, his hands shaking from fear and excitement. He grabbed his phone and tried to text Germaine. The device shuddered in his hands. He fought with it, almost texting three other people before his fingers cooperated and allowed him to select Germaine's number. He tried to type, but auto-correct fought him every step of the way. He surrendered and deleted the text. He held the voice assistant button, "Text Vincent Germaine," he ordered. When it asked what he wanted to say, Frank replied, "It's done," and sent the text.

At just the same time, another text message floated through cyberspace. Marc Cunningham heard his phone dance across the table as it vibrated. Picking it up, he saw the new message was from Nichols. He turned his phone to the side and played the video. When it was done, he sent his response, "Finish it. Make sure it cannot be traced back to you." Then, Marc put his head back and closed his eyes, steeling himself for what was about to happen.

Chapter 37

The Duel

Frank opened the door from the garage gingerly. His plan was simple. He would slip inside and hurry upstairs. The gun needed to be cleaned and returned to his father's office down the hall. That could take some time. Still, Frank intended to be in bed before anyone knew he had been out. It would all be over soon.

He crept up the stairs and into the empty office. He sat and cautiously cleaned the weapon. This tool had solved the biggest problem he had ever faced. Frank appreciated its effectiveness. He had thought he would feel guilty, or sad. Instead, he felt powerful, almost limitless. When he finished, he locked the weapon away and shut the door quietly behind him. He walked down the hallway towards his bedroom, knowing full well he would never be able to sleep.

The dull light of a television spilled out into the silent hallway. His mother probably fell asleep with it on again, he thought. Frank tip-toed into the room, looking to turn the screen off. He gasped at what he saw.

His mother sat watching the news, the phone on her lap. He could hear her sobs in between the words being spoken. "Frank Macintyre is wanted in connection with the murder of Brett DiVinceo. Anyone with information concerning his whereabouts is encouraged to contact the Mount Collier Sheriff's Department."

He heard, more than felt, the gasp that came from somewhere deep inside his chest. The problem was, so did his mother. She turned to face him. Red puffy eyes, blurry with tears stared at him. "Is it true?" she seemed to choke on the words.

Frank stood as if he had been turned to stone. He could not move; could not speak. He just looked into the eyes of his mother and saw her disappointment and confusion. Suddenly, her brow furrowed. The muscles of her face tightened. Varied emotions seemed to congeal into anger. She raised the phone and began to dial. Within minutes, the sirens blared in the distance.

Frank remembered yelling. He remembered pleading. He remembered running. He ran as fast as he could without thinking of where he could hide. It was panic, plain and simple.

Frank found himself hiding in some brush in an unfamiliar yard. He needed a plan. He needed to escape. Frank skulked further into the bushes as the sirens grew louder. He couldn't go home. Frank considered going to Meagan, but quickly decided against it. She wouldn't want to help a killer and even if she was willing, she had no ready cash to aid his escape. There was only one person Frank knew that had enough cash lying around that could get him far away from Mount Collier.

Frank waited until the shriek of the sirens and lights faded into the distance before he emerged from cover. Marc Cunningham would have no reason to help him. Still, Frank felt he was the best available choice to turn to. Marc might not have any reason to help Frank, but maybe he had reason to help him disappear. "With me out of the way, he can have Meagan all to himself," Frank thought, "He is welcome to her, for a price."

He moved carefully on the streets, avoiding any movement. Frank didn't run anymore. Walking was more normal and far less likely to attract attention, he felt. It took him longer than he wanted, but eventually he arrived at Cunningham's house. Marc lived in a massive mansion that was set far from the road. All the better, Frank thought, to hide him from the growing manhunt. Frank rang the doorbell.

Moments later, Jacob answered.

"Is Marc here?" Frank panted, looking over Jacob's shoulder.

"He is asleep," Jacob explained as if to a child.

"It's urgent. I need to see him," Frank's voice cracked. His need mixing with his disdain for speaking to a servant.

"You can wait in the library," Jacob conceded.

~

"He is here?" Marc said, stunned.

"In the library. He looks terrified," Jacob replied, pointing downstairs.

Marc paced across the bedroom floor. "He came to me for help," he laughed at the thought. "Well, I will not deny him," he said, shaking his head. "I will help him on his way," Marc added ominously.

"Let me send him away," Jacob begged. "None of this can be tied to you. You can walk away from it."

"Impossible," Marc declared, pulling on a pair of athletic pants. "Stay up here. Keep our guest safe."

"She is waiting to meet you," Jacob said frustration clearly evident. "How much longer do I have to lie to her?"

"She is the final part in all of this," Marc explained. "When I am done with Frank, it will be her turn," he added, heading out the door and down the stairs.

"Frank," Marc said as he entered the library, his hand rubbing his face, feigning fatigue at this late hour.

Frank was on the wrong side of the desk, as if he had been searching through it. "Marc!" Frank exclaimed. "I need help!"

"How can I be of service?" Marc replied, looking down at a half open drawer.

"I need money. Cash," Frank blurted, his eyes darting around the room.

Marc followed his eyes. Frank looked at the eighteenth century sword, then to the nineteenth century bayonet. He was seeking more than cash. Marc moved around the desk and sat. "Tell me. What is going on?"

Frank thrust his head back in frustration. "There is no time," he yelled.

"I cannot help if I do not understand," Marc replied calmly.

"I have been betrayed!" Frank screamed.

The muscles in Marc's jaw grew taught. "By a friend, I would imagine. Someone close to you?" he asked, barely above a whisper.

"Yes!" he agreed. "It was Brett!" Frank held his hands in front of him.

Marc rose from the desk and walked towards the sword. It was a basket hilt claymore. A broad slashing blade with a metal cage to protect the hand. It wasn't overly ornate. It was a weapon designed to hack and slash the enemy. To stab them. Marc picked it up and examined it. "How did he stab at you?"

"Brett broke in here. He tried to blame me. He told the police things," Frank trailed off, not wanting to add anything further. "Please, Marc! You have to help me get away."

Marc put the sword down and returned to the desk. He unlocked a wooden filing cabinet next to it, reaching inside and removing a thick manila envelope. He began to count out cash onto the desk.

"Where is Brett now?" Marc asked, having already seen the video of the murder.

"I don't know," Frank responded quickly, easily selling the lie.

"Do you honestly believe Brett is smart enough to ensnare you in this way?" Marc suggested, just as Abraham Feinstein had helped him to assemble the pieces of his own betrayal.

Frank shook his head. "No. Germaine, maybe?" he said, trying to lay out the puzzle. "That can't be, though."

Marc stood and slammed his hands on the desk. "You always were a good liar, Frank." He walked to the door and locked it. "This is the end for you," Marc added coolly.

"What are you doing?" Frank asked desperately.

"Edric Davies sends his regards," Marc spit the words at his enemy; to the man who was once the best friend he had in the whole world.

"What?" Frank muttered, still confused.

"Years ago, it was I who could not see the enemy that stood before me," Marc seethed, "Now, you are blind to him."

"How do you know Davies?" Frank demanded to know.

"Oh, I know him!" Marc raged. "I know what it is to be betrayed by a friend. To be left alone and desperate. To hope and have that hope crushed."

"Who are you?" Frank moved cautiously around the room, closer and closer to his target.

"I am balance! I am vengeance! I was Edric Davies!" Marc swore.

Frank was aghast. His skin went the color of milk and he stared silently into Marc's eyes. There was no denying the truth.

"You have nothing to say now, do you?" Marc prodded his enemy, screaming and spitting the words.

Frank reached out and grabbed the sword. He pointed the blade at Marc. "Get away from the door!" Frank ordered. Marc and Frank moved in concentric circles keeping the distance between them equal. Soon Frank found himself at the door. He felt for the lock with his hand and could not find it. Frank glanced behind him and found the bolt and pulled it open.

That was all the time Marc needed. He took up the bayonet from the shelf and lurched across the room. He was in front of Frank before the door was half way open.

Frank slashed the long blade at his oncoming enemy. Marc parried the strike with the smaller bayonet, but it wasn't enough. The tip of the sword dug deeply into his arm, opening a deep wound across his triceps. He let out a loud groan and stumbled backwards, the smaller blade clanking to the floor moments before Marc joined it.

Frank seemed to hesitate between running and attacking. He lurched towards the door and then thought better of it. With sword raised, Frank came right at Marc as he struggled to his feet. The two fought with blind fury. There was no banter. No words of any kind could express the depths of their hate.

The blade swished through the air and landed with a thud against the floor where Marc had been. A second thud crashed into Frank's head. Marc delivered a kick to the side of his face sending Frank careening across the room.

He slashed the sword wildly, fending off any further attack by Marc. Then, Frank regained his feet and charged, the blade clearing a path before him.

Marc dodged to the left and missed with an elbow strike. Frank turned and whipped the blade just over Marc's head. Marc ducked and struck into his ribs with a quick blow. The sword fell to the floor and Frank leaped forward, bringing both of them to the floor. His hands slithered upwards, finding Marc's throat. They tightened around his neck, squeezing with every ounce of strength he had.

Marc used his leg to turn Frank and put him underneath. Still, Frank would not let go of him. Marc tried to peel away the thumb from his throat, but his arm, injured and bleeding, lacked the strength for it. Instead, he reached for the bayonet on the floor a few feet from him. His fingers grasped it, pulling it closer until he had the handle.

He put the tip against Frank's chest. Marc felt the blade slip forward. Frank struggled harder as he felt the tip of the bayonet slip between his ribs. There was a scream that turned to a moan and then a gurgle before it fell silent. Frank's hands slackened, falling away like dried leaves from an autumn tree.

He sat against the wall and looked at the results of his vengeance. Frank's eyes stared lifeless at the ceiling. Marc felt his own blood pooling on the floor as it rushed down his arm. He was woozy and tired. He just wanted to close his eyes and rest. He wondered when the last time he felt truly rested had been.

"Edric!" he heard in the distance. "Edric!" a faint, familiar voice called. The world seemed to narrow and then go dark.

Chapter 38

The Suspicion Confirmed

"I repeat, the video you are about to see is disturbing and not recommended for younger viewers," the perfectly manicured newscaster said in a somber tone.

"Thank God for DVR," Meagan thought as she rewound the video again on her living room screen. It was the third time she watched it. The first time, she had barely paid attention to it until she had heard Frank's name as the person wanted in connection with murder. It had been mere background noise then.

The second time she watched it in horror, tears streaming down her cheeks. She watched the two young men that she had known all of her life. Meagan could not hear it all. They talked, voices stern, but not overly angry, she thought. She had seen them have these types of conversations a thousand times. She watched in abject horror as Frank drew a gun from his sweatshirt and fired. The muzzle flash seemed like fireworks. It all felt fake, like a special effects show at an amusement park. Tomorrow, everyone would laugh at themselves for being fooled by it. Frank would have proven to himself, once again, that he was smarter than everyone in this town and they would all have a good laugh about it.

Meagan needed to know if she heard what she thought she heard. The sound was muffled at times. Words grew louder or softer, seemingly at random. The wind interfered with even more. Despite the whipping gusts, she could have sworn she heard it. Meagan turned up the volume on the television to the max and craned her ear to the speaker. It was Brett's voice and it was clear enough for her. He said, "Davies," she was certain of it.

She thumbed the DVR again and again, listening to a single moment just before Frank pulled the trigger. "Davies," and then she could make out, "what we did," before the world went crazy again and two bullets ripped through Brett. Worse, they were put there by her boyfriend! "Why?" She wondered over and over. Meagan could think of just one person; Edric Davies. Brett and Frank had done something to him. They were behind whatever happened to him.

She let the video run as the newscaster spoke, "Anyone with information concerning the whereabouts of Frank Macintyre is encouraged to contact the Mount Collier Sheriff's Department."

Meagan grabbed her phone and called Frank. It went straight to voicemail. The next person she would have called to find him would have been Brett. The thought of that brought tears to her eyes and bile to her throat. Meagan dashed to the bathroom and made the toilet just in time for the eruption. She clung to it like a precious friend she feared she might lose.

When Meagan was certain that her stomach could offer up no further grief, she cleaned herself up and prepared to go out. There was one person she was sure would know what to do. Meagan put on a light scarf to deflect the cool night wind, grabbed the keys to her car and steered towards the home of Marc Cunningham. She didn't quite understand it, but she was now certain that he was the boy she once knew as Edric Davies.

Meagan arrived at the house ten minutes later. The drive had been an emotional tumult. Her mind raced with a million thoughts. What had happened to her boyfriend? Was he alive? Where had he been? She realized that she wasn't thinking about Frank as her boyfriend, but rather Edric. She cried and smiled at the same time.

Meagan slammed the car into park and ran to the front door. She didn't knock or ring a bell. There was no time for that. Her need to know, to understand, became an inexorable missile on a one-way mission. Meagan had become a juggernaut and she would not be denied.

She did not call for Marc. "Edric!" she yelled, every second that passed feeling more desperate to confirm her suspicions. "Edric!" she called again, looking every direction, seeking for light or movement inside the house. Then, she saw the library door ajar and a light on. She thought she heard a groan. Meagan dashed into the room and found blood and death.

Chapter 39

The Ladies

Meagan paced back and forth on the cheap tile in the waiting area of the emergency room. It was going on three o'clock in the morning but her nerves would not allow her to rest. She was not alone. Jacob rose every ten minutes like clockwork to check on Marc's status. The answer was always the same. "He is in surgery. When the doctor is finished, she will update you."

She had screamed, she remembered that vividly. As much as she had grown to resent him, the site of Frank lying on the floor with a knife in his chest was more than she could bear. There was so much blood. She had never seen a floor so covered in red. Beyond that, she had little recollection of anything afterwards.

She surmised that she must have fainted. When she awoke, she was on the floor in the foyer of Marc's house. A paramedic, one of the school bus drivers, was hovering over her and taking her pulse. She had never thought of the bearded man as anything more than a driver. He smiled at her and called her Sweetie.

She watched the wheels of the gurney pass by her. Meagan had no idea if it was Marc or Frank. She knew Frank was dead. She had seen the knife in his chest. What had happened to Marc was still a mystery to her. Then, the thought of Frank dead, of Brett shot dead by him, overwhelmed her and she sobbed.

Jacob had fought with the paramedics. "I'm going with you," he demanded.

"Sir, you are not a direct relative," they had tried to explain.

"His parents left him in my care!" He yelled, but to no avail. Instead, Jacob would follow the ambulance to the hospital.

"Take me with you," Meagan had pleaded.

He never really answered. She just got in the car and he never argued with her. Funny thing was, Meagan wasn't alone.

Jennifer Kelly was there. She was an old friend of Edric's. She had gone off to college someplace Meagan couldn't recall. Now, she was here at Marc's house, in the limousine with her going to the hospital. It was all so confusing. Her head felt foggy and slow.

"Is he Edric?" Meagan asked no one in particular.

Jennifer glanced at her with a confused look, but said nothing. Jacob stayed focused on the road and the flashing lights that he was following.

"Is he Edric?" Meagan asked again.

Jennifer Kelly tilted her head and looked hard at her. "Are you Meagan?" she asked.

Meagan nodded.

"Is who Edric?" Jennifer asked, leaning forward and putting her hand on Meagan's knee.

"Him," Meagan said without intimating who. A blank, thousand-yard stare dominated her face. Slowly, she added, "Marc Cunningham."

The rest of the trip was spent in silent, pensive reflection. Both women sat with furrowed brow and tucked lower lip, working out everything that was going on. Not much had changed since they had hit the waiting room.

It was Jennifer that had returned to the conversation first. Jacob had just returned from his regular check in with the frustrated receptionist when she started in on him. "Do you want to tell me what is going on here?" Her tone was unmistakably angry.

"Later," Jacob quipped.

"No," Jennifer stood and demanded, "Now!"

Meagan was impressed by her. She was a strong, intelligent girl and clearly, she knew something wasn't quite right with all of this. Inspired, Meagan asked again, "Is he Edric Davies?"

Jacob squirmed in the seat and said nothing.

"Frank Macintyre is dead," Jennifer said, pointing a finger as if she were counting off the evidence. "Killed in Marc Cunningham's house. He was Edric's best friend."

Meagan nodded angrily, encouraging the woman to continue.

"Brett DiVinceo played with Edric on the basketball team. He was murdered earlier today," Jennifer continued, though she had no idea where she was going with the information she had. "You bring me here. I was Edric's babysitter. He was my friend," she added solemnly. "Then, Edric's girlfriend is at the house when Marc and Frank fight to the death," she paused at that and ordered Jacob to explain. "Tell us the truth!"

"Can we please just focus on Marc's health?" Jacob pleaded.

Jennifer railed at Jacob, "This has something to do with Edric Davies. No one ever knew what happened to him. Why he was sent away. Tell us what this has to do with him!"

"Excuse me," a small framed Japanese woman in blue scrubs said. "Your friend is out of surgery."

"How is he?" Jacob blurted, popping from his chair as if someone had hidden an air bag underneath it.

"He's doing fine. He is in recovery now and already awake."

"Can we see him?" Jacob asked quickly.

"Actually, he asked to see just one of you," the doctor explained. She turned to the girls and asked, "Which one of you is Jennifer?"

Jennifer stepped forward and followed the doctor down the hallway. Meagan shrunk in her chair and did not pursue the conversation further, instead lamenting the fact that she had not been chosen.

Jennifer entered the recovery room where Marc lay. She sat in a guest chair and looked intently at the man in the bed. He was puffy with the excess fluids of surgery. Jennifer tried to remember Edric's face. It was thin, an innocent smile and bright eyes. This man's face was strong and stern, not at all what she remembered of Edric. Meagan was wrong, she thought. This may have something to do with him, but they were not the same people.

"Thank you for seeing me," Marc said groggily. "I know you must be very confused."

"That's the understatement of the year," Jennifer retorted.

Marc chuckled, "You were always quick witted. You never let me get away with anything. I should have expected that."

"Oh my God!" Jennifer blurted.

"Long time, no see," Marc smiled.

"Edric?" Jennifer asked.

"In a way," he said, "Though not as you knew him."

"What do you mean?" Jennifer asked, confusion cutting across his face.

Marc tried to shift up in the bed. He felt no pain yet, but he did realize that his ability to move had been compromised. Jennifer rose and helped pull him up, tucking his thin pillow behind his head.

"Thank you," he said earnestly.

Jennifer sat and waited.

"Do you remember the night of the homecoming game? When I saw you coming out of Germaine's office?" he asked, not bothering to hide his identity any longer.

Jennifer bowed her head in shame, "I do."

"That is where this all began," Marc explained.

"What did he do to you?" Jennifer asked, tears pooling at the corners of her eyes.

"They took everything from me," Marc said and then told his story.

Chapter 40

The Final Conspirator

When Jennifer consented to this, she had not thought it through. Marc's horrible story had been enough to get her to agree to almost anything. Now, standing at the large glass entranceway to Mount Collier High, she felt the heat flushing her face. She looked up at the sun, a toddler in the sky, and grimaced in anger. "Why did I agree to this?" she wondered aloud. Students were still streaming in; many would be late to their first period classes if they didn't hurry. Jennifer didn't miss any of the heat or the stress. Every decision she ever made here was made in the heat of passion. Jennifer shook her head in disgust at herself. "You need to make better choices," she muttered.

She signed in as a guest and slapped the sticker used to identify her on the top of her dress in just the right spot to call attention to her ample assets. Jennifer understood what would distract Germaine and she wasn't afraid to use what she had to get what she wanted. She checked the small purple clutch she was carrying. A small wire hung limply from it. Marc said it would allow her phone to record the conversation more clearly from inside the bag.

Jennifer walked towards the center annex offices, deep in the bowels of the school and her past. Memories flooded her mind. She remembered the first time she had seen him, truly seen him as a man of power and influence. Vincent was a force of nature. That, of course, was the problem. He was a hurricane, powerful and full of bluster. Vincent Germaine was exciting to be around, but terrifying to stand against.

She pushed through the door and was greeted by a familiar, though unfriendly face. Mrs. Harris scowled at her and Jennifer didn't know if it was recognition or a simply a natural state for her. "Is Mr. Germaine available?" Jennifer asked, in a forced, friendly tone.

"Do you have an appointment?" Mrs. Harris asked. The old, used up voice brought back a flood of memories for her.

Jennifer wanted to respond with, "You know I don't. You keep his schedule you old hag!" Instead, she went with, "No. I wanted to surprise him."

"And you are?" the old woman didn't bother to hide her impatience.

"Please tell Vincent that Jennifer Kelly is back in town and would love to see him," she deliberately chose the familiar rather than the formal.

"Have a seat," the woman said and seemed to wait purposely and for no reason before she buzzed into Germaine's office.

Jennifer waited almost ten minutes before Germaine emerged from his office.

"Ms. Kelly, won't you come in?" he said, gesturing to his office.

"Thank you for seeing me without an appointment. I know how valuable your time is," Jennifer replied. She dropped the clutch bag she was carrying and bent low at the hip to pick it up. A quick glance confirmed that Germaine appreciated it.

Once they were seated in the office, Jennifer waited and allowed Germaine to begin the conversation. "What are you doing back in town?" he asked.

Jennifer wondered if her presence made him nervous at all. If it did, he didn't show it. He was calm, confident, and seemingly unflappable. He had not seemed to age at all, where Jennifer could not say the same about herself. She was a full-fledged woman now. Still, Vincent was a man of strength and intelligence. That was what had attracted her to him in the first place. College boys were just that; boys. In almost four years, she had yet to meet a man who compared to him. They were not assertive or decisive. They waffled and whined. Vincent would crush any of them.

"I came back for the funerals," Jennifer said, feigning sadness.

"Here I hoped it was for me," Germaine quipped.

"I'm in your office now, aren't I?" Jennifer flirted back. She was surprised how easy it was to fall back into the old routine.

"You look great," Germaine observed, allowing his eyes to travel places they shouldn't.

"Thank you," Jennifer demurred. His predatory inclinations reminded her of how dangerous he was. She was right that he was unlike the boys at college. He was deceptive and cruel. A user that destroyed other's lives any time it suited his needs. "Time to get focused," she thought. She uncrossed and then immediately crossed her legs again. "We should have dinner. Relive old times, don't you think?"

"I am not a fan of public meals," Germaine retreated.

"Sorry. I should have remembered that," Jennifer tried to recover. "Maybe we could get together? Maybe someplace a bit more private?" she suggested.

There was a long pause before Germaine responded. "Is your number still the same?"

She knew she had him now. "Let me give you the new one," she offered. Jennifer leaned over the desk and took the pen out of his jacket pocket, despite having several other available ones on the desk. She wrote the number down and then walked to the door. "Don't wait too long," she said and walked out.

Jennifer sat in the car and felt her heart pound. She had done what Marc had asked. The hardest part was still ahead of her and she was beginning to think she would not be able to do it. "One step at a time," she said aloud to herself, trying to calm her nerves. She took out her phone and sent a quick text to Marc. "Trap is set."

~

"Thank you for coming in," Collins said, rising and extending his hand.

Marc shook it and nodded, "My pleasure." When Collins had called him and asked him to meet, Marc's curiosity was piqued. Collins had offered to come to the house or meet someplace private. Marc said he would come to his office at the station.

Collins offered him a chair. Once Marc sat, Collins followed suit. "Have you ever heard the name of Edric Davies?" the detective asked, getting right to business.

"No," Marc lied. "May I ask why?"

"His name has been popping up in my investigation," Collins replied.

"How so?" Marc asked, curious as to how the detective came to hear that name beyond the video that was making the rounds on the news and social media.

Collins shifted a bit in his seat. "It is an active investigation. Not something I can share, you understand," he proffered.

"I understand your hesitation. I promise you that I would like to get to the bottom of this as much as anyone. You may need to trust me if I am to be of any help," Marc spoke soothingly.

"How well did you know Frank Macintyre?" Collins asked, evading Marc.

"Not that well. After all, I am new in town," Marc shrugged.

"He had recordings. Hundreds of recordings," Collins offered. "The kid must have recorded almost every conversation he ever had."

Marc felt every nerve in his body alight. He reached instinctively to his arm, still in a sling. If Frank had recorded him the night of the fight, Collins may well know more than he was letting on. Marc's mind seemed to follow dozens of pathways, working out the information he had, following each to their own logical end. No, Collins could not know what transpired that night.

"May I assume that the recordings implicate this man, Eric Davies?" Marc asked.

"Edric," Collins corrected him. "No. In fact, there seems to have been a conspiracy to ruin the boy."

"Germaine," Marc said, knowing the answer.

"You are smart," Collins said, sitting back in the chair and folding his arms.

"One does not have to live here long to understand who that man is," Marc observed.

"His influence is . . ." Collins hesitated, then added, "expansive."

"He has something on you?" Marc asked, suspecting he understood Collin's reticence. It would explain so much of what had transpired four years ago.

Collins immediately got defensive, "What are you insinuating?"

Marc understood what he was about to do was a risk. He was confident that he knew what Collins was facing and that he could entice the man to some long awaited action. "I apologize. I want to destroy him as much as you do, for reasons of my own. If he did not have leverage on you, you would have used the recordings to arrest him. That was all I was suggesting," Marc explained calmly. He understood Collins position and his desires. Marc had no fear of Collins asking too many questions now. The two men had common purpose and the will to act.

Collins sighed. He felt that Marc could see right through him somehow, as if he knew things he shouldn't. Still, Collins felt that Marc was telling him the truth. "I had an affair years ago. It was a mistake. I love my family and I didn't want them hurt by something I did," he explained. "If I bring him to court, he will use that to impugn my integrity. The whole case could collapse."

"What if there was another way?" Marc suggested.

"I'm listening," Collins replied, curiously.

"Let me go to the school. I'll present the evidence as if I had stolen it from Frank. That would explain his presence at my home, even the fight," Marc laid out his plan. "Germaine will be terrified by that because he has no leverage on me."

"And then what?" Collins asked. "What happens then?"

"Then, Germaine flees. He runs like the coward he is. You, and this town, will be free of him."

Collins considered Marc's proposal for a few moments. "It's the best of a series of bad options," he remarked, thrusting his hand forward so the two could shake on it. "How does tomorrow morning, say ten o'clock, work for you?"

Marc grinned, "It would be my pleasure."

~

Marc walked out of the station. The two men had worked out the details of the meeting, deciding who would play what role and how they envisioned it would go. Collins had Marc record several pieces of evidence on his phone for use against Germaine. It had been easier than Marc had ever imagined.

He glanced at his phone and saw Jennifer's text. He went to text her back and decided against it. Instead he put the phone to his ear and called her. Several long rings led ultimately to voicemail. "Jennifer, there has been a change of plans. Call me as soon as you get this message," Marc said, excitement creeping into his voice. He would no longer need to put her in a difficult situation. Marc dialed another number. This time he made contact.

"Hey, buddy," Nichols said as he picked up the call.

Marc went straight to business, "I need you to get me a handgun. Something that cannot be traced."

"I can get you a Glock by this afternoon. How many rounds?" Nichols replied.

"One. I only need one," Marc said and ended the call.

Chapter 41

The Last Shot

Marc stormed into the office. Collins had ensured that Germaine would get no advanced warning from the front desk at the door. It was amazing what a badge and a gun could do to intimidate someone from doing their job.

"Can I help . . ." the decrepit old woman who had done nothing to help him said.

Marc ignored her and headed straight for Germaine's door.

"Excuse me!" the secretary demanded, but Marc ignored her. She shuffled forward in her chair and went to pick up her phone to call in to her boss's office, but a big hand reached out and stopped her.

"No," Collins said quietly, but firmly.

Jennifer stood beside him, a big grin on her face. She gave a finger wave. "Hello," she said smartly. "Did you miss me?"

Marc flung the door open and it slammed shut almost as quickly as it had opened.

Germaine turned from his computer, stunned by the unexpected entry of this student. He regained his composure quickly and demanded that Marc leave. "Get out of my office before I have you expelled," Germaine ordered, pointing and waving his finger at him.

"I think not," Marc said, taking a seat.

Germaine grabbed the phone and pressed the call button for his secretary. Marc assumed that he would tell her to have the school resource officer come and escort him out. That was just one of the many things Collins had ensured Germaine would not have access to. As the phone rang incessantly and without response, Germaine grew more frustrated at his impotence. He slammed it down hard and got up from his desk.

Marc said nothing. He had already queued up one particular recording that he knew would get Germaine's attention. He pressed play on his phone where he had stored three such recordings that he and Collins had agreed were the most damning.

It was Frank's voice that spoke first, "How much heroine do you think we can push?"

Germaine's voice responded, "I really wish you would say product, rather than naming it aloud,"

"We are in your office. Who could hear us?" Frank's voice asked with an air of supreme confidence.

Marc let the recording go for a few seconds more, just to prove that he had more and then cut it off. "It is over for you," Marc stated.

Germaine's face had gone ashen. The color had slipped away and even the vaunted Vincent Germaine was left speechless. Marc wondered how many children he had done the same to in his tenure here. The white of the man's face brought an unexpected warmth to Marc.

"Jennifer Kelly is in the hallway. She has already given her statement to the police. The statute of limitations may have passed on what you did to her, but I am certain it will encourage others to come forward," Marc laid out the case. "Then, there is the matter of these recordings. Drug trafficking, endangering the welfare of minors, conspiracy to commit murder are just a few of the charges you will be facing."

"Why?" Germaine asked, still suffering from shock. "I don't understand."

"Of course," Marc said smugly. "You are so certain of your success against your enemies, you cannot fathom that one might return."

"Who are you? A cop?" Germaine demanded to know.

"Maybe I shall send you to your doom without the knowledge of who was behind it?" Marc proffered. Then, he seemed to reconsider. "Doesn't that remind you of someone?" he asked.

Germaine looked utterly confused.

That only served to fuel Marc's anger. How the man could not connect, could not remember what he had done, enraged Marc. "Mr. Germaine," he began, "Edric Davies sends his regards." He laid a large clear plastic bag on the table and waited.

Both men gazed at the contents of the bag, one in shock, the other in satisfaction. "There is only one, so make it count," Marc added as he turned and walked out of the office.

Germaine slumped into the chair, a puff of plastic air wafting around him. He stared at the bag. A handgun, flat black and menacing, stared back. Marc's words echoed through the office. "There is only one, so make it count." One bullet, Germaine thought. It would be enough to kill Marc. One bullet wasn't enough to erase the evidence though. It couldn't cut through the net that he was ensnared in. Vincent Germaine raged against the cage he was in. He smashed his fists on the desk, waging a war against the office. He picked up the coffee mug and flung it, ceramic shards filling the room like shrapnel from a grenade.

Marc stood a few feet outside the office in front of Germaine's secretary's desk. He remembered being here, at another time and another place. He was trapped then. He had no idea of what was happening or why. Marc remembered the sense of powerlessness and desperation. How he reached out for help and none came.

Detective Collins stared at the door, like a hyena salivating over a wounded lion. Where once Germaine had been the alpha of the pride, his power had waned and then suddenly collapsed. Collins had been ensnared in those teeth for far too long. Now, it was his turn to bite and the anticipation was torturous.

"Give him a moment," Marc said, suggesting patience as if the man deserved mercy. Collins leaned towards the door, willing his feet to stay put. Marc put his one good arm on the man's shoulder. "Trust me," he said, soothing the beast within him. Detective Collins body seemed to sway again, this time away from the office.

Jennifer watched Marc. He was a commanding presence; powerful, but patient. He was less than half of

Collin's age and yet he confidently controlled the man and everything around him like a general on a battlefield.

A loud bang ripped through the office. Jennifer shuddered, her whole body tensing. Collins grabbed for his sidearm and took a step toward the office door. The only one who seemed not to move, not to react at all, was Marc. That was untrue really. Marc did respond to the sound, just not the way anyone else did. Marc Cunningham breathed deeply and smiled. It was finally over.

Chapter 42

The Price of Vengeance

Jacob drove back to the mansion with Marc and Jennifer seated in the back of the limousine. Marc was still uncomfortably sore from his wound and the subsequent surgery. The two sat trapped in an uncomfortable silence.

Marc had made Jennifer an offer. At first, she seemed interested, even excited. Then, suddenly, she became sullen and morose. No response had come and Marc continued to wait for one. For Jennifer's part, she seemed to be stuck in a decision making loop that ran the gamut from exhilaration to terror and back again.

Jacob pulled the car up to the front door and time seemed to expire on Marc's offer. Marc got out of the car and made a show of holding the door for her. Jennifer thanked him with a smile and a nod. They walked towards the door as they had ridden, in thoughtful silence.

Marc opened the grand entryway door, allowing Jennifer through. She seemed to quicken her pace, as if she could run from whatever Marc had suggested. Suddenly, Jennifer halted, her back going ridged.

Marc saw her stop short. Suddenly, he realized that someone was standing several feet in front of her. He moved quickly towards her and put himself between Jennifer and the unexpected guest.

"The door was unlocked," Meagan explained, her head lowered slightly, whether to hide tears or embarrassment, Marc did not know.

"You are always welcome," Marc replied warmly.

Jennifer gave him a long, cold stare. "I will give you two a moment. I have to pack anyway," she said icily. She stormed off, up the wide staircase.

Meagan kept her head low while Marc looked at her. Neither of them spoke. Neither of them moved. A door slammed loudly upstairs and sent a jolt through Meagan. Still, she seemed unable to begin.

"May I offer you something?" Marc asked, ever the proper host.

Meagan shook her head.

"Would you like to sit?" Marc motioned to the side, towards the library.

Meagan shook her head again, more vigorously.

Marc scolded himself for the callousness of the offer. The last time Meagan had been in that room, she had seen the body of her dead boyfriend. "I apologize. I did not mean to hurt you," Marc said sweetly.

"Then why didn't you tell me the truth?" Meagan finally spoke, a sudden strength in her voice.

"What do you . . ." Marc began, but she cut him off.

"Oh, don't stand in front of me and pretend you don't understand what I mean!" Meagan screamed at him.

Marc retreated. He looked around the room as if he were searching it for something. "This," he motioned to it all, "This is the truth." Marc said. "This is the life I have been given, for better or worse."

Meagan looked disgusted. "So, you have become the thing that you once hated?" she asked sarcastically.

Marc hardened. "They made me into this!" he spat. "Do you think I chose this? Do you think I wanted everything they did to me? Everything you did?"

"I did?" Meagan asked defensively. "What did I ever do but love you?"

"Love me?" Marc scoffed. "Don't pretend you didn't know what he was capable of."

"He was your friend. Did you know?" Meagan asked reigning in her emotions.

Marc ignored the question. He had no answer to it. "Did you even try to find me?" he asked, his voice tinged with ancient pain.

Meagan was utterly wounded by that. She seemed to falter, her knees quaking, "I asked everyone. Your father wouldn't speak to me. Mr. Moore tried over and over. Oh, Edric, I am so sorry for what you must have been through."

"You have no idea what I have been through. What I have done!" Marc responded angrily. It seemed the softer Meagan became, the more incensed he grew.

"You are right," she admitted. "Please Edric, let me in."

"Stop using that name. He is long gone," Marc snapped.

"I see that now," Meagan said, choking back tears. Marc watched as she fought with herself, struggling to control her emotions.

"I am sorry," Marc said, apologizing again and bowing his head.

Meagan walked towards him. She stood in front of him, their faces mere inches from one another. She reached out with her fingers, finding his hands at his sides. Meagan entwined their hands. "If, by chance, you ever see Edric again, even for the briefest moment," Meagan sniffled and fought to continue, "tell him that I loved him, would you?" It was all she could do to hold back her tears.

Marc could not meet her gaze. Meagan was the past. A part of a life that had been stolen. Could it be recovered? No, their love for one another was tarnished; stained by those decisions that survival had dictated. He had known that, somewhere deep in his soul. Still, to hear Meagan speak those words tore at a wound he had thought long healed. He left his chin burrowed in his chest and spoke in low tones, "He is gone. The dead cannot come back."

Meagan let her hands fall away from his. "Then I must suffer losing someone wonderful twice in a lifetime." She stiffened, trying to gather her strength. She tenderly removed the faded band from her wrist and held the small silver heart in her hand. "Best of luck to you, Marc Cunningham." She placed the heart gingerly on a shelf. Then, Meagan turned away and walked out of his life.

Chapter 43

The Future

Marc looked up for the fifth time, his eyes scanning the corners of the pier. At least it had been five times since Jacob had started counting. He knew what his friend was watching for. Like his friend, he hoped and doubted at the same time.

Marc returned to his work, loading boxes of supplies into the pantry aboard the yacht. It was a massive floating palace that barely dented the man's finances. The instructions Jacob received were exacting, as always. A staff of four, three bedrooms and the ability to stay at sea for months at a time. Despite the presence of a crew to do the heavy lifting, Marc wanted to do the work. Ever since his revenge had been achieved, there was some primal need for physical exertion on his part. Jacob had a theory about that.

"You think pain and exhaustion will help you forget?" He called out to him, sarcasm dripping from every word.

Marc ignored him. He had been doing a great deal of that lately. There was a vast well of emotion deep within Marc that no one ever got to see. Jacob was probably the only one in this world who had even the slightest clue of what direction that underground river was running. When all of that knowledge of Marc Cunningham was tallied, it amounted to almost nothing.

But, he was learning, always learning. Jacob had known very little about boats before meeting Marc. He knew very little about real estate or construction, but he figured it out. He learned how to hide things from people, to be deceptive. He began to understand the depths of human generosity and the length and breadth of human selfishness. Marc had saved his life and Jacob liked to think that maybe, just maybe, he had saved Marc's. Beyond the adventure and mystery was a loyal and giving young man. Underneath that layer was a person so deeply hurt, so scarred that it was a wonder how they endured getting up each day.

That Marc was defined by his pain, Jacob had no doubt. He had been betrayed, imprisoned, and tortured. Never given the opportunity to fully understand why, Marc was left to despair. Yes, his vengeance had been cruel and Jacob had tried to move him beyond the need for it. Still, it was hard to argue that it wasn't just. Marc called it balance. Jacob had helped him to balance the scales with good and bad people alike. As an accountant, the need to balance the ledger was something that Jacob found easy to understand. It was the human side of those actions that was something else entirely. People's lives were ruined. Two young men are dead. Jacob didn't know how to settle those accounts.

Marc paused again; seeking, searching. Still, nothing came. Jacob didn't know how long they would wait, just that they would. After all, where they were going, there was no urgency. At that thought, she rounded the corner.

She looked nervous. Her shoulder was burdened with a heavy bag and she dragged an even larger one behind her. Jacob smiled as Monster rose to greet her. The Labrador tangled himself among the girl's feet, wagging his tail indiscriminately. Jacob jogged over to her and took the bag from her shoulder.

"Hi," she said meekly, using her newly freed hand to placate the dog's unquenchable thirst for attention.

"Hello," Jacob replied, taking the other bag from her. "He'll be happy to see you." Jacob motioned towards the ramp, inviting her aboard.

"Jennifer!" Marc blurted and dashed down the ramp towards her. They hugged awkwardly like two people who didn't quite know the terms of their relationship.

"Let me show you to your room," Marc offered, taking the bags from Jacob.

"Thank you," Jennifer replied timidly, brushing her windblown hair from her face.

That evening, the strange crew of the luxury yacht, the Mad Priest, sat down to a fine dinner of filet mignon, fresh green beans and loaded baked potatoes. The awkward silence became oppressive and then finally unbearable.

"So, Marc, what's the plan?" Jacob asked, his voice sounding louder than he intended as it carved through the silence. He knew the plan, but Jennifer did not. Plus, it would give them something to talk about. The only shared experience they had was not one any of them cared to relive.

"I suppose I should show you," Marc said to Jennifer. He left the table and opened a cabinet, taking out a box. He returned to the table with a journal.

"This is the journal of a brilliant historian, teacher and friend," Marc began. His fingers caressed the cover lovingly. "He is responsible for all of this. For everything I can share with you." Marc opened the journal to a hand drawn map. It was detailed, carefully drawn in a simple script. There was a compass rose in the lower corner, lines denoting various paths and geographic points and a large X near the mouth of a small, hand drawn cave. "We are going to find his cave and the rest of the treasure that he left behind."

"And after that?" Jacob asked.

Marc looked pensive. He reached out to Jennifer and she took his hand. When he finally answered, it was with a firm conviction, "Then, we chart our own futures."

The next thrilling novel by David W. Gordon

Amelia O'Brien and the War for Time

Also by David W. Gordon

The Outhouse

Winner of a CIPA EVVY for Best Historical Fiction, Honorable Mention awards in the New England Book Festival and The Great Southern California Book Festival.

"A gritty, visceral, page–turning, emotional roller coaster."

". . . will leave you turning the page with one eye closed wondering what is going to happen next."
Onlinebookclub.org

&

An Absence of Faith

Honorable Mention recognition by the Florida Book Festival.

"An intense, terrifying journey into the mind-set of a murderer . . ."
Onlinebookclub.org

". . . disturbing, in the most entertaining and gripping way possible."
Seriousreading.com

Book Club Questions:

1. Would you recommend *The Count of Mount Collier High* to other readers? Why or why not?

2. With which character did you most closely identify? Why?

3. Do you think Edric was justified in his actions? Would you have sought vengeance or do you believe you could have forgiven and moved on with your life?

4. If you are familiar with the novel or film iterations of The Count of Monte Cristo, did you feel this novel stayed true to the source material? What was missing or what do you feel could be discarded?

5. Like the characters in the novel, are we the sum of our experiences or our choices? What events or choices in your life may have influenced your answer?

6. Themes of betrayal and vengeance are often considered universal. Does this hold true for you? Why or why not?

7. Has there ever been a moment in your life when you felt betrayed or sought vengeance? How is Edric's journey a form of wish fulfillment for those of us who have had those experiences?

8. If you had written a different ending to this novel, what would you include or exclude and why?

9. What do you think the future holds for the characters?

10. What literary character might you want to insert into the story? How would their inclusion alter the storyline?

1/02